JANE WATSON is a Melbourne writer. She is part of an extended Indian–Bengali family living in Australia, the United States, Britain and India.

Hindustan Contessa

a Novel

Jane Watson

PICADOR
Pan Macmillan Australia

First published 2002 in Picador by Pan Macmillan Australia Pty Limited
St Martins Tower, 31 Market Street, Sydney

Copyright © Jane Watson 2002

National Library of Australia
cataloguing-in-publication data:

Watson, Jane, 1952–.
Hindustan contessa.

ISBN 0 330 36361 1.

1. Australians – India – Fiction. 2. Kidnapping victims – Fiction.
3. Identity (Psychology) – Fiction. 4. India – Fiction. I. Title.

A823.4

Typeset in 12.5/15 pt Bembo by Post Pre-press Group, Brisbane
Printed in Australia by McPherson's Printing Group

This book is for Sanjib

ACKNOWLEDGMENTS

I wish to acknowledge the Australia Council and the Victorian Ministry of the Arts for their financial support without which the writing of this novel would not have been possible.

I would like to thank Le Musée de la Contrefaçon de l'Union des Fabricants situated at 16 rue de la Faisanderie, 75516, Paris, for their kind permission to use material regarding the Counterfeiters' Museum described in this book.

My gratitude for kind permission to quote from *Hindu Myths* translated by Wendy Doniger O'Flaherty (Penguin Classics, 1975). Copyright © Wendy Doniger O'Flaherty, 1975.

I thank Museum Victoria for their kind permission to use material from their website.

Thanks go to my writing friends, particularly Paddy O'Reilly and Gina Perry, for their encouragement; to John Marsden for his Tye workshops, as a result of which this book found a publisher; to Anna McFarlane for her taste in choosing this book; to Nikki Christer for taking me through the process as a guide and mentor; and to Jo Jarrah for her sensitive editing.

My gratitude, also, to Verna, my mother, and to Arati and Sanat Roy, my mother- and father-in-law, and to Sanjib for everything.

PROLOGUE

When you enter a cave first you must stand at the entrance and look forward into the dark. Then, with your first few tentative steps you start down the steps into the underworld. The first thing you notice is the change in the air. It grows colder. Then, as you proceed, you may notice stalactites hanging down like icy teeth from the roof. By now, you have realised that the sounds of the outside world have diminished and you are locked into silence. You cannot go back even though you may have wished it. You are driven, like Persephone— into the arms of death.

But you do not die. Suddenly down here in this strange atmosphere you can breathe and your eyes become accustomed to the gloom. You begin to make out, in the dark, the outline of your captor. His dark alien eyes become appealing to you. But still you cannot speak to him. Your language is unintelligible to him. You try to communicate with hand gestures but what meant certain things in the other world seems to have no credence here. Still you come to find this way of life pleasant and seductive. You crack open the hard shell of a fruit and find inside the myriad red seeds which spill out on your hand like jewels. You eat its contents before you realise that accepting such a gift makes it impossible for you to go back.

ONE

MAN AND WOMAN IN A CAR
Man and Woman in a car
Artist unknown, Maharashtra.
Opaque water colour and gold on paper. Circa ?

CAPTURED
It is dark but I can see the outlines of the others. Milan is next to me. I can feel his cotton shirt rubbing against my arm. I cannot tell if this is a house or some natural structure like a cave. Does it really matter?

There is a sobbing sound. The aunt is crying. She has high blood pressure. On the journey she was worried because we had no air conditioning. There was supposed to be air conditioning in the car. We had arranged the hiring through Milan's uncle, Pralad. He said everything would be as it should be. Is this what he meant?

There is a strong smell of cardamom. And a sound like a tap dripping. They will not want to keep us long. We will be a lot of trouble.

I am not used to sitting on the floor. It will be harder for me, perhaps, than for the others to adapt here. But what a prize they must see in me. A Western girl dressed up like an Indian bride.

'What is this?'

The tallest speaks quite good English. Under other circumstances I would find him a striking man. He wears a skullcap and has large eyes. He is very calm and speaks very slowly and deliberately. He is addressing Milan.

'It is my passport.'

'Are you sure? You are an Indian. Why are you carrying an Australian passport? I think you are lying to me.'

'I was born in India. But my family all live in Australia. I am an Australian citizen. You must let my aunt, me and my wife go.'

The tall man snorts and says something very quickly in a language I cannot understand. I can tell that it is not Hindi.

'Who is your wife?'

Milan gestures towards me.

'She is not your wife. She is a tourist. Why would you marry a tourist? You are not low-born. I can tell. You are too light-skinned. Your parents would have not allowed such a match. What sort of game are you playing here? Do you think that I am stupid?'

WHO IS YOUR WIFE?
'Who is your wife?'

It is a good question. I have often wondered myself. Every time my in-laws speak to me I wonder if they really see me as they should—their *bo*, the wife of their elder brother and son—or as they would like to: a stranger who has entered their family inappropriately. When my sisters-in-law look at their own or future Indian husbands, so carefully chosen by my mother-in-law, what must they think of who their brother has chosen?

The morning of our marriage Jyoti, my eldest sister-in-law, wept. I wore a sari for the wedding, much like the one I have on now, except that the wedding sari was sent by Milan's Takuma, his paternal grandmother. I will tell more of that later.

But for now I will only say that it is unfortunate that someone who has tried to bridge the gap between two cultures is being seen as an impostor. And I would like to say that my intentions were good.

THE JEWELLER'S HANDBOOK
They have left us some books and an oil lamp. I lie down next to Milan and try to read. It is very hard in the gloom of the cave. I do not know for certain that it is a cave but that is what I have decided to call it. You must forgive me. I am disorientated and it is not uncommon for those who have been confined to become delusory. I have a guidebook,

several maps, some art books and a book on gems and precious stones.

Along the way Milan has complained about the books I have collected and their weight. But the book on gemstones has taken his interest. The book is called *The Handbook of Gems, Glass and Precious Stones*. Occasionally when the need arises we have consulted it to discover the origins of some piece of jewellery or ornament. From time to time he reads out something from this that he finds appealing:

> *Real diamonds repel water, fluoresce blue under X-rays, have a brilliant lustre known as adamantine and cannot be chipped or scratched.*
>
> *Hardness, crystalline structure, fractures, cleavage and lustre are some of the features that help the gemmologist detect the true stone from the fake, the original from the synthetic.*

I put *The Handbook of Gems* down and open up a small book covered in black cloth that I carry with me everywhere. I take up a pen I keep with it and I begin to write. I call this book my Book of Travel but it is really an exposition of everything that has happened to us. It is full of sadness and fractures. A writer who keeps a notebook, I am told, will always be prepared for what lies ahead.

If they find us dead this book will remain to tell the tale.

THE QUEEN'S NECKLACE

It began in Bombay, or should I say Mumbai? Our captors would prefer I did.

If at night you stand at the top of Malabar Hill overlooking Bombay you will see a string of lights along the esplanade at Nariman Point. These lights, on high steel lampposts, illuminate the coastal road of the city and shine out over the bay. They are called by the locals The Queen's Necklace.

The necklace is best seen on a clear night and on such an evening at twilight Milan and I are standing on the walkway looking down.

'Whose necklace is it meant to be?' I ask.

'Queen Victoria's, I imagine,' Milan says. 'It must be her diamond necklace. She stole everything else from us—why not the view as well?'

On the opposite side of the road a small boy and a dog are balancing on a plank which is resting on a petrol drum like a seesaw. They appear to be defying the laws of gravity. As I watch them Milan sees my astonishment.

'They're performers, but sometimes, you know, the trick is just another kind of illusion,' he says.

I look at the pantomime group of boy and dog again to see if they are genuine but I cannot tell.

On the corner of the hill our driver waits next to our hired car. It is a white car shaped like a Japanese model but on the boot the make is written in silver letters: Hindustan Contessa.

Our driver's name is Ranjit. He is a self-opinionated man. He collected us from Mumbai airport an hour ago and now he is taking us to our hotel. We did not ask him to take us via Malabar Hill but this has not stopped him trying to fit in a small tour. In two days time Ranjit will take us on a car trip to a small town outside Bombay. He has taken the job because he has relatives in the town, he tells us. Otherwise who would want it—one day on the road and a bad road at that?

While we are standing admiring the view I get out my Pentax and take a few wide-angle shots of the bay, then I swing my camera around and point it at the Hindustan Contessa with Ranjit standing by the bonnet.

CLICK, CLICK.

Ranjit grins shyly, then says half boastfully, '*Acha*. You have me on your camera now. So now you have my face. It is yours.'

SHOPPING

A night haze has begun to spread over the city through which a vulture wheels, its wings spread out like hands in the sky.

'We won't see much more now, let's go back,' says Milan.

As we climb into the car again Ranjit turns in his seat and says, 'Excuse me, madam, are you wanting to buy very good jewellery or clothes? If so we can stop at these shops before we leave and you can purchase them.'

On our right just visible in the gathering dusk are some depressed looking buildings with signs hung up outside which say: *Nazim's Saree Emporium* or *Gopal's Astrology—All Sarts of Reading Done*. Next to these is a blistered, dilapidated two-storey building with a large billboard over the front which says: *Happy Teacher Academy*.

Ranjit turns the wheel sharply and pulls the Contessa in beside a small shop owned by *Naral Singh*.

'What are you doing?' Milan demands.

'Stopping, sahib, so you can make your pur-chases.'

'We don't want to make purchases. We want to go to our hotel.'

'This is very good shopping, sahib. Much cheaper than in the city.'

As he says this he turns to look at me, as though he expects me to respond. He obviously believes I will be delighted at this opportunity. I am, after all, a woman.

'No,' says Milan. 'We don't want to stop here. Or anywhere else, unless I tell you. Start the car.'

Ranjit looks sulky. He shrugs and does as he is told. I feel sorry for him. But I know who *Naral Singh* must be. He is more than likely his cousin. If we give in now our whole car trip will be a series of Singh family visits.

A voice wails up over the landscape. A woman down below is singing. I recognise the tune and its meaning even though I cannot understand the individual words because I have heard a recording of this song at my mother- and father-in-law's home in Melbourne. It is a Bengali song:

I wait by the shore,
O Lord dark as night,
Take me across to the other side . . .

She is singing a song to Lord Vishnu, asking him to take her across the water to the land of the dead.

We look down at the boulevard that runs along Nariman Point and see the ocean at a distance gleaming like black oil in the gathering dark. As I look from the window of the car at the waters I expect to see the moon reflected in them but they are so dark and opaque I can see nothing.

THE GONDOLIER

We descend Malabar Hill and re-enter the outskirts of Bombay and I suffer for a moment from another illusion. I look at the old two-storey Italianate Victorian villas with iron balconies and climbing jasmine and suddenly for a moment I feel I am back once again in Europe, in Rome, or even Venice. It is only a fleeting glimpse but it hurls my mind backwards to another time, another place.

On this day Milan is walking with me. I am

conscious of his movement: the noise of his leather jacket, his gait, the way the light sometimes changes the colour of his hair. When you travel all of your senses come alive. What may have seemed ordinary and commonplace at home suddenly seems interesting in a way you have never noticed before. The effect can be painful. As you are walking down a Venetian street you are conscious of every cobblestone, every turn and twist of the narrow road.

We are on our honeymoon. And like every tourist in Venice we have come to take a gondola ride. The water is like green glass. Our black gondola cuts through the green glass as we sail off from the jetty.

Our gondola has a small gold ornament on it, a mythical creature, half-horse and half-fish, named after the seahorse, the hippocampus. The seahorse-shaped hippocampus in my brain shares its name—it lies there, recording experiences and storing memories.

There is another couple in the boat with us. We take turns to photograph each other. We are polite and well meaning, anxious for the other couple to see us as happy and content.

Halfway around the route it begins to rain. It pours down in sheets. There is no roof to the gondola but Milan discovers a yellow tarpaulin which we pull up over our heads. The other man joins us but his wife sits on a gilded seat in the rain and refuses to move. She says there is not enough room.

It is at this point I realise that our gondolier is drunk. He has pulled a half-empty bottle of alcohol out from under the stern of the boat and is swigging from it with abandon. When he sees me staring at him silently from our watery shelter he grins as the boat bumps against the wall of a house we pass.

I have a camera with me and as I raise it to my eye the smile on the gondolier's face goes.

'No, no, signora.'

The smile returns but now it is weak and manipulative. He does not want his picture taken, not with a bottle in one hand. There are rules. I hold the camera steady for a moment, conscious of my power as a voyeur, the unwelcome observer. Then I lower it and the gondolier laughs.

Two

IN THE HINDUSTAN CONTESSA

The Hindustan Contessa wheels dangerously around the long curving esplanade that flanks the bay of Bombay. Should I call the road Marine Drive, or by its more recent nationalistic name, Sri Netaji Subash Road? I ask Ranjit.

'You may call as you wish, but we prefer the name given to it by us,' he says somewhat stiffly.

The name of the car adds to my confusion. Surely Contessa by Ranjit's definition is an inappropriate name for an Indian car? Trying to make an Italian Contessa into an Indian by calling her Hindustan does not seem to work either. Nor does the ambivalent design of the car itself. It is an Indian idea of what a Toyota should look like. As if to echo my thoughts Ranjit suddenly finds fault with the car also.

'I don't think,' he says as the car does a sharp turn, 'that this is the right choice of car for a long journey. You should have taken an Ambassador. This car is not made for the Indian road.'

I imagine he is about to add: 'This is the sort of car you drive a memsahib in.' And I am grateful that he doesn't. Then he asks Milan why we are not travelling by aeroplane.

'Plane is very good for people of your class.'

He looks pained as he says this, as though he personally would rather see us flying even if it meant he would not have a job.

'I have promised my mother that I will not fly from Bombay to Shundarpur. My mother had a dream. She thinks the plane may blow up,' Milan says.

'*Acha*,' Ranjit says, nodding his head wisely. 'The mother.'

He turns the key in the ignition and stops the engine. The car is now stationary outside a hotel and, despite the fact that I am half hidden by suit-cases, people on the outside are peering in to catch a glimpse of the foreigner and her Indian husband.

'And where is your mother?' he asks Milan.

'My family is in Australia,' says Milan. 'That's where we have come from. But my grandmother is in Shundarpur. That's where we are going.'

'I knew,' says Ranjit, 'when I saw you that your parents were born in India. I could tell. You look like a Hindi-speaking kind of person.'

THE IMPERIAL HOTEL

The foyer of the Imperial Hotel is paved in marble. A pattern of jewel-like tiles set in the floor radiates out from the centre of the room. As we approach the reception desk I see two men whispering and looking at us. In particular they are looking at me. When I go up to the desk and speak in English they lapse into Hindi.

Milan smiles but he looks nervously at me.

'What are they saying?' I ask.

'I don't think you want to know just this instant,' he says. 'I'll tell you later.'

'Tell me,' I say. 'What sort of interpreter are you if you won't interpret for me?'

'They said that the master has come with his fair dessert.'

'What?'

He looks unhappy.

'They are talking about *sandesh*, the sweet my mother sometimes makes.'

'Really?' I say. 'I've become dessert. And you said nothing to them?'

He looks at me.

'It doesn't matter what they think, Tilly. Just ignore it.'

I know he is right and I should laugh but I turn away and look out the large doors of the hotel into the street. There is a collection of street players milling around the entrance. A man balances on one hand as he tries to collect money in a tin.

When we reach our hotel room I open the curtains and look down into the street. Below us is the chicken market. Thousands of chickens are cooped up in straw cages which are shaped like triangular hats. I can hear their distressed cackles and see their white heads bobbing up and down trying to escape from their prisons.

'We're not going to get much sleep,' I say.

Milan peers down into the street. He sighs.

'We'll ask if we can shift.'

We ring reception and ask for another room. The night manager comes to the door and speaks to Milan.

'Will you be requiring a room with two beds or one, sir?' he asks.

'We require a room with a double bed,' Milan says.

'Is your wife with you, sir?' the young manager asks.

'Of course she is,' Milan says. 'You can see that.'

'I am thinking, sir, that your wife is not with you.'

He smiles and shows me his teeth. I want to take out my passport and show him my married name but Milan stops me.

We accept the room. It has two single beds. The room overlooks an internal courtyard with an ornamental pool. Milan stands by the window and looks down into the courtyard.

'You're not enjoying yourself,' he says.

'I am,' I reply.

'Then why is everything not right? Why are you so anxious?'

I say nothing.

'It's me,' he goes on. 'If you were happy with me none of this would matter.'

'Of course it's not you,' I say. 'Don't talk like that. Travelling makes me nervous.'

THE COUPLE

At the end of our room there is a set of French doors which lead out onto an enclosed balcony with wicker armchairs. I go out and sit on the balcony which is still warm from the daylight sun and look down at the cold pool in the dark. As I sit there I see another Western couple who have just arrived. They are putting down their bags at the door of one of the rooms on the other side of the pool. Under the floodlight I see the woman bang down her suitcase and turn angrily to the man.

'It was your idea,' she yells. 'I didn't want to buy it. You said you knew what to do.'

The man turns his face from her for a moment. The sound of her voice rings out around the pool. The man finds the key, fits it into the lock and jerks the door open. The woman marches through the rectangle of dark made by the door. The man follows her. Then the door closes behind them and the rectangle vanishes.

◆

A GLASS BROOCH

I bought a glass brooch when we were in Venice. One afternoon I went for a walk on my own in the Jewish quarter. The houses were small and looked out over a canal. It was a beautiful day and every now and then a snatch of conversation would drift down from an open window. It was the noise of families sharing a late lunch together. A small piece of their lives floated down like a gift to me.

As I was walking along Calle dei Frati, I saw a young Venetian with his girlfriend. My senses were so on edge, so exposed, that they drew me in. They were looking in shop windows. The girl laughed and he turned and moved his arm from around her shoulders to her waist, where he held her against himself for a moment then kissed her. The girl pointed at something in the window of the shop they were in front of and he said a few words to her. She shook her head and laughed again.

After a few moments the couple walked off down a small side street. I went over to the shop window and looked in. It was a cluttered dark window but something in the front, a Murano brooch, caught my eye. The brooch was dark green with circles of red and blue flowers, millefiori, embedded in the glass. The circles seemed to coil around each other in a spiral. As you stared at the centre of the spiral you felt like you were being drawn into the pattern. Around the rim of the brooch there were small diamonds. A leaflet next to the brooch said:

The glass-making technique of millefiori, whose name means 'a thousand flowers', uses patterned rods which are cut up, assembled in an iron ring, heated and finally encased under a bubble of clear glass, whose purpose is to magnify the design.

I went into the shop and asked the price of the brooch. It was four thousand lire. I bought it. The shop assistant wrapped it up in blue and gold paper and I walked out of the shop with this piece of beautiful jewellery in my coat pocket.

FISH-SHAPED EYES

When I go back into the bedroom Milan is already asleep. His face has a gentle expression. His eyelids do not quite close when he sleeps. They are elongated and lift up at the corner like the sudden flick of a fishtail. Beneath the lids the bottom of the whites can be seen as though he is in a kind of ecstatic trance.

Milan has fish-shaped eyes. In India fish-shaped eyes are considered beautiful. I did not know what they were until one day Milan traced the outline of an oval fish on the eyes of a woman in a painting on our lounge room wall at home. The woman in the picture is a goddess who is riding on a lion with her eight arms outstretched. The picture has no perspective. It is a flat, one-dimensional representation. The goddess has enormous eyes.

'In India these are considered beautiful eyes,' Milan said.

Milan's mother, Gita, has large black eyes just like her son's. Gita often says that our children might have eyes like this. My mother always says that our children will have blue eyes and red hair.

'We're going to have red-haired children with black fish-shaped eyes,' I told Milan once, and he laughed.

The goddess came to our house one day rolled up in a pair of pantyhose to keep her clean. She was a gift from Milan's parents. We took the painting to have it framed.

When the framer unrolled the rough cotton paper drawn in bright blue and red pigments he was surprised.

'Unusual,' he said. 'Not like anything I've seen before. Where'd you get it?'

'It comes from the village where I was born,' Milan said. 'It's a small village just outside Bombay called Shundarpur. The name means Beautiful City.'

The framer tested the paper between his forefinger and thumb and then he got out a large ruler and measured the dimensions of the painting.

'Not quite regular in size,' he said. 'How were you planning to have it done?'

'I thought perhaps just under glass with clips so when it hangs on the wall it will look like it has been painted on it. That's how it would have looked in the village,' said Milan. 'They used to decorate the walls on special occasions. Then when the colours faded they would whitewash over and begin again. Later on the women began to do them on paper like this.'

The framer peered even more intently at the figure of the goddess.

'She's packing a few.'

I realised that he was referring to the weapons in each of the goddess's hands. I wondered if Milan was going to tell him the story of how the goddess came to be such a lethal fighting machine but the framer had suddenly found something else of interest.

'I didn't know they had lions in India!' he said, screwing up his face to look closely at the stylised lion that was being ridden like a horse by the terminator goddess.

'You do realise, of course, that eventually the dust will get under the glass and the pigment may fade in the light here also? But I guess if it's what you want then it will have to do.'

DIGHT'S FALLS

From her vantage point the goddess on our lounge room wall can look out the window of our house in Clifton Hill. She can see the Yarra River and could ride her lion, if she wanted, along the road past our house into Johnson Street.

What the goddess can see is something that ordinary residents would find difficult to view owing to the number of factories that line the banks of the river in this area which is known as Dight's Falls. There are two stretches of water that come together at Dight's Falls. The Merri Creek meets the Yarra River as they both flow into Yarra Bend Park. After they are joined the swollen stretch of calm water they form meanders towards the falls. The river is brown and opaque. When it reaches the weir it surges over the artificial causeway and through its viaducts to create the effect of the falls.

Melbourne Parks and Gardens have erected a sign on the grass near the weir. *Danger*, the sign says. *Do not walk on the weir. Strong currents prevail on the weir wall which is slippery.*

The water which rushes over the lip of the weir is only inches deep. It is tempting to imagine walking across the concrete causeway. It looks deceptively easy but a loss of balance could prove fatal.

THREE

THE SWIMMING POOL

In the early morning a woman of an uncertain age
walks round and round the swimming pool of the
hotel. The floor of the pool is indigo. On the sides
there is a mural of twisting lotus leaves which seem
larger when viewed through the lens of the water.
From the balcony of our hotel room I can see her
speaking to herself.

At the end of the pool there is an alcove. Inside,
a squat obelisk of black stone, a shawl of silver foil
wrapped around it, stands alone. On the rock
someone has painted two red dots with black cen-
tres to represent a pair of eyes, and placed a garland
of flowers at its feet. Suddenly the woman misses a
turn at the end of the pool and walks over to the
black stone where she puts her hands together in a
gesture of worship.

'They're leaving a lot to the imagination,' I say, laughing as I point out the stone obelisk to Milan when he awakes. 'If this is supposed to be the goddess.'

'That's the whole idea,' he says. 'To be too definite, too precise, would limit the viewer. There must always be room for interpretation.'

There is an Indian breakfast set out on the coffee table: little rice dumplings with coconut chutney, delicate *dosai* pancakes stuffed with potato, baby donuts made out of chick-pea flour, and strong black tea. Milan sits down to write postcards. He spreads out on the table a pile of tourist images: the Taj Mahal, the Gateway of India, the Golden Beach. I sit silently sipping my tea, locked out of this private greeting card world.

We're having a wonderful time,
Wish you were here,
The food is marvellous,
Hope you are well.

It is a complex feat of balance. Just enough to make the receiver feel they are being kept informed, not enough to tell them anything of real importance. His hand speeds across the white squares of card, possessed.

Before leaving Australia he wrote to his grand-mother to tell her of our coming:

Sri choron komol leshu Takuma . . . the letter began

with the traditional Bengali greeting: 'Dear grand-mother with lotus-like feet . . .'

A letter came back in English from one of her sons. *My dear Milan,* it began, *I have come to know that you are not spending time with us when you visit India.*

'Aren't we staying the day with your uncle and grandmother?' I asked Milan. 'In Shundarpur?'

'Yes, but that's not considered staying with them,' Milan said. 'That's a stopover. They will be hurt that we are not staying longer, preferably several weeks or even a month. We are dealing with Indian time here. It's not the same. If they could keep us prisoner there in Shundarpur, they would. Separation for them is terrible.'

'Have some tea,' I say to Milan. He shakes his head.

'Don't talk to me until I've finished these,' he says.

As though it is important that our friends receive their greeting from this city or the next. I watch the knot in his jaw clench and unclench.

LADY WITH A YOYO

While Milan is writing the postcards I go for a walk on my own in the hotel. There is an internal court-yard at the back and some small shops surrounding it. A shop called Chuckles sells stationery and books. There is nothing funny about the premises and I cannot help wondering why it has such an unlikely name. The owner is a small owl-like man. I can see him observing me. Inside there are art books, a collection of Indian prints on glossy paper and an Indian calendar that catches my eye.

I flip through the calendar until I come to January, which says:

Lady with a Yoyo—Artist unknown.

The painting is of a young noble woman standing on a red footstool on an expanse of grass in the open air. In one hand she dangles a yoyo. In the other she plays out the length of string to its end like a fisherman reeling in a fish. Behind her a young manservant stands holding a fan of peacock feathers and a posy of flowers. In the foreground there is a small tree with orange flowers and in the background an endless field of green meets a turquoise sky through which two white cranes fly.

I am struck by this depiction of courtly life, which shows how a young woman spent her time: playing with a yoyo. I think of something my mother-in-law once said.

'A girl is lovely to have around the home. She is so decorative.'

The morning of our wedding I put on a red Banarasi sari with medallions of gold embroidered upon it. The sari had come from India wrapped in cloth in a brown envelope covered in stamps that showed scenes of rural India. It was a gift from Milan's Takuma.

At the wedding there was a photographer named Al who was Sri Lankan. When he was about to photograph me, Al held a meter up to gauge the available light like a priest holding up a cross to the infidel. Then he looked at me very seriously and said, 'You don't look Indian.'

And I could see he had been waiting to say this.

'I'm not,' I said, 'but my husband's parents are. I thought it would be nice to get married in a sari, for their sake, you know.'

Al nodded. For a moment I imagined he understood what it was like to walk across that narrow strip of land between two worlds.

With the wedding sari I wore my mother-in-law's gold *tikkli*—a headdress of gold chains woven in an intricate pattern that draped down over my forehead.

'Looks nice, the sari. You look just like an Indian girl. Especially with the headdress,' Al said.

'Do you really think so?' I said to Al. 'I think I look like Theda Bara.'

Al looked confused He was trying to be friendly but I could see he wasn't sure if what I had just said was complimentary or not.

'Yes you look very nice,' he replied.

When Gita saw me she said, 'Please don't tell me that is all the jewellery you have.'

With the *tikkli* I wore a gold pendant and a pair of gold earrings which she had given me.

'Please don't tell me my son is too mean to buy you proper jewellery. I can't bear to think it.'

I looked around at the other Indian women among the guests who were at that moment beginning to arrive. They were dressed in diaphanous evening saris and draped with gold jewellery like exotic Christmas trees. My mother-in-law took my arm.

I will lend you my crown,' she said. 'I brought it just in case.'

She took me into the cloakroom and out of a canvas bag took an object wrapped in blue tissue paper. It was a high gold metal crown shaped like a party hat.

'Every Bengali girl wears a crown at her wedding. This is because the goddess wears such a crown and on this day you become a goddess too,' she said.

As I stood for the photographs I saw my reflection in a pane of glass opposite. I wondered if I looked decorative enough. The crown was enormous and overpowered my face. *The Bride's Book of Beauty* recommends that an Indian girl use kohl on her eyes to make them appear larger and to increase the depths by colouring the lids blue with the juice of the wild plum. I had used some blue eyeliner and an eye shadow called *Arctic Mist* bought from the chemist that morning, but the effect was not the same.

As the photographs were being taken Milan's elder sister, Jyoti, wept. She convulsed quietly into a handkerchief. She whispered to me, 'He's such a wonderful brother. So kind, so thoughtful. When I was pregnant I had a craving for chocolate éclairs. I asked Kishore, who wouldn't get me any'—she gestured coldly toward her husband—'but Milan arrived at my front door with a box of éclairs. I was so moved.'

She began to sob again, apparently made even more miserable by this fresh memory. Jyoti had two children. When I explained to my mother that several of the guests would be children she looked alarmed.

'I don't think that small children have a place at this sort of function. This is an adult reception. The children should be left at home with baby-sitters,' she said.

'But they're important members of the family,' I said. 'That means if they don't come some members of the family will not be there.'

I saw the look in my mother's eyes harden.

'We can't have children running all over the place,' she said. 'Everyone knows that children do not attend weddings.'

But I knew this was not what she meant. I saw the vision that she had before her. Small children ran in and out of the festivities. The whole scene was chaotic. Worst of all it was foreign. This was not an Australian wedding.

Our marriage celebrant was a small woman in a long silver gown who looked like a cabaret singer. She stood up the front of the hall with a microphone in her hand and spoke to the guests: 'Dear friends and family of the bride and groom, we are gathered here today to celebrate the marriage of Matilda and Milan.'

The cabaret singer made a gesture with her hands as though she was performing a conjuring trick, and Milan and I exchanged garlands of orange marigolds and yellow chrysanthemums.

Tied to my right wrist was a white horseshoe decorated with tiny wedding bells. As we were leaving for the wedding that morning my neighbour had come out of her house waving the good-luck charm. Her face dropped when she saw me in the sari.

'Well, something old, something new, something borrowed, something blue,' she said in a flat kind of voice which trailed off as though she was not sure what to say next. I thanked her and tied it onto my wrist.

Al took more photographs at the end of the ceremony. We all lined up outside the RACV Club and smiled. My grandmother waved from the sidelines.

'You look lovely, dear, but don't you think the crown is a bit much? You don't want to look cheap. Why don't you take it off for the camera?'

♦

THE PEN

In the hotel bookshop under the watchful eye of the owl-man I buy the calendar, some books, a fountain pen and a bottle of ink. The pen is an old-fashioned Sheaffer made of green bakelite with a gold nib.

'Does this really write?' I ask the man.

He looks at me quizzically.

I motion as though to write with the pen.

'*Ha,*' he says, 'Sheaffer.'

He wraps the books in newspaper and ties the bundle with string. He wraps the pen in a piece of white cotton cloth and puts it in a small cardboard box. Then he takes a square of newspaper, places the ink bottle in the middle and twists the top up to fasten it like a bonbon. As he is handing me the bundles he taps on the side of the ink.

'Madam, *hara.*'

I have no idea what he means but I smile and nod my head as I walk away.

THE ABYSS

'Are you angry with me?'

As he says this Milan puts down his postcards and looks up. I have just piled my parcels up on one of the beds. We have not been able to talk about some things. Our words mean different things. The week before our wedding Milan asked if I had enough jewellery to wear with the sari.

'I have more than enough,' I said.

But it seems that we forgot to talk about what enough really meant.

'Why didn't you tell me,' he said later, 'that you needed more jewellery? The bride should have outshone the other women. My mother feels humiliated. And she blames me.'

'Then why didn't you tell me what enough meant?' I replied.

The Handbook of Gems talks about the ways in which a jeweller defines a gem and what tools he uses to do this:

> *The tools commonly used to identify a gem are the lens, the spectroscope and the refractometer. With them the jeweller can examine a gem to determine its identity by means of its crystalline structure, specific gravity, index of refraction, lustre and hardness.*

But what tools do we have to examine our lives? Mostly I have tried to be direct. That is how I have been taught to think. Milan has always found it hard to be direct. He moves round an issue like a hawk circling its prey. When he tells a story he does not follow the narrative in a straight line. He moves forward by small degrees, always going back to touch on its beginnings. It used to drive me mad. I used to tell a story that went straight to its target like an arrow shot from a bow. But if I tried to make a straightforward point about an event, Milan would find this crass.

'No, no, no, that's not what happened,' he always replied.

I had always thought an event was an event and a fact a fact but now I realise that I was wrong. The events change depending how and from where you view them.

Milan tells stories like his father. Once I complained to Milan about his father's storytelling technique. We were driving home from their house in Park Orchards.

'Why is he doing this to me?' I asked. 'Why does he keep on going round and round in circles and why does the story start so far back? When does he ever get to the point?'

'But don't you see?' said Milan. 'That is the point. The way my father tells a story is a classical storytelling method. In India my father would be considered a superlative storyteller. This is the proper way to tell a story and he is making the effort to tell it this way because you are his daughter-in-law.'

One of my father-in-law's stories is about an earthquake. I call this story The Abyss. The story begins some years ago when there was a terrible earthquake in India. There was a report in the newspaper. The report was at the bottom of the front page and next to it was a map of India. Three towns had been damaged by the quake. They were drawn on the map: Bishnupur, Manbazaar and Shundarpur.

We took the newspaper to my father-in-law and showed him.

'Oh my God, another earthquake,' he said.

'It's a very bad quake,' we said. 'We also heard about it on the evening news.'

The television had shown the broken buildings, the people without shelter, standing in the dust, the children screaming.

'Oh no, it couldn't have been anything like the first one. You can't imagine what the first one was like,' he said.

'When was the first one?' I asked him.

'In 1934,' he said. 'I will tell you about it.'

And he did. He began in 1870, when the British took away the family lands to build a railway. One evening they went to bed landowners. The next morning they had nothing. This was in Bengal near Durgapur. Then he went on to describe how the family left and travelled to Shundarpur to be near their relatives. They knew that the place that they had come to lay in an earthquake area. It was only fifty kilometres from a large fault. They were frightened but they had no choice.

So the story is built up, layer upon layer. Then, as in all my father-in-law's stories, he would go on to describe some small detail that would give the story more interest. In this case it was the mango orchard.

'Behind my father's house there was some land and on that land there were some mango trees.

Actually there were twenty-five different varieties of mango. All sorts; red mango, green mango, yellow mango. You could just go out there and pluck what you wanted. In spring it was very beautiful.'

With the power of the storyteller he evoked the scene for us so we saw in our mind's eye a mango tree covered in a profusion of waxy pale green flowers. A sweet and delicate fragrance hung gently in the air. Gradually we were able to make out tiny green fruit hanging like teardrops from the branches.

'The earthquake came at mid-morning, which was lucky because if it had come at night we would have all been killed. But as it was daytime the people were awake and knew what to do because the people in this area actually have earthquake engraved in their minds.'

Then he began again in 1910 with the story of a boy who, seated in a classroom, heard the familiar rumbling sound, which could warn of a quake, and without stopping, jumped out of the window two storeys to the ground breaking both his legs, before discovering it was the sound of a distant storm.

I realised then that this group of people had catastrophe bred into their bones; they were walking human sensors, always measuring the amount of turbulence there was in case of danger.

The boy's story was followed by another about the mayor's wife who, having left her disintegrating house during the quake, realised that her jewels were still inside and, despite the efforts of others to stop her, rushed back in and was pulled out later crushed to death, her jewels clasped to her breast.

'That's dreadful, but what happened to you?' I said.

'I'm coming to that, but first I must tell you about the orchard. After the quake had stopped all the ripe fruits had been shaken off the trees onto the ground and many of the trees had been uprooted and destroyed. The whole orchard was a mess. My father was upset. But he was even more upset when he woke up the next morning and looked out the window.

'"Rupa!" he called to my mother. "Bring my gun."

'When my mother looked out she saw the whole field was full of elephants, about twenty of them, and what were they doing? Eating the mangoes. There were so many of them you could hear the sound of them chewing on the luscious fruit. Because you see elephants love mangoes. And they were very angry with my father for chasing them away.'

He laughed as though this was the most enjoyable and important part of the tale. Then he stopped for a moment like a diver before he plunges into the water, and looked at me.

'As for myself, I am lucky to be alive.'

He waited a moment for the impact of this to sink in.

'When the earthquake was going on, I was

running with a group of others when, suddenly before me, the ground opened up into an abyss.'

He stopped again so we could gauge the full horror of this.

'I couldn't stop myself. It was fifteen to twenty metres deep with straight sides. I fell down and would have been gone forever but a man running with me saw me go and at the last minute grabbed my hand as I disappeared over the edge.'

He waited again.

'He was able to pull me up out of the hole. I was very small because I was a very young boy. I was only nine years old.'

He stopped again. Then, with the storyteller's flourish, he fixed us with a look of satisfaction as we too were pulled up out of the bottomless depths of the story.

HIS BLACK JEWEL-LIKE EYES

From the parcels on the bed I pick up the newspaper bonbon and twist it open to look at the bottle of ink I have just bought. I hold the bottle up to the light. The ink is green. So this is what *hara* means. It shines like poison.

'If you are angry with me I am sorry. Travelling in India is hard and I may be asking too much of you.'

Milan is still addressing me even though I have not responded. Perhaps because of the colour of the ink, I have been thinking of the brooch I bought in Calle dei Frati two years ago. How strangely the mind works. My seahorse brain remembers. The heat is oppressive. Even the breeze through the window is sultry. Carried through on a waft of the breeze I hear the sound of a woman's voice outside singing.

Lover, you say I am blind, the singer wails, *but I have seen your black jewel-like eyes.*

I try to look into Milan's eyes but he lowers his gaze.

'No, why should I be angry with you?' I ask him.

'Perhaps I am neglecting you, perhaps you're not enjoying the trip.'

Both of us know this is not the real reason. We hear his voice echo in the large slate-floored room, joining up the words one by one like threading beads on a string.

'I am. I really love India. I'm glad we came,' I say.

He gives me a quizzical look. He moves closer and I feel him pressing against me urgently. He touches me tentatively. He places his hands on my shoulders. We lie down together on the other bed, one dark body, one white, on a quilt of Indian paisley. He circles my body with his arm.

'I need to be inside you,' he says.

He holds me in his arms and I sit on him and I feel him like a lotus opening up in the midday sun.

◆

THE GODDESS OF THE DACOITS

The aunt has sore feet. Milan sits beside her and offers to rub them.

'I'm not complaining,' she says, 'for my feet. It is coming from the blood pressure. That is what my body is saying: swell up feet because I have nowhere to send the fluid. I do not have all of my tablets. The rest of the bottle is at home.'

'Perhaps if you put them up in the air?' Milan says. 'You can rest them on my knees.'

'*Acha*, there's no need to make yourself uncomfortable,' she replies.

She leans over towards me.

'He's a good boy. I have always found that boys who grow up in the village are better. More traditional. In the village life is beautiful. You learn to enjoy simple things. Not like these modern city rascals. All boom, boom and no respect.'

She turns and faces me again. In the half-light of the cave her face seems ancient. For the first time I begin to really worry if she is well enough to withstand this ordeal. We have only been here for two days but already it appears that for the aunt it may be too long.

There are two dacoits in the cave. Up close the tall one is very handsome. It is impossible to ignore his charisma. There is a small gap between his front teeth which makes him look like Omar Sharif. The other dacoit is not immune to his charms. He always defers to him and calls him Muni, and sometimes 'our leader'. The other dacoit looks Kashmiri. He has a long woollen cloak. His hair is brown, and he has striking green eyes. He looks like Jesus but I do not trust him. It is impossible anymore to know who to trust.

Ranjit sits in the corner a little removed from the rest of us. He is uncharacteristically quiet. I feel sorry for him. He has obviously ended up here by mistake. He is not of the right background to interest the dacoits. His family has no money— they cannot rescue him. But he was in the wrong place at the wrong time, driving the Contessa. If he could, I wonder if he would run away and leave us to our fate.

At the end of the cave there is a small altar that the dacoits have set up. There is an upright stone like a phallus with several bowls of oil with burning wicks in them. On the altar there is a poster picture of the black-faced Kali, her bright red tongue protruding from her mouth dripping with blood.

We watch the tall dacoit go over to the altar and speak to someone, presumably the goddess. The dacoit's voice has a tone of authority to it as though he is giving the goddess orders.

'Oh Ma, hear my request. I need your help.'

'At least,' Milan whispers, 'they don't appear to do sacrifices. The dacoit movement developed from the *thuggee* movement. The *thuggees* used to tear people's hearts out and give them to Kali. But these people don't seem like ordinary dacoits. They are too educated, too sophisticated. Something else is going on here. I think they are playing for higher stakes.'

He puts his arm gently around me. While it may seem strange to want to embrace, I feel an urgent need to. As we lie together so close in the cave it would be comforting to feel the other body next to your own quicken in response to your need, but we do not dare. Our captors will be watching. They will not approve of our desire.

GRAND LARCENY

I wonder if there were any warnings that we could have heeded and whether doing so would have prevented our capture.

Indians usually take predictions and warnings very seriously. When an Indian child is one year old a special ceremony is held to predict his future occupation. The child is placed on the floor in the presence of priests, and a number of objects that symbolise future work are placed before him. There might be a pen, a calculator, a wallet, or a prayer book. Sometimes the parents place the object they most want the child to grasp within easier reach than those they don't. In Milan's case his parents pushed a book towards him but he ignored it. He just sat there and watched them. Even at that age, I tell him later, he was wary of tricks.

My parents would have laughed at this because

for them there was no secret life. The strange way that things were linked up beneath the surface in the deep unconscious was completely unknown to them.

In India, however, such things are taken very seriously. There is a story about Milan's birth that contains a prediction, a warning perhaps. Milan's father told this story to me after we first met. For some this would seem like the story of Sleeping Beauty, a fairytale; for an Indian it would seem very real.

It takes place in the village of Shundarpur. To understand this story you must imagine the village as it was. A beautiful lush place with thatched huts, some brick houses, a girls' school and a boys' school, a river nearby and a village lawyer. I am taking you into the home of the lawyer where a baby boy has just been born. A boy, of course, a Brahmin boy, is a cause for rejoicing. But this child wrapped in cloth, lying in a crib suspended by a rope from the ceiling, is even more important.

This is the first boy child born into the Chaudhuri family in five generations whose grandfather has ever lived to see his face. This family, the locals say, has suffered under a curse. Hitherto whenever the daughter-in-law became pregnant with a boy, her father-in-law would sicken and die suddenly just before the birth.

So this child, swaying gently in his cradle, had within him the potentiality for breaking a curse. As for his mother—well, things could have gone either way for her.

When she became pregnant the villagers began gossiping about this girl. If the grandfather lived, they said, it was because the girl was a good person, a saint, a manifestation of the goddess. If he died, well, then, they said, she must be a demon. In this case the girl got lucky but you can see that the goddess and those that wish us to become one have a lot to answer for.

I have to tell you, however, that after the boy's birth a rumour went around the village that he was not a boy after all but a girl and that the family were too ashamed to admit it. The overjoyed family, feeling the weight of centuries of bad luck lifted from them at last, paraded the child through the streets naked from the waist down so everyone could see his genitals.

To celebrate the occasion of his grandson's birth the grandfather threw a party for the whole village. Food was prepared. Every guest was presented with a gift as they entered the house: a length of white cloth to make a dhoti for the men, a length of sari material for the women. Everybody should have been very happy.

But there came to the party an old woman, a wicked crone, who went to grandfather and said: 'Babu, now you are so happy give me a loan of one lakh of rupees so I may buy some land.'

Now what could grandfather do? He could not

afford to give one lakh. One lakh is 100,000 rupees. But he should not refuse a guest in his home on such an important occasion. Naturally he became angry at this woman's trickery and told her not to ask for such a thing. Then the old woman flew into a rage.

'Curse your family and curse your grandson. One day he will suffer from your meanness. There will be a grand larceny. He will be held to ransom,' she shrieked.

The old woman was thrown out of the house in front of the shocked guests.

'Such things are superstition,' people murmured. 'Just ignore her. She has no right.'

But the evil seed had been planted. How do we draw the distinction between an old woman's anger and the voice of the gods? How could people be so sure this woman was not in contact with karmic forces?

The girl whose child it was took the prediction to heart and thereafter went to the temple to pray to the goddess to deliver her child from this curse. This woman, my mother-in-law, was fearful of anything placed in her son's way that could steal him away from her. Many years later, when Milan and I were about to go overseas, she fell at his feet and begged him not to go. When asked why, she simply said two words: 'Grand larceny', and wept.

FOUR

AN IMPORTED MODEL

Hindustan Contessa—Silver Grey, Price: Rupees 60000. Scratchless Body, Stereo attached with Air conditioner, Good Condition, Single Hand Driven, interested persons kindly contact on the phone number listed below.

The notice is stuck on the back boot of the Contessa with sticky tape. I look at it silently.

'You're selling this car?' I ask Ranjit as Milan and I get in the back seat. 'But it's not your car. It belongs to the hire company. Milan's uncle arranged the hire for us.'

He turns around and looks at me. We are about to go for a drive around Mumbai.

'The company of your uncle's acquaintance have

asked me to be open to buyers. If I should find one on my drive they will pay a commission.'

'You think that is likely?'

I feel more than a little annoyed about this. It seems that our hire car is about to be hijacked.

'Perhaps yes, perhaps no. I am neither ruling it in nor ruling it out. Not that I am saying that this is not a fine car but there have been certain problems with its deportment—which explains the desire to sell. The Ambassador is more convenient. What you see is where you are with the Ambassador but this one . . .'

He shakes his head and makes a slight tutting sound. 'It could go either way.'

'Then why did the company buy it in the first place?' I ask.

'Very popular with tourists, madam,' he replies. 'Looks like an imported model. Very important to look up to date, I am thinking.'

THE PLANETARIUM

Ranjit drives down a series of streets on a tour which seems to have no defined purpose. As we go I try to read the street signs. Down Dr Dada Saheeb Bhadkamar Marg which connects up with Dr Anandrao Nair Road. Through Jacob's Circle. Along Dr E. Moses Road turning left into Dr Annie Besant Road, by which time I am beginning to wonder why there are so many doctors in Bombay. But I am too nervous to ask Ranjit.

'You will be seeing Nehru Science Museum very soon,' says Ranjit.

Another ten minutes passes with no sign of the museum.

'Smog very bad today, but planetarium coming up instead,' he says.

Suddenly to our left a large building with a dome on the top, as though a flying saucer had landed on its roof, comes into view. The building has six sides which are clad in a concrete fretwork that seems to belong to the sixties.

'You can go there, see lots of shows,' says Ranjit. 'You can see the nine planets of the solar system.'

'Have you been there?' I ask.

Ranjit smiles shyly. 'No, madam, I have five children. I cannot afford it.'

He looks slyly at me.

'I think it is for people like you. You have a planetarium in Australia?'

'Yes we do. Several. There is one in Melbourne.'

'Ah,' he says, squinting out the windscreen. 'That is good.'

I could have added that I had been there with Milan. I felt Milan move slightly beside me, indicating that there was something left unsaid. I was sure he remembered as well as I did our last visit.

WHEN WE LOOK AT THE STARS
On a beautiful spring day in Melbourne I walked with Milan down the corridor of the old museum.

The planetarium was in the basement. A strange place, you would have thought, to find the temple of the stars.

We went into a circular grey room with rows of cinema seats. The night sky was represented by a high concave ceiling lit up by pinpricks of light. The lights came from a large machine in the centre of the room called the star projector.

We had been given a brochure:

The H.V. McKay Planetarium's 10 metre dome is made of solid fibreglass and amplifies a cone of sound. Upon its surface the different hemispheres can be displayed exactly as they would appear in the night sky at certain times of the year. The seats in the planetarium are arranged in a circle facing the star projector in the centre of the dome so that each viewer can see the night sky. At each end of the GOTO optical star projector a lamp shines through 15 lenses. Attached to each lens is a shell on which the position of the stars has been etched. Light streams out through the shells to create the star images.

The room suddenly went dark. A shadowy figure of a woman turned on the projector but it was a man's voice that spoke.

'Welcome to *The Secret of the Cardboard Rocket*,' the voice said.

The night sky manifested above us in the black bowl of the dome. It was a perfect illusion of space.

The narrator asked us to imagine that we were two children in a cardboard rocket setting out to explore the heavens. How wonderful it would be to leave everything behind like children, I thought, to set off in a vessel of discovery into the unknown.

I looked up at the blackened ceiling lit by pricks of light and saw the shapes in the stars. I recognised some, particularly the constellation of Perseus, who rescued Andromeda. How many women, I wondered, were captured in the sky—Cassiopeia, Electra, Venus, Andromeda? The list seemed endless—and what torture had they been put to there? Cassiopeia was tied upside down to a chair and sent into orbit around the pole star, Andromeda chained to a rock and left to face the dragon.

Milan leant over and said to me in a quiet voice: 'Look up there on the right, the *krittikas*, the wives of the seven *rishis*.'

I followed his eyes and saw, rising above the sword of Perseus, a brilliant coronet of stars and I recognised them immediately—it was the Pleiades.

How strange. For Milan it was a constellation of holy women, the *krittikas*, from the land where he was born, a land where people still traced their descent from one of the seven *rishis* who went with their wives to live in the stars. For me it was the constellation of the seven sisters who were put there by the gods to protect them from a jealous lover. When we looked at the stars we saw different things.

The voice of the narrator interrupted my thoughts:

'On your right you can see the Horsehead nebula—a gaseous formation of cloud and dust formed by the remnants of a dying star. Its presence was first detected by radio telescope which picked up its electromagnetic radiation long before scientists could detect it visually.'

The night before Gita had rung our home and I had picked up the telephone. Milan was at work. He was meeting with Stephanie, a town planner who was also one of our friends. They were having a discussion at a restaurant which was close to the architectural firm Milan had just begun to work for.

'I'm sorry, Ma,' I said. 'He's not here. He's out with Stephanie.'

There was a silence on the other end of the telephone. Then a sound like a drawn-out but stifled cry of dismay. It was impossible to respond to this noise because the intention of the person who made it was not clear. It was almost as if Gita had made it to see what kind of response she would get. If I began wailing too, perhaps that would have been a confirmation of her fears. But being unused to this level of enquiry I stumbled into the conversation blind to its threat.

'He's very late,' she said.

'Not really,' I said. 'There is a lot to discuss. This is a great opportunity for Milan. The firm is giving him a real chance to show what he can do.'

A radio telescope can pick up invisible micro-waves from outer space. One day, perhaps, someone will send us a message, communicating across the distant galaxies and solar systems, sending out minute pulses, almost undetectable across the ether and we will understand them. But I was unable to pick up the coded message my mother-in-law was sending me down the wire.

'I feel so sorry for you,' she said. 'At home alone. Jyoti did tell me that whenever she rings, Milan is at work. Why must he work so hard?'

I refrained from telling her that a black man living in a white man's world would always have to work hard.

There was an edge to the way she said the word 'work'. And a quiet restrained tone in her voice as though she knew what was going on but was too tactful to say.

'Do you know exactly where he has gone?'

'Not exactly.'

I began to feel annoyed. Why should I be made to feel that something was wrong?

The deciphered message was beginning to come through. Perhaps it was my fault. Perhaps I was sending out messages to her that she could not understand.

'It's perfectly all right,' I said. 'Stephanie is an old friend and he needs to see her for his work.'

'You must be feeling very lonely. You know you can always come over here for dinner when Milan is out. Why should you spend the evening alone? If not, Jyoti can bring the children and come and stay with you. Jyoti feels very worried for you.'

'There's nothing to worry about,' I said. I could hear my voice becoming icy. 'I could easily go out with a friend too.'

There was a pause, then I heard her voice speaking softly as though, now, she was really frightened. I saw her, in my mind's eye, standing at the phone in Park Orchards, trying to preserve a world that was already thousands of miles away and in another time.

'Well,' she said. 'I feel sorry for you.'

Across the planetarium sky a brilliant supernova has exploded, its overheated core expanding and erupting, throwing off its protective crust and sending its debris of meteors and dust for miles out into the universe. Its cast-off pieces have flown off into the unknown.

That evening when Milan returned, I recounted the conversation between Gita and myself. He laughed.

'I think Jyoti's been telling lies about us,' I said. 'I think she has persuaded Gita that you are having an affair.'

'Just ignore them,' he said. 'They don't have enough to do.'

But the next day sitting in the dark I found that I could not.

There are black holes in the universe. At the

centre of a hole the gravitational pull is faster than the speed of light and the light rays are bent back upon themselves and cannot escape. At the centre of this void time does not elapse. Once caught there you do not change or evolve, you remain as you were the moment you entered.

'She doesn't mean it the way you think,' Milan said. 'She's just a lonely old woman who misses her son and who is caught in a time warp. She misses you too,' he said. 'You're special to her too. She doesn't really believe all the stuff she says. It's just a way to get our attention.'

I saw him struggling, trying to balance the pull of both bodies, trying to establish some stasis which would allow for both to remain in his orbit. We sat in the dark, and in the dark he leant towards me almost imperceptibly, as though he was drawn but unable to connect. I looked up at the stars and I had to remind myself that they were not really there. This was all a story.

We had reached the outermost limits of the solar system now and were heading back to Earth. As we approached our rocket should have burned up in the planet's atmosphere but it did not. It was, after all, magical.

'A perfect landing,' said the narrator, and the children in the audience clapped and shouted with excitement. Then it was all over, the lights went on and we were left staring at a white concrete ceiling.

Outside, in the foyer, the museum shop sold the

artefacts of our journey, a miniature rocket, a telescope, a map of the solar system, and a star chart
which was called 'A Map of the Southern Skies'.
The star chart was a black disc of cardboard with
blobs of white painted to represent the stars. You
turned the wheel around and it showed the stars
visible at any time of the year. If you had a compass
you could use the chart as a navigational aid. I held
the chart between my thumb and forefinger and
turned the cardboard slowly: a miniature galaxy
revolved in the palm of my hand.

'Look, there's the Southern Cross,' Milan said,
peering over my shoulder.

We both saw the shape of the constellation laid
out on its side, pointing to the Pole.

Suddenly I said, 'I really would like to go to
India. Just so I know what it's like. So I can understand why people say things. So I can feel more a
part.'

THE BLUE DEVIL

After taking us for a car ride through Bombay,
Ranjit arrives unexpectedly at a large bazaar which
has a cloth market next to it.

'Why have you brought us here?' I ask.

Ranjit smiles.

'I am thinking, madam, that you may want to
buy silver jewellery and maybe saris. I have a cousin
who sells such things. He works in one of the shops
here.'

His cousin, Rizvan Singh, is a small man with a moustache. He takes out several trays of earrings and rings. The jewellery is modern in style with Westernised settings. There are diamond earrings and gold bracelets, pearl necklaces and ivory bangles and pendants.

'Don't you have any traditional styles?' Milan asks.

'These are very modern, sir,' Rizvan says. 'This is the best jewellery in Mumbai. Everyone is wanting to buy these,' he says with an offended air. 'They are very much sought after.'

He brings out a pair of earrings made in a flower design with pale red petals and a deep blue sapphire in each centre.

'No, not sapphires,' Milan says. 'We don't want any blue stones. You understand?' He gestures impatiently at the man, who nods his head sympathetically from side to side.

'Don't you like sapphires?' I ask.

'Some stones are not right for certain people,' Milan says. 'You must never wear a stone unless it has been properly checked out by an astrologer to make sure it is the right stone for you. And sapphires, in particular, are considered a very dangerous stone. Blue stones are connected with Saturn, the malevolent planet. That means that they can bring the wearer either very good luck or very bad luck.'

◆

THE KOH-I-NOOR

The first time my mother went to my mother- and father-in-law's house for dinner she wore a pale blue sapphire ring surrounded by tiny red garnets.

On that evening she was nervous of the food. She toyed with the tandoori chicken on her fork.

'My word, this is a lovely pink colour.'

'From the tandoor,' said my father-in-law. 'We rub it with all sorts of spices and yoghurt and then bake it in the oven. I myself made this tandoor especially. I knew you would like it.'

'But you're not eating it yourself,' said Mother, giving a little nervous laugh.

Milan's father politely giggled back.

'My problem, you know, is that I can't go past the crab curry. Whenever Gita makes this curry it's all I want to eat. Sometimes she says I will turn into a crab if I am not careful.'

He deftly picked up a crab by its body and crushed the shell with the fingers of his right hand. Then he put his fingers into the cavity and dug out the soft flesh. One of the large pincers lay on the serving plate in front of Mother, its serrated claw half open, looking expectant.

'I believe that you are very fond of art,' said Gita.

'I draw,' said my mother. 'Landscapes mainly. I belong to an art group which meets on Saturdays. We sketch in the Fitzroy Gardens.'

The Indian woman looked impressed. A woman of culture, she was no doubt thinking.

'And do you sing?' she asked. 'Perhaps you would like to sing something. In India we always ask a guest to sing after dinner.'

'People don't do that here,' Milan said hastily. 'I'm sure we won't be offended if you decline.'

'I'm not a singer,' Mother replied.

'What a pity,' said Gita, and we all sat for a moment in silence.

'I'm admiring your ring,' Gita began again. 'It's very pretty.'

Mother held her hand up so we could all see.

'This was my grandmother's ring,' she said. 'When she died she left it to me.'

Mother's thin hand looked like a claw with the oversized ring loosely threaded on it. She turned her hand so the ring caught the light.

'I've just had it valued.'

'Are they rubies surrounding it?' asked Gita.

'No, they're garnets, but they're not cheap ones,' replied Mother.

'Oh, that's very good,' said Gita. 'We believe the garnet is a very lucky stone. It protects the wearer.'

'What does it protect him from?' asked Mother.

'Oh, all sorts of things—indigestion, lightning, poisoning.'

'Really?' said Mother. 'Poisoning?'

'Yes,' said Gita. 'And the wearer of garnets, like the ruby, can always tell if they are in danger. When trouble is near the stones will change colour. They will go from red to almost black. You will see when you are in a bad situation that this will happen.'

'Well, I've never noticed it before,' said Mother, and gave the ring a glance.

'Jiban gave me a set of diamond flower earrings when we were married,' said Gita. 'I don't have them with me at the moment because Jyoti has borrowed them but they are very fine earrings. India, you know, is a very good place for diamonds.'

'Is it?' said Mother. 'I didn't realise.'

'Surely you must have heard of the Koh-i-noor?' said my mother-in-law, scooping up some rice and crab and forming a small ball with them in her hand before swallowing the ball whole.

Mother gave one of her dazzling smiles and then nodded. 'Oh yes, doesn't it belong to the Queen or something?'

'Exactly,' said Gita. 'Your Queen has it. But it used to belong to India. And until your Queen gives it back there will be no end to the bad luck she will be having. That is why her children are all getting divorced. That is why that poor girl died in the car. It is the kismet of the stone if you come by it through dishonest means.'

'Perhaps you would like some more chicken?' said Milan. 'And then perhaps you could tell us about your paintings. Tilly tells me you are doing a self-portrait.'

Gita went on unperturbed: 'Four hundred years ago Babur said that such jewels cannot be taken.

They must be sold or passed on as an honourable gift. The Queen pretends the Koh-i-noor was presented to her family as a gift but this is not true. She stole it. When her grandmother was Empress of India she owned it because she was the Empress and the stone belonged to the state, but when we achieved independence it should have been given back. Don't you agree?'

She fixed her large eyes on Mother's face. Mother returned her gaze mutely.

'Well, I wouldn't know,' she said. 'I don't know much about Indian history.'

CEYLONESE SAPPHIRES

'Well, I guess that explains anything that has gone wrong in my family,' I say, pointing at the sapphire earrings that Ranjit's cousin had laid on the counter. 'Both my mother and my grandmother wear sapphires—and I doubt they have had them checked by an astrologer.'

On special occasions my grandmother used to wear a large choker of blue sapphires. It had been handed down to her from her own mother, whose family had acquired it in Ceylon before they came out from England to settle here.

On my eighth birthday I had a party at home. I invited all my friends, including a boy in my class at school called Jamil, whose parents came to pick him up afterwards.

Jamil's mother spoke very little English. She

wore a type of silk pyjama costume and she had a gold stud in her nose. She smiled broadly at my mother and grandmother. Her teeth were cracked and her skin was pockmarked; around her there was an aura of garlic. My grandmother had on her sapphires. They sparkled against her pure white skin and she smelt of lavender.

'It must be hard for you to mix with people who are not your kind,' Grandmother said.

THE SAPPHIRE THIEF

'My mother had a sapphire ring once but she threw it away,' Milan says, leaning on the jewellery shop counter.

'You're joking.'

He laughs. 'No, you'd be surprised how seriously she takes this. She would not give the ring away in case she passed the bad luck on to the new owner. But according to my mother, the sapphire did not always affect her badly. When she first acquired it she kept it in a jewellery box with another ring that had a large diamond in it. One evening a thief broke into our house and stole the contents of the jewellery box leaving the sapphire ring, despite its obvious value, behind because, you see, the thief was also superstitious.'

'This is a widespread thing then?'

'Oh yes. Many people are wary of sapphires. Some astrologers tell the person who owns a sapphire ring to place the ring under their pillow at night. Then the person must observe their dreams. If they have good dreams then the sapphire will have a good effect on them but if the dreams are bad, for them it is a malevolent stone and they must leave it alone. My mother believes that while the diamond was there, in the jewellery box, it put a check on the effect of the sapphire. But when the thief stole the diamond ring there was nothing to stop the sapphire spreading its influence and wreaking havoc on the wearer.'

I have a vision of the sapphire lying there in the box like a blue devil waiting to be freed from the protection the diamond cast around it.

While we are talking the jeweller is sitting on a stool at the end of the counter busying himself with arranging some rings on a tray. I go over to the tray and pick up one of the rings. The stone in the ring is a deep plum colour and it is surrounded by small diamonds.

'What type of stone is this?' I ask Rizvan.

'It is a star ruby, madam,' he says. 'I am selling it for two thousand rupees.'

'Is it a type of ruby?' I ask.

'No, madam,' says the jeweller. 'It is another kind of precious gem. If you hold the stone in the light you will see the star flashing in it.'

I turn toward the door and rotate the ring until the white crucifix of light dances in the purple dome in my hand.

'It's wonderful,' I say. 'I've never seen a stone like this.'

'Let's get it,' says Milan.

'We can't afford it,' I say.

'Yes we can,' he says. 'It's not expensive.'

I could not help feeling how pleased Ranjit's cousin would be that he had sent him some real customers. How would this affect Ranjit's behaviour with us, I wondered. Was it a wise thing to do? Were the stones genuine?

Milan turns to the jeweller.

'We'll have the ring, and I would like the flower earrings but not with sapphires. Do you have any others with a different stone?'

The jeweller shrugs. 'Unfortunately, sir, I do not have. But I can change the stone to rubies for you while you wait. It will take maybe one hour. Come back at two and they will be ready for you.'

'That's fine, but we do not need them today. We will come back in seven days' time. In four days' time we are travelling to Shundarpur. When we return we will collect the earrings from you.'

I grasp Milan's arm.

'You're going too far,' I say. 'I don't need all this jewellery. Stop now, please.'

But already I can see from the expression on his face that he is not going to. It is set, grim, determined.

♦

AMULETS AND PASSKEYS

On our arrival back from Venice at the end of our honeymoon, I gave Gita the brooch that the happy couple in Calle dei Frati had led me to. It seemed to me that by making a gift of this to my mother-in-law it would act as a kind of passkey for me. An amulet, if you like, that would open up the door to the family for me. When she pulled open the blue and gold Venetian paper and lifted the lid of the box Gita exclaimed with pleasure.

'It's very pretty,' she said. 'It must have cost a lot of money. You shouldn't have spent so much money on me.'

She pinned the dark green brooch on the veil of her sari. The diamonds glistened.

'I have so little jewellery now,' she said. 'We sold most of my dowry. And now we have been humiliated by such a bad purchase.'

The purchase she was referring to was the acquisition of two rubies from overseas by my father-in-law. One was slightly smaller than the other. The larger one had been ordered and paid for by a family friend. Sometime after it had been handed over Gita came to our house with a dejected look.

'We are quite humiliated,' she said. 'The ruby we obtained for the Martins. It seems that it is not as valuable as we were led to believe. They have had it valued and it is not worth what we thought.'

'What do you mean?' I asked. 'Have you taken it to be valued yourself?'

She shook her head. 'We have no family jeweller here,' she said. 'We know no-one we can trust.'

I took both the stones to my mother's jeweller, who reported that although one was not so valuable, the loss from that was more than made up by the value of the other.

'You can have them set yourself,' said Milan. 'Forget about the Martins. Give them back their money and keep the stone. You can make up two rings and for your birthday we will buy another smaller stone for a third ring. That way there will be a complete set for your daughters after you die.'

I knew he was thinking of Jyoti, Priya and myself. I did not know whether to feel flattered or alarmed that now I was considered a daughter of the family.

THE MANUFACTURING JEWELLER
My mother's jeweller had an office in the city. I took my mother- and father-in-law there one morning. The door opened after we pressed the bell. The jeweller's assistant led us into a small room where there were a table and chairs. The room was small and intimate and lined with wood. We sat there for some time as though we were in a doctor's waiting room. No-one said anything. Gita looked anxious.

'Good morning, ah Mr and Mrs Chaud . . .' The

man who came in wore a white coat. He was old and distinguished in appearance.

'Mrs Chaudhari,' I said. 'My mother-in-law. I have brought her because you did the alterations on my mother's diamond ring. Perhaps you could offer her some advice for her rubies.'

The jeweller smiled. He held his hand out as though receiving a wounded bird. Gita took a small brown envelope out of her purse and passed it tentatively to him. Deftly, expertly, the jeweller tore open the top and allowed the contents to spill out into his hand. The two rubies, one light and pink, the other dark and bloody, rolled around the Mount of Venus and the Line of Fate amongst the spider work of creases on his palm.

Detoxification of the blood, lethargy, nightmares are just some of the complaints that rubies can address. Did the jeweller know anything of this?

'What is it you are planning to do?' he asked Gita.

'I'm thinking of making some rings,' she said. 'Two, with one of these rubies in each, and a third with a stone my son shall purchase.'

The jeweller nodded. He took out a small jeweller's eyeglass and examined the rubies in his hand. The eyeglass was made of black plastic and looked like a mini telescope.

'I will leave you for a little while to look at these catalogues then I will return and we will discuss the possibilities,' he murmured.

Then the jeweller went to one of the cupboards in the wall and he took out some large plastic-covered books. He set the books down on the table in front of us.

Gita opened one of the books and began to turn the pages slowly. My father-in-law and I watched over her shoulder. There were hundreds of photographs of rings in a variety of settings. Some were just simple stones, others were surrounded by diamonds like haloes of light. There were matching ring sets and there were gigantic gems with enormous feet holding them in place like Sinbad's Roc bird clutching onto its egg. It was amazing the illusions that could be created by a particular setting.

After the jeweller returned another stone was selected and Gita chose settings for the rings. The jeweller took out a rod made of metal with grooves cut along its length. Then he produced a set of steel rings of different sizes all held together on a chain like a bunch of keys. He placed several of the rings on Gita's finger and then measured their sizes on the rod.

'You are an *I*,' he said. 'That is the size we will make the rings. Most satisfactory. An *I* for the Indian lady.'

FISH BRACELETS
There are several more jewellery shops at the other end of the shopping complex in Mumbai. We go

into one and stand at the glass counter. The jewellery under the counter is the traditional jewellery which we have been looking for: silver bracelets and silver neck rings, nose studs and ankle bells.

'Do you have any Bengali pieces?' Milan asks the man.

He looks at us with a glazed expression.

'Do you have coral and shell bangles?'

The man shakes his head. 'No, sahib. I only trade in silver.'

I know what coral and shell bangles are for—one red coral, one white shell and one plain iron bangle tell the observer two things about the wearer. That she is Bengali and that she is a married woman. I wonder at Milan's desire to get me a set. To whom does he wish to demonstrate that I am married?

High on the wall of the shop there is a locked glass case. In the case spread out on display is a silver necklace and two bracelets. I see Milan looking at them.

'Can you show us those?' he asks the man.

The man's upper lip curls as he smiles. 'These are very old, sir,' he says, making no move towards the cabinet.

'Yes, I can see that,' says Milan. 'I'd like to see them.'

The man grins again and takes out a bunch of keys. He unlocks the cabinet and carefully takes out the pins that hold the jewellery in place on its hessian backing. The necklace is a heavy circle of silver with small individual jasmine buds of blackened silver hanging down from it. The bracelets have a circle of fish which meet up face to face at the clasp.

'Yes, this is what we want. Kissing fish bracelets,' says Milan.

'They are over seventy years old, sir,' says the man. 'They are very precious.'

He gives us a meaningful look, as though to say: 'Surely you cannot want these. These are of no interest to tourists.'

Then he says, as though to finally convince us: 'The bracelets are two thousand rupees each. The necklace is three thousand rupees. I cannot charge less.'

'I'll give you three thousand five hundred for the lot,' says Milan.

The man looks wounded.

'They are too precious, sahib, for such a low price. I have five children.'

'I'll pay in overseas currency,' says Milan. 'Australian dollars.'

The man bites his moustache.

'I'll be ruined,' he says.

'You won't get another buyer for something like this who can pay in dollars,' says Milan.

'OK,' he says.

There is a silence.

'But please don't buy anything else. It is only

because of your sweet temper and your wife's beautiful face that I am letting them go so cheaply.'

I put the necklace and bracelets on for safekeeping. I love them as much as anything I have ever seen. The bracelets are large and heavy and slightly worn. At the clasp there are two ornate fish with gaping mouths giving each other mouth to mouth resuscitation. As I look down at my own arm I imagine another darker wrist. These bracelets must have been worn by several women before me. They would have been handed down from mother to daughter. What tragedy, I wonder, had occurred in the family that the fish bracelets found their way to the shop?

In one of the photographic books I bought from Chuckles there is a washed-out sepia-coloured photograph of a mother with two girls. *An unknown family from West Bengal*, the caption underneath says. The date is 1850. The mother and the eldest girl both wear shell bangles. Their saris are white like those worn by widows. They all have, even the smaller girl, who clings to her mother's sari, a ring pierced through their nose. This is their only ornament of value. The expression on the mother's face shows a loss. Her look is one of hopelessness and despair. The elder girl leans her head on her mother's shoulder. Her arms and neck are bare. There is no fish bracelet on her wrist. I wondered what had attracted the nineteenth century photographer to the group in the first place. Perhaps it was a voyeur's interest in capturing so much pain, so evident, and so exposed in that moment by the camera.

'Sorry,' I whisper as I look down at my own wrist. The fish are gasping for breath.

The last shop we visit is a gift shop where we buy an oil lamp for my father-in-law. The shop also sells jewellery. As I lean my hand on the counter the owner grabs my wrist.

'Where did you get these?' he says, pointing to the bracelets.

I pull my arm back quickly.

'Why?' I ask, annoyed at his intrusion.

He looks at us both and narrows his eyes. For one awful moment I think he is going to say that he knows the previous owners. Then he smiles a toothy grin.

'They're very valuable,' he says. 'Genuine pieces. Very old.'

'Yes I know. That's why we bought them.'

'I see you are buyers of excellent taste. Perhaps I can show you something.'

He leans down under the counter and brings out a small box. It is made of mother of pearl. He opens the box and puts the contents in front of me. There, lying on a bed of red cloth, is a silver ring with a large blue stone in it. The setting of the ring is Victorian and ornate, and the silver has oxidised with time.

'This is over one hundred years old,' he says. 'A stone of exquisite beauty and with a glorious past.

This ring once belonged to the Nizam of Hyderabad's mother.'

As he says this he fixes me with a steady gaze.

'And what type of stone might this be?' I ask, giving him back the gaze.

'Why, madam, this is a genuine sapphire.'

I pick the stone up and look at it. It is beautiful. A perfect cloudless blue. The wrecker of how many lives? The destroyer of how many families? Milan watches me.

'Do you want to buy it?' he asks.

'Of course not,' I say. 'Let's go.'

'Madam, just try it on and you will see.'

But I am becoming superstitious too.

'No,' I say, and I throw the ring down on the counter and walk out.

BEDI'S

The cloth market in Mumbai has a shop famous for its saris. On our way there we meet many beggars. We have gone only a few metres before the game begins.

'Madam, madam, look this way!'

A string of beads rattles in my face.

'Hello, my name, Zafar. You buy postcards now? Maybe later? I see you later. Remember my name, Zafar.'

'Hello, madam. You want to see cobra? You want to see cobra dance? You want to see mongoose? You want to see mongoose fight with cobra?'

Milan takes my arm and begins to guide me through the crowd. I see the look of anxiety on his face. As I go up the steps to *Bedi's Saree Emporium*, I look down. There is a small child on the step.

'*Ma, mujhe do.*'

Such a small voice. I can hardly hear what she says.

'*Ma, mujhe do*'

'Mother, give me.'

She holds out a hand. She is about five years old. There is no expression in her voice. Someone has taught her to say this like a parrot.

'*Baba, mujhe do.*'

'Master, give me.'

She holds out a metal tin.

'*Ma, mujhe do.*'

A crowd is beginning to form. Milan grabs my arm and says, 'Come inside. Don't look at her. Walk past. You can't afford to help her. It's child exploitation. They're forcing her to do this.'

He turns to the child.

'*Bhago!*' he yells. 'Go away.'

Then he drags me into Bedi's.

In the dark cool wood-lined shop the saris lie in carefully folded stacks. It is quiet. The salesmen take out the bolts of cloth and with a series of flicks spread them deferentially on the counter. The raw silk shimmers and eddies in the light. We buy two silk saris. A bright green Kanchipuram and a traditional Kashmiri style with small flowers on it. The other customers are wealthy Indian women.

As we are leaving Milan takes out a five rupee note.

'What's that for?' I ask.

'The child,' he says.

She is still there on the doorstep. He hands her the note. She looks at it as if she is not sure what it is. It is clearly more than she has ever been given. We start to walk towards the meeting place we have arranged with Ranjit in the bazaar.

'Bhai, bhai, mujhe do.'

It is not the child's voice. It comes from a tall woman with one eye.

'Bhai!'

She smiles and holds out her hand to Milan.

'I've already given,' says Milan.

'Mujhe do, bhai, baksheesh!'

The child is now in her arms. Her mother follows us, chanting the request, over and over.

'Go away!' Milan yells at her. 'Leave us alone.'

He turns to the woman. He hands her another five rupees. His face is terrible. She sees this and laughs. She cleverly chooses the words she addresses him with. She calls him *bhai*, meaning 'brother'. She has captured him completely. He stands there, wretched, a prisoner of his guilt, and she winds him round and round with invisible chains of kinship.

ENGLISH FOLK SONGS ON THE PIANOFORTE

We have a list of gifts that we must buy to take home. Various members of Milan's family have put in their orders. Gita requires some miniature musical instruments. She will put them on the sideboard at home. I am at a loss as to why she needs a tiny sitar, a set of *tampura* and a miniature Indian violin, but she must have her reasons.

The first two shops we enter as we walk back to the bazaar have no miniature instruments. In fact the shopkeeper is bemused when we ask for them.

'We were keeping such things many years ago but there is not much call for them now. People only want modern things. The very latest. All up to date and imported.'

In Gita's lounge room in Melbourne there is a piano. It is an English piano with a fine walnut case. Shortly after we were married Gita took me aside and, indicating the piano, said: 'I am keeping this for your child.'

The piano sits in the lounge room, its lid shut to protect the keys, and on its top are several statues of Shiva and Ganesh. Occasionally, at family gatherings, Jyoti will encourage her daughter to play a tune. Cherie takes lessons from a well-known piano teacher and Jyoti has great hopes for her as a pianist.

In Jyoti's home there is a china cabinet in the lounge room. The china cabinet has claw feet and a lockable glass door. Its wood is mahogany. Jyoti could have filled the cabinet with Kashmiri boxes, fretted sandalwood carvings and Indian marble dishes inlaid with precious jewels, but none of these had ever appeared there. Instead, one day she brought home a small box full of ornaments from the local antique shop. The ornaments were old pieces of Staffordshire and Royal Doulton china. Some of the pieces, however, had not been properly packed and had fallen over in transit and been damaged. Two Dresden shepherdesses emerged from their tissue paper to reveal that they had both been decapitated. A Staffordshire dog had also lost its tail but this did not seem as bad as the sight of the two shepherdesses in tiered dresses of frothy lace, their delicate porcelain hands about to shade eyes that were now non-existent. Bewildered, Jyoti put the pieces in the cabinet. They remain there still, the severed heads placed carefully alongside the bodies awaiting repair.

One evening, when the entire family had gathered at Gita's place, Jyoti asked her daughter to play on the imported piano. The child played 'Moonlight Sonata' in a jerky, halting way, her thin brown fingers straining at the keys. I watched her dark aquiline profile bent over the instrument. As her daughter played, Jyoti raised her eyes anxiously to me as though looking for an opinion.

'That was lovely,' I said as Cherie placed her hands demurely in her lap after the performance.

'Oh, thank you,' Jyoti said, as though she herself had just played. 'Cherie will be so happy you think so. She needs to hear from people like yourself.'

'But you can't rely on my opinion because I cannot play,' I said.

This did not seem to affect Jyoti. After an inter-
mission she asked me to turn the pages of the
music book while Cherie played another piece. I
pointed out to her that I could not read music.
Jyoti's dark eyes opened until the pupils were
rimmed with white.

'Just turn the page when she finishes it,' she said.
'I have to make the coffee.'

'I'll make the coffee,' I said. 'You can turn the
page. I can't follow a music score. I've never studied
music. I cannot read music. Don't you understand?'

I could see from the look on Jyoti's face that she
did not want to understand, that the information I
was giving her was unpalatable and unacceptable.
All memsahibs played and read music. Surely that
was so? They sat in airy, light-filled rooms in muslin
dresses and played English folk songs on the
pianoforte. So shaken was my sister-in-law that she
said nothing but she gave me a look of despair.

The evening of Cherie's performance was also
the birthday of Milan's youngest sister, Priya, and
Jyoti had brought for her a present wrapped up in
red cellophane. She made Cherie present it to Priya.
Cherie made a little curtsy as she handed over the
red package. Priya smiled and took it. She opened it
with one long purple and gold-specked nail.

'Gee, thanks, you guys.'

Priya always referred to everyone as 'you guys'.
Priya was going out with a bikie named Bill. Bill
called his girlfriend 'mate'.

'G'day, mate,' he always said when he arrived at the house to pick her up.

Once Gita told me that she wondered why he did that and as she said this she gave me a worried look. She did not approve of Bill and she had previously tried to divert Priya's attention from him. She had offered Priya a trip back home to India to stay with relatives. She wrote to her sister in Calcutta instructing her to send a list of eligible young men with pictures. When the photographs arrived, Gita laid them out on the dining table for us all to see.

'This is a nice young man,' she said, looking at Priya. 'A dentist, I believe. And this one, the son of Mr Mukerjee, a very well-known family in Calcutta, related, I believe, to the Tagores.'

Priya did not pay attention until her mother said: 'I'm not suggesting you should consider any of these, Priya darling. All I'm saying is: keep an open mind.'

Priya picked up the photograph of the dentist and ripped him in half. Gita said nothing. She held the rest of the photographs for a moment and looked at them. Her eyes were very large and dark and I was scared to look at her.

Once Gita showed me a photograph of herself. It was an engagement photograph. In the black frame I saw a young girl with a happy face. Her hands were folded demurely in her lap; she wore a silk sari and there was a string of pearls around her neck.

Priya had come to the birthday party in a black leather jacket and tight blue jeans. In her ears she wore a pair of gold razor blades dangling from chains.

'You should see what Bill gave me,' she said. 'A pair of black knickers with pink hearts on them. Isn't that sweet?'

'Look at your present,' said Cherie, pointing to the red package which lay with its belly ripped open waiting for Priya to reveal its contents.

Priya pulled out a set of table napkins embroidered with little flowers.

'Oh, that's nice,' she said in a kind of flat voice.

'For your glory box,' said Jyoti. 'You need some things for when you get married.'

'I'm not getting married,' said Priya. 'Bill and I have decided that marriage is outdated.'

'What about when you have children?' said Jyoti.

'Ugh, yuck, I won't,' said Priya. 'No kids.'

'Then I won't be able to leave you any gold jewellery. I have kept some gold for my grand-children,' said Gita. 'If anyone is without children then their family will not be able to get any.'

She looked around the room at all of us as she said this.

'Why should we wait until you die?' said Jyoti. 'You don't go out. You don't need jewellery. And I have had two children. Why won't you give me some jewellery now? I demand you do.'

There was a silence in the room. As though someone had already died. Gita looked embarrassed.

'What do you want?' she said.

'Show us what you have,' her eldest daughter said. She smiled and looked at Cherie. 'Go and get Grandma's jewellery box from the bedroom,' she said. The child went off solemnly and came back with a large wooden box. Jyoti took it and, placing it on the table, opened the lid.

'Anyway,' she said, 'if you're not wearing them why don't I borrow some just for now? Kishore and I often have to go to important functions. You don't realise the pressure on someone who works at an insurance company.'

She stopped for a moment and pulled out something round and shiny. It was the millefiori brooch.

'I'll take this,' she said. 'It will look well on my pale gold Banarasi.'

I waited for Gita to say something but she didn't.

'And I will borrow this.'

She held her hand up for us all to see the pigeon-blood ruby ring on her finger.

'It is very pretty,' Jyoti said, admiring it. 'And there is one for Priya here and one for Cherie also.'

She smiled at them both. She took out the other two ruby rings and handed one to her daughter. I looked at Gita. She looked panic-stricken. I turned to look at Milan but he did nothing. Then finally he spoke.

'That's fine,' he said. 'I bought that ring for Ma

but Cherie may like to borrow it. I am sure it will look nice on her hand. The ruby is only small and it suits a young girl.'

I sat back in the chair. I wondered if Jyoti even knew what millefiori meant.

MILLEFIORI

'Do you mind my sister taking the brooch you bought my mother?' Milan asked me as we drove home that night.

'Of course not,' I said. 'I gave it to your mother. She can do what she likes with it. It's hers.'

We did not talk about the ruby ring.

At the end of our shopping trip in Bombay, as we drive back to our hotel, we pass some roadside stalls. In one shop there is a small business making clay figures to use on festivals. It is surrounded by a mud-brick wall. On top of the wall I can see two life-size heads with no bodies, as though they have been severed, placed there to dry in the sun, upside down.

You are never honest when you first begin a relationship. How can you be?

FIVE

THE LEFT HAND

A small stove has been set up in one corner of the
dacoits' cave. One of the dacoits makes flat bread
on it. Each night the meal is the same. Dhal with
chapatti or roti. Sometimes there is rice. Then
white tea. The tea is boiled up with milk and ghee
in a large pan. I cannot drink it.

'Why you are not drinking?' the Kashmiri who
looks like Jesus enquires.

'I can't drink tea with milk,' I reply.

He gives me a suspicious look. I am too frightened to tell him that the food, too, is making me
sick. There is too much ghee in the dhal. In fact it
is nothing more than lentils with butter fat and a
small amount of spices. Spices must be hard for the
dacoits to get because they are very sparing with
them. I see Jesus opening up pieces of newspaper

that are made into little pouches with a twist at the top and inspecting what remains in each before he cooks the evening meal every night.

There are no utensils to eat with and we must eat the meal with our fingers Indian-style, scooping up the sloppy lentils and gravy with a scrap of bread or some rice. Everyone eats with their right hand. I know it is considered unclean to eat with the left hand so I try to use my right hand even though I am left-handed. I do not want to give the dacoits any more reason to criticise Westerners. Milan tries to help me.

'Just form a small ball with the rice, then wrap the food up in it and place the whole in your mouth,' he says.

But I do not have a great deal of dexterity with my right hand and the morsels I pick up are usually very small. This seems to be insoluble. It will always be unacceptable to eat with the left. I will always be left-handed.

MAHDU SWEET SHOP

On the way back to our hotel Ranjit stops near a sweet shop.

'This is the famous Mahdu sweet shop near the Hanging Gardens,' he says. 'Many tourists have heard about it. They sell the best packed Indian sweets—*gelabi, rasgullah*, *halwa*, *sandesh*. Perhaps you would like to try some of these for yourself. We will get down now for a few minutes.'

It seems that we have no choice because he has already jumped out of the car and is opening the door for me. I do not dare ask him if it is owned by one of his cousins.

'Would you like to try some?' Milan says.

'Is it safe?' I ask.

'Quite safe,' he says. 'Everything is cooked.'

We go into the shop. There are trays and trays of sweets. There is *sandesh* cut into small lozenges and studded with pistachios.

Milan is overjoyed when he sees them.

'See, here they have *sandesh*, real authentic Bengali sweets.' He pauses. 'But these are not *bhaper sandesh*.'

'What is the difference?' I ask.

'These are not steamed,' he says. '*Bhaper* means steamed.'

Steamed *sandesh* resembles cheesecake. Making steamed *sandesh* is a time-consuming task. I have watched Milan preparing it in our kitchen at home. First he puts some evaporated milk into a wide pan and stirs it over the heat as it reduces. When the milk has lost most of its moisture content it becomes a soft tacky yellow cream called *kheer*.

Then he makes fresh cheese by boiling a pot of milk on the stove and pouring a cup of vinegar or lemon juice into the pot until the curds separate. After draining the fresh curd in a colander lined with cheesecloth he puts the curd under a weight and places it in the refrigerator for twenty-four hours to dry out. When it is dry, the curd, *kheer*, some cracked cardamoms, some natural yoghurt and some icing sugar are all placed in a food processor. The mixture that results is poured into a large dish ready to be cooked in the microwave without water or put over a saucepan to steam in the traditional manner.

We have served *sandesh* at dinner parties.

'It's fabulous!' our guests always exclaim. 'Indian cheesecake! You must give us the recipe!'

'First you make your own cheese,' I tell them with a smile.

'Forget it,' they say. 'It's too much trouble.'

Milan only learnt to make *bhaper sandesh* by trial and error. When he asked his mother to give him the recipe she refused.

'My recipes are not for your eyes,' she said.

Her recipes were secrets, handed down in an unbroken line from mother to daughter for three hundred years. She would not even allow Milan to watch her cooking.

'This isn't for your eyes,' she would say. 'Get out of my kitchen.'

THE SECRET PHOTOGRAPH
And yet the real secret my mother-in-law kept was hidden in a photograph no-one saw.

Before we arrived in India I had seen very few pictures of Takuma because there were very few available. One photograph showed a middle-aged man with a woman standing in a field. The woman was tiny and child-like. She wore a plain cotton sari and she had a toothy grin.

'This is Takuma,' I was told.

But there was another photograph. No-one was allowed to see it. It was referred to as the 'terrible photo' by my mother-in-law. When photograph albums were brought out, the secret photograph was hastily removed and put away. I was almost embarrassed by this. I had to hold my imagination in check, to forbid it the pictures it could have conjured up. Until one evening, when, quite suddenly, when we were looking for some slides, the familiar oblong of black cardboard wrapped up in white tissue fell out of a box we had just upended.

'Perhaps you would like to look at this, Tilly,' my mother-in-law said, picking it up. 'If you do, you will see something really terrible.'

I took the piece of flat cardboard from her. Through the thin skin of tissue paper I could just see the dark and light shapes of the picture. Slowly, I folded back both sides of the tissue paper and looked.

What I saw surprised me. It was a picture of a happy family, a black and white portrait of middle-class India taken about thirty years earlier. The men wore dark suits, the women wore their best saris. The composition of the group had been carefully arranged by the photographer so that it resembled something of a painting rather than an informal group. Each person in the picture had a look of happy expectation on their face. Or so it seemed at first. Upon looking closer, however, I saw on the right-hand side of the picture the figure of a young man, whom I recognised as my father-in-law. Next to him was a young girl with a sad face.

'Ma, is that you?' I asked her.

'It is, and your Baba is next to me. Do you recognise anyone else?'

I scanned the picture. It was hard to know who the people were because the photograph was so old. On the opposite side of the photograph there was an older woman holding a fat baby.

'Who is the baby?'

'Why, Milan, of course. Can't you recognise him?'

'And the woman?'

'That,' she said, 'is Takuma. And you can see what she is doing.'

'She's holding the baby,' I said.

'Precisely.' My mother-in-law's mouth was set in a hard line. She raised her eyebrows as though to say, You see what I mean?

But I was not sure I did.

'Why is it so terrible?' I asked.

The abyss opened before me.

'Terrible? Terrible?' said my mother-in-law. 'Oh Ma, what pain I have been through! And all because of that she-devil.'

She put her hand to her throat as though at that moment the she-devil might grab her there.

'It is not a natural photograph,' she said slowly, as though she was explaining this to an idiot. 'Things are not as they should be. I should not be standing there, empty-handed, while another woman holds my baby.'

She stopped for a moment.

'She took my child. It is, if you like, a kind of kidnap, a kind of theft.'

A BENGALI LESSON

I first tasted some of Gita's *sandesh* when I went to visit her for a Bengali lesson. My mother-in-law had given me a book called 'Teach Yourself Bengali in a Month'. On the first page there was a vocabulary list.

Amar nam Ram: My name is Ram.

Apni kamon achen?: How are you?

Ami bhalo achi: I am well.

I had asked Milan to teach me Bengali.

'It would be better if you got my mother to teach you because I can't read Bengali as well as her,' he said.

'Why do you want to learn Bengali?' Jyoti asked me with a horrified look on her face. 'Such a useless language. No-one in Australia can speak it.'

'Because you can speak it and I can't,' I said. 'When I visit India I may want to talk to people.'

'You're going to India?' she said. 'It's a dreadful place. Filthy and dirty. I wouldn't waste my money.'

'But you're Indian,' I said.

'I'm not,' she replied, holding up one hand to inspect her rings.

'I was born in Britain. When Ma and Baba were overseas. I've got a British passport. I'm British.'

Gita invited me over on a Sunday for the first lesson.

'Come, Tilly,' she said. 'Sit here and we will begin.'

There were Bengali primers laid out open in front of her. They had pictures in them that looked like nineteenth century Victorian illustrations. She picked up a small blackboard on which she had written the vowels.

'Repeat the sound after me,' she said. 'I will be listening.'

'O, I, U, AU . . .'

I found it difficult.

'That's good.' She smiled. 'Now we will do the consonants.'

I found this even more difficult.

'Now we will do some reading,' she said.

Ram amar chele: Ram is my son.

Ma amaye khabar dao: Mother, give me food.

Ma amaye ekta golpo bolo: Mother, tell me a story.

The order of the words in the sentences was different from English. A literal translation would actually have been: 'Mother, me one story tell' or 'Mother, me food give'.

The structure was circular. In the sentence the

verb at the end referred back to the object at the beginning: a language of circuitous thought, like my father-in-law's stories.

'Now we have done some reading, we will have some tea,' my mother-in-law said.

She went over to the counter and brought back a plate covered in plastic wrap.

'I have made some *bhaper sandesh*,' she said.

She peeled off the plastic to reveal a large flat circle of cream which looked like a cheesecake.

'This is a secret recipe handed down by my grandmother to my mother and then to me. I will teach you the recipe if you like and then you can make it. It's not like ordinary *sandesh*. This *sandesh* is steamed.'

'Thank you,' I said.

She cut a wedge and gave it to me on a plate.

'It is a necessary accomplishment in Bengali families to be able to make a good *sandesh*.'

'Perhaps you can write the recipe down for me,' I said.

She looked offended.

'It has never been written down,' she said. 'This recipe is three hundred and fifty years old and it has never been written down. I must show you.'

'Has Jyoti learnt how to make it?' I asked.

She gave me a sad look. Her eyes were large.

'Jyoti isn't interested in these things. She thinks Indian cooking takes too much time.' Then she went on enthusiastically, 'When you have a child, the child will appreciate these things. All children like *sandesh*.'

I thought about this. The goddess who had children and made *sandesh*. The vehicle of my mother-in-law's desires. I plunged my spoon into the soft white texture of the sweet. It was flavoured with cardamom.

'Of course,' she sighed, 'it's difficult to make sweets such as these in Australia. The milk here is not good. There is no cream. It is not mature. The milk for *sandesh* should come from cows which are more than five years old. Your carton in the super-market does not specify the age of the cow.'

I agreed with her that it did not.

After the *sandesh* Gita made another pot of tea. The tea was Tippy Flowery Orange Pekoe, the best West Bengal tea. I looked down at the open Bengali primer.

Bring fruit and flowers, it said.
I travel to Calcutta in two days.
You and I will go together.
Bring hot tea.
The peacock dances.
Grandma is going there too.

'The problem with Takuma,' said Gita suddenly, as though this was a subject we had just been dis-cussing at length, 'I will tell you frankly. The problem is that she is an *ojha*.'

I must have looked bewildered.

'An *ojha*,' said Gita. 'A woman connected with

snakes. This is a very old and fearful power. She is immune to snake bites and she can cure snake bites. The powers of the *ojha* are hereditary. With the inner eye they can cast spells. They are passed down the female line. Even if they are not used they lie dormant and can be unleashed at any time. We may not be certain that Takuma has the powers. They are unpredictable in whom they choose. But because there is a possibility, people must be careful with her.'

I had a picture in my mind of an old woman stooping down on the back doorstep of the house with a saucer of milk and calling to the snakes as you would a cat.

'*Esho, esho*: Come, come,' and the snakes slithered up with glittering eyes to wrap themselves affectionately around her ankles.

Gita gave me a look of satisfaction. She could see that I was impressed.

'And there is something else I must warn you about,' she said. 'Do not wear any gifts that she gives you. She also has the evil eye and she means to do me harm. She will know that you are dear to me and she will put a spell on any object that she gives you.'

I did not know what to say. How had we descended into this black hole of malice? My wedding sari had been sent by Takuma. Surely Gita remembered this?

'Here,' she said, 'Try some *naan-ka-tai*.'

She went to the counter and came back with a plate of small biscuits. They were golden in colour like shortbread and each was studded with a slice of red cherry. She held the plate out to me.

'Come,' she said, trying to tempt me. 'Just try. One won't do any harm.'

I picked up the golden biscuit. It smelt strongly of ghee. The top had formed into a shining dome and seemed much harder than shortbread. I put it slowly into my mouth and bit. The hard crust gave way and imploded in my mouth. Beneath it was nothing, just a hole, an empty hollow of air.

KALI'S BLOOD

The terminator goddess who hangs on our lounge room wall holds many weapons in her hands. The disc, the bow, the spear, the thunderbolt, the trident and the noose are just some of those which are visible; four of her hands hold invisible weapons which create the magic power of illusion. They are all an essential arsenal for a fighter.

There is another figure in the painting almost obscured by the border of flowers in the left-hand corner. This is the figure of Kali out of whose mouth there protrudes a thin red line. Her power comes from the fact that she is the final form of all other goddesses, created one day when the side of the golden-skinned goddess split open and out sprang a coal black woman upon whom Brahma, the creator, looked down and said: 'Behold Ma, your true form.'

Milan says that this figure in our painting is a depiction of the Great One when she slew the buffalo demon whose every drop of blood, when it fell to the ground, gave birth to a new demon. Before this catastrophe happened, however, the goddess Kali put out her phenomenally long tongue and lapped up the buffalo demon's blood.

If you continue to feed something with blood, to nourish it with your being, it will stay alive. Even an inanimate story can flourish in such soil. The soil might be fed from different sources but it will remain fertile. The story of Takuma has been fed by many different people. My mother-in-law has told one story. Milan will soon tell another.

The day we announced our intention to visit India my father-in-law was not pleased.

'The weather will kill you,' he said. 'This is the wrong time to visit India.'

Then he went on to say that I would find India too difficult a country to travel in because I was not used to the privations of its everyday life.

'In India, in 1954, I was travelling from Jaipur to Jaisalmer. My God it was hot. We were in a bus that took tourists. There were a lot of other Indians. One English woman became very sick. I said to the bus driver, "If you don't stop she will die". But he said to me: "Stop? Where can I stop? There is nothing here. It is hard to find any shade at all. Surely you know that travelling in India is hard. In India everything is hard!"'

Milan was annoyed.

'Well, we're going anyway. This is the best time for us. It will be early summer. Tilly wants to go.'

They both turned and looked at me. The memsahib. Progeny of a mad race who used to wilt and die in India in days gone by.

My mother-in-law said nothing. She was very quiet. Finally she said to Milan: 'And will you be visiting your Takuma?'

The air around us was still. Through the open window of the kitchen where we were sitting I could see the branches of a tea tree leaning in against the house. Its bark was peeling off in strips like skin.

'Of course,' Milan said. 'I will take Tilly to Shundarpur. Takuma would like to see her.'

His mother got up and went to the stove where she was frying some onions and chillies. She took a spoon and stirred the mixture, which popped and hissed terribly as the acrid, vengeful smell of the chillies filled the small kitchen space.

SMALL AUNTIE

In the hotel Milan and I wait in our room for Milan's aunt and his uncle Pralad to come to visit. Uncle Pralad is a successful businessman who has arranged the hire of the Hindustan Contessa for us. I wonder if it is his choice of car.

When she arrives Milan's aunt is wearing a pale blue chiffon sari with a transparent blue veil. Uncle

Pralad, a short squat man with a moustache, is in a
suit. But, according to Milan, I am not supposed to
call them Aunt and Uncle. For me, he explains, they
must be Chotopisho and Chotopishi: Small Uncle
and Small Auntie. Uncle Pralad is married to the
youngest girl in Milan's father's family. Hence the
name 'small'. If he had been married to the eldest
he would have been called *boro*, which means big.

Milan explains to me beforehand, 'What one
calls a relative depends on their position in the
family and whether the person addressing them is
on the paternal or maternal side of his family. So
one person may have a number of titles depending
on who is talking to him. Everything changes
depending where you view it from.'

'Your Chotopishi and I are very pleased to see
you,' her husband says to me, shaking my hand as
we stand awkwardly at the door. 'Your Little Auntie
is very pleased to see you.'

I take a photograph of them sitting together on
our bed. Then we go out to dinner. Small Auntie
and her husband are taking us to the Military Club.
We follow them through a slum street until we
come to a Victorian portico. Through the portico
we enter a lounge and bar. On the side wall of the
lounge there are stuffed tiger heads and crossed
muskets. A large painting of some British battle
covers the end wall. The waiters are dressed in
white costumes with red sashes and red turbans and
they carry silver trays.

'This is an exclusive club,' Small Auntie's husband says. 'It used to belong to the British, then certain Indian families were allowed in. We enjoy it very much.'

I order a glass of soft drink because I am terrified of the whisky. I have read in the papers of people dying after drinking bootleg liquor:

Today in Andhra Pradesh two villagers succumbed to the poisonous effect of locally distilled spirits. There were also several cases of blindness and one of paralysis.

Small Auntie has powdered her face a strange white colour and is wearing a blue *bindi* on her forehead to match her sari. Small Auntie has been ill. She has leukaemia. I notice that she keeps the sari veil draped over the arm that is swollen by the insertion of the needles. Her only hope is a bone marrow transplant but in India a compatible match cannot be found. With Small Uncle she has travelled four times to see Sai Baba in the hope of a miraculous cure. She tells me of the way Sai Baba can produce magic ash and tiny pictures of himself for the faithful, as if out of thin air.

'I will take you to the hospital if you like,' she says when we are seated at the club. 'I will show you what they do to me.'

I find it odd that she thinks I would enjoy this. Perhaps the sick become totally self-absorbed and that is the only way they can survive.

'That'd be nice,' I say. 'I'd also like to see the caves on Elephanta. I've heard you can get there by boat in half an hour from the Apollo Bund.'

She suddenly clutches my arm.

'Tell me, Tilly, please,' she says. 'How do I look?'

'You look very well,' I say. 'I think your health must be improving.'

'It is,' she says. 'It is. Did you know I can sing some English songs?'

She begins to sing *Twinkle Twinkle Little Star* in a high falsetto voice.

'What do you think?' she says when she has finished. She looks at Milan coquettishly and giggles.

'It's wonderful,' I say. 'Just wonderful.'

'I remember Milan,' she says, 'when he was a child standing in his white singlet outside our house in Shundarpur. He had a small suitcase full of stones. I always remember those stones. He used to play with them. They were his only toys. His parents, my Boroda and his wife, had just come back from Britain. They had been overseas for four years. Milan, I believe, stayed behind with Dadu and Ma. They kept him, like a kind of hostage, so that they would have to return. Ma was frantic that her son would leave and not come back.'

Suddenly I see before me a little boy in baggy shorts with a battered old case in front of him. Gravely, he lifts the case's lid and lays out its contents, one by one—a piece of granite with flecks of mica, a limestone with one face smooth as glass, quartz with threads of yellow through it and a piece of volcanic basalt, heavy and dark as pitch.

'Jyoti came back with them. She had been to school in Britain. She didn't like India at all.'

A little girl wearing a sunfrock and buckled-up sandals comes into my mind. Her hair is brushed back and caught with plastic clips in the shape of pink butterflies and around her neck is a string of baby pearls.

'How she laughed and laughed when she saw her brother's toys. She said that her brother was such a backward little village boy that he only played with stones!'

Small Auntie giggles once again. Milan says nothing. I am sure Small Auntie means well but he obviously does not enjoy her story. I wonder if she knows how to laugh properly.

In our hotel room that night I question Milan.

'Why is your aunt so immature? She was behaving like a small child today at the club. I couldn't believe it.'

'She is treated like a small child,' he says. 'That's what Indian men do to their women. That's what happened to my mother when she was forced to leave me in India and follow my father to Britain. She had no choice. The men would have decided for her. She was treated like a child.'

We are lying in bed. Milan's naked chest is smooth and dark. I caress his nipples which are like hard black buds. He does not have a sacred thread, made of white cotton, slung across one shoulder and worn over the breast. He is not a real Brahmin. He has not been through the initiation which would make him one of the twice-born. Perhaps my mother-in-law's rage at the theft of her son by the grandmother had persuaded her to make him an outsider, to isolate him from the family who wanted to keep him.

'When my parents came to Shundarpur to collect me,' he says, 'I didn't know my mother. I thought my grandmother, my Takuma, was my mother. It was such a shock to me to see my mother, this sophisticated lady with bright lipstick, strange perfume and high-heeled shoes. I thought she was a demon. I crept into my mother's room and took some of her make-up and gave it to my grandmother. "Put it on," I told her. "Then you will look as pretty as her".

'I didn't understand what was happening. I was too small. My parents put me in a buggy in front of my grandmother's house and my mother handed me a new toy—it was a Hornby train set. I had never had a toy like this in my life. This was the sort of toy I had dreamed about.

'"If you come with us", my mother said, "there will be more toys like this. These are not things you will get here in Shundarpur".

'I remember taking the train-set box in my hands. I was mesmerised by the picture on the front of a beautiful red and green train. I just wanted to look, to see what such a toy might be like. But as I held it in my hand, the driver gave the pony a flick of the reins and suddenly we were off at a quick trot.

'As the buggy moved off my Takuma clung on to the wheel and would not let go. She screamed at my mother and father: "If you take him away we will die".

'It was only when we reached the station just around the corner and I saw the real train waiting to leave by the platform that I realised what I had done. I stood on the railway platform and I could hear my Takuma screaming two streets away.'

THE DREAM
In the middle of the night our door bell rings. I get up to answer it. A waiter stands there with a tray of cooked food.

'You ordered,' he says.

'No,' I say. 'We didn't.'

'I am bringing you the food you ordered now,' he says.

'But I didn't order any food,' I say. 'It's the middle of the night and I was asleep.'

He raises one eyebrow as though to say, You memsahibs do such strange things—I know what you're like.

'Good night,' I say and close the door. I hear him shuffle off down the corridor, with the tray of food, muttering.

On my way back to bed I pick up the star ruby ring which is lying on the bedside table. I look at the purple dome which fractures into a star as I turn it in the moonlight. Then I place it very carefully under my pillow. When I go back to sleep I have a dream. In my dream I am with a boy with dark blue skin the colour of ink and eyes like fish. We are sitting on the bank of a river. Then we slip into the water and intertwine our bodies to see what they will look like together under the water. The boy is dark like a water snake and I am pale blue-white like a ghost trembling under the surface.

SMALL UNCLE

The next day Small Uncle takes us shopping, but with an air of sufferance. Small Auntie does not come.

'My wife is unwell,' her husband says. 'Tell me what you would like to buy.'

'We would like to look at some *patolas*,' says Milan. 'Is that possible, do you think?'

Small Uncle looks at Milan. With one hand he strokes the ends of his moustache.

'Do you know how much a *patola* costs?' he asks. 'Why, even I cannot afford to buy one.'

'Just take us to see them,' says Milan.

We go to a shop in Grant Street. The proprietor watches as his assistant pulls out the bolts of material from the shelves and spreads out the saris before us on the counter. There are several *patolas*.

'These are double ikat saris,' Milan says. 'They're traditional wedding dresses. We call them *patola*.'

I pick one up and read the piece of paper attached to it:

Various traditional symbols are used in this type of sari such as 'The Tree of Life', and the design known as 'The Nine Jewels'. The colours are derived from natural sources which include: indigo, madder, saffron, larkspur, the pulp of the jojoba berry and the rind of the pomegranate. Following the double ikat method the warp and the weft thread are laid out and dyed separately in sections according to their place in the pattern. This time-consuming process is responsible for the high price of these saris. They are an item of valuable worth. You are asked to respect this. Please do not beat the sari.

There is one special *patola*. It is red with a black and yellow motif. It is hard to tell what the motif is because it is so stylised, but it seems to resemble a kind of rounded fruit like a pomegranate with large blossoms. The effect of the bright motif on the red background is to produce a modern-looking, almost abstract pattern.

'This is stunning,' says Milan. 'Let's get this.'

'I don't know if we can afford it,' I say. 'Remember what Chotopisho said.'

'He's just trying to stop us buying it because he hasn't bought one for Chotopishi. He's just too mean. He could afford to buy her one if he wanted.'

Small Uncle stands at the back of the shop, just out of earshot, his arms crossed in front of his stomach, a small embarrassed smile faintly visible under his moustache. The sari is seven thousand rupees. We do not have that much cash and the proprietor will not take credit cards. When Small Uncle sees that there is a problem he comes up to the counter.

'I will lend you,' says my Small Auntie's husband.

He leaves the shop and goes outside to the Contessa parked on the kerb, where he takes a grey hard-sided attaché case from Ranjit. He walks back into the shop, places the case on the counter and flips the locks open. Inside there are neat bundles of one thousand rupee notes piled one upon another. It looks like a kidnapper's ransom. He takes out several bundles of notes.

'Will ten thousand be enough?' he asks, and he places the stack of notes on the counter.

'More than enough,' says Milan. 'We'll repay you back at the hotel.'

Small Uncle nods his head in silent agreement.

As the clerk is wrapping the sari up he looks at me and smiles.

'Very nice sari,' he says. 'We use it for weddings.'

Then he looks at me and at Milan and falls silent. I know what he is thinking. I want to say we are married, but I cannot.

In our room, back at the Imperial, Small Uncle sits on a chintz sofa and drinks a glass of whisky. I notice that he wears a large sapphire ring on his little finger.

'For my health,' he tells me when he sees me staring at the ring. 'I have consulted an astrologer who has advised me that this stone will bring me good health and a happy life.'

Then he goes on: 'Your Chotopishi wants me to arrange a tour for you to visit Elephanta.'

He wipes his moustache slowly and looks at the ring thoughtfully. 'I will see what I can do.'

We offer him the money which we owe him but he looks thoughtful again and does not take it.

'Actually,' he says, 'what I need is foreign currency. Give me the same in American dollars.'

'We can't,' says Milan. 'We don't have it.'

He looks surprised and raises his eyebrows. I can see the expression in his eyes which says, these children don't know how to play the game.

The next morning there is a knock at our hotel room door. I open the door in my dressing gown and find two strange men standing there in embarrassed silence.

'Yes?' I say.

They shuffle their feet and grin.

'Mr M. Chaudhari,' one of them says with a nervous smile.

'Just a minute,' I say.

Milan is in the shower.

'There are two strange men at the door,' I yell.

Milan gets out of the shower, goes to the door in a towel and comes back.

'Chotopisho must have sent them,' he says. 'I think they're the tour guide for Elephanta and the driver. I'll take them downstairs and give them a cup of tea while you get ready.'

He leaves to go downstairs. Through our hotel window I can see the Indian Ocean. Somewhere in the far distance beyond the horizon lies Elephanta.

Downstairs in the cafe, Milan and the two men are drinking tea. As I approach they stand up and shake my hand in turn, still grinning. They seem at ease sitting at the table.

'Are we running late?' I ask Milan.

He gives me an anxious look.

'Not really,' he says.

The two men suddenly lurch to their feet, bob up and down several times, grin at me again, shake our hands, thank us in a profuse and embarrassed fashion and then say goodbye.

'Goodbye,' I reply, not knowing what else to say. I watch their backs disappear out the glass doors and down the hotel corridor.

'What's happened to our tour?' I ask Milan.

He says nothing but hands me a small white card.

Dilip Kapoor. Judo Instructor, Mumbai School of Judo.

I stare at the white card for a long time and then look at him.

'Do you know them?' I ask.

'Never met them in my life,' he says.

'What did they want?'

'They wanted to make contact with other judo schools in Melbourne.'

I think this is a joke.

'Who gave them our names and our room number?' I ask.

The question dangles. We both know the answer.

'Chotopisho,' he says.

We sit in silence and drink our tea.

'I've come halfway around the world and I'll never see the caves of Elephanta,' I say.

The tea is spiced with cardamom and has a strong flavour. It is not like the tea we drink at home. I look at Milan's face. It has an apologetic look.

I wonder why he continued to be polite when he realised who they were. Perhaps he could not bear to confront them directly. Instead he skirted around the issue like a hunter stalking his prey. I would have fired a bullet straight at their hearts: 'Sorry, we're not interested in judo. Thanks for calling.'

Outside the tea room window there is a tree with large blood-red flowers. Everything blossoms with extravagant beauty here and then quickly fades, its sap drying up in the sun. In one Hindu legend, Sita, the good wife, was imprisoned by a demon in a grove of red trees where she remained cheerful and faithful to her husband. Since then all good wives have tried to emulate Sita. I remembered Small Auntie sitting with her husband, her head bowed meekly.

'What type of tree is that?' I ask Milan.

'It's a *palash* tree,' he says. 'Some call it "Flame of the Forest". It has no fragrance. In fact, it is a totally useless tree. All show and no good qualities. There is a saying about it in Bengali. When we suspect someone is a rotten person we say he looks like the *palash* flower and tastes like the *makal* fruit, which is very bitter.'

Palash, Pralad—the two names run on in a meaningless chant in my head. Outside in the red tree a small eagle has just taken off. It flies in ever widening circles outward.

That evening Small Auntie rings us at the hotel. When I answer the phone the voice at the other end sounds unreal and very far away. It is hard to imagine that the crackling telephone line is connecting me to someone who is only a few miles away on the other side of Mumbai. She may as well be calling from another country, another world.

In her high girlish voice, Small Auntie says how sorry she was that she was unable to see us in person again, before we left.

'You know, Tilly, my husband needs me at home. It is very hard to get out nowadays. I have not been able even to have you to my house. Next time you come you must visit us.'

I thank her. Will there be a next time? How long will she live? Her voice has a strained note in it. Appearances have to be kept up. Virtue and devotion to the husband must be shown to survive through every ordeal.

I have the photograph of Small Auntie and Small Uncle developed in the hotel photo shop and I post a copy to her. In the photograph Small Auntie and her husband are sitting in our hotel room. The curtains have been drawn by her husband to protect his wife from the heat of the sun. She sits in gloom on the chintz bedspread in an expensive blue sari. He sits next to her, a glass of lassi and an ice bucket with tongs on the table by his side. They look like any other well-to-do Indian couple posing for their picture, but when I look at the photograph again later I begin to wonder if it is all an elaborate hoax to fool her family—if the mild solicitous look he gives her, a gentle smile playing on his lips as he twists the sapphire ring on his finger, is the bravado of the gangster. A child bride, possibly, had she come into this marriage willingly or had she been taken against her will? I wonder what life she is leading that this photograph does not show.

Six

FEELINGS OF FEAR

When you are held prisoner in a cave, each day is not always the same as the one before. Some days you wake up and look down at your arms and legs and you are aware that you are still alive and your body feels much as it did before you were captured, except for a certain cramp in the calf or a twinge in the elbow. The mere existence, the corporeality of your own flesh, becomes something you can find comfort in. Perhaps this is the same sensation a child feels when they count their toes. So, in this marvel of small sensations you become a master. Your existence becomes an existential one, you feel each moment, each nuance, in such a zen-like way that you wonder that you have not been able to find comfort like this before. In this state you look through a keyhole, as it were, at the horror around you. You see your lover lying beside you and you forget that you are not in bed together, for surely if your body does not lie about your existence then the facts as you see them must be real. The terror becomes part of a dream world and it is only yourself that is not a dream.

THE CHILD SAINT SAMBANDAR

If no-one comes for us, what will we do? Will we be driven to desperate measures if our health or our sanity begins to fail? I feel, myself, that I would rather die by my own hand than give the dacoits the satisfaction of killing me.

Once Milan said to me, 'Do you ever worry about dying?'

'Sometimes,' I said.

'When I was five I wanted to kill myself.'

'Five year old children are too young to even think like that,' I said.

'You might think so but they're not. When my parents came and took me away from my grandmother I felt hopeless.'

We were at the National Gallery. In the foyer a series of log coffins stood up like totem poles in clusters that marked out the path of a river. The log coffins were the containers for the bones of the Aboriginal dead.

There was a silence. It was broken by a mother who came into the room with a tearful child in her arms. We turned away from each other and concentrated on this domestic scene because to contemplate each other was too difficult. Then the relevance of this scene to the pictures in our mind apparently dawned on us both together and we turned back to each other again.

There was a statue standing in the forecourt of the gallery and a sign in front of it. The sign said that the statue was of the child saint, Sambandar, who wandered throughout India in the seventh century singing praises to Lord Shiva until, suddenly, vanishing without a trace at the age of fifteen. Witnesses of the disappearance described how, at the crucial moment, his body evaporated into a cloud of light created by the god Shiva.

The boy stood at the entrance to the Nomura Court in the Asian Art collection. In his left hand he held a cup filled with the milk of the goddess. Around his neck was a tiger claw worn to protect him from evil. His limbs were slender and his face was round. On his plump neck there were two delicate folds in the skin which looked like necklaces. How must his mother have felt when he disappeared? Did she believe that her son had been abducted by Shiva?

I thought then, for the first time, of Gita, waiting to return to India, wondering every day how her son, who had gone from her life, was. Surely she had not wanted to leave her only son behind? To abandon him? Hoping he still remembered her. Praying to the gods to restore him to her. I looked at the figure of Sambandar with his plump, ringed neck. An auspicious sign. The necklace of the gods. I looked at Milan and at his own brown neck, with the same telltale creases, even though he was now an adult. What had Gita been told when her child was taken from her while she and her husband travelled overseas for so many years? Which god had been blamed for this or, worse still, which goddess?

THE GIRL IN THE CROWD

When we were in Venice I saw a girl in a crowd. One minute she was there, the next she had just vanished into thin air. I noticed her because she reminded me of Stephanie.

I was walking along the narrow dark streets trying to find my way. At every turn when I expected to see the daylight I came across another dark alley. Eventually I hoped I would reach somewhere, find something that would indicate the way more specifically. The signs around Venice were vague: *To The Rialto*, they pointed with an arrow, or *To San Marco* or *Ferrovia*. What happened if you had another destination in mind?

Then, suddenly, without warning, the space opened up and I found myself in a square filled with pigeons and tourists. There were such contrasts of dark and light here that it seemed as if I was looking through a prism.

One woman was standing apart from the

tourists. She had green eyes and fine bone structure. Her skin was like creamy paper with a hint of an olive watermark bruising the surface.

I turned to look at a church on the corner with a large bell tower and when I looked back she was gone. There was just a swarm of people and none of them looked like her.

THE MISSING DAUGHTER

Just before we left for India, Priya went missing.

'We have not heard from her for four days,' Gita said. 'First she rings us nonstop, and now this. Something terrible has happened to her. I know it.'

Milan and I were seated in the family room of his parents' home when she said this. Gita was sitting at the head of the large family table, her eyes wide with terror. Jyoti had come to offer advice.

'Perhaps she has just gone off somewhere for a holiday,' suggested Milan. 'You know what she's like. She never tells anyone what she is doing or where she is going.'

There was a strange silence in the room, as though someone had died. After several cryptic telephone calls the week before, in which his sister had announced her intention to leave Bill, Priya had disappeared. Not even her close friends knew where she was. She had left a note on the kitchen table at Bill's place telling him she was leaving.

'What I know is that if my daughter is unhappy living with Bill, she should come home. After all, where else can she go? Here, with her family, is where she ought to be. I cannot believe that she is all right if she has not contacted us. He has done something terrible to her,' said Gita.

'She's so irresponsible,' said Jyoti. 'You just can't decide one day you've had enough and leave without telling anyone where you are going. It's not *Shirley Valentine*. This is real life.'

I thought I detected a note of bitterness in her voice, as though she wished that there was an escape as dramatic for herself.

'Perhaps she needed some time to herself,' I said. 'You know, she may feel that she has to work out what she is going to do next before she tells us what has happened.'

The two Indian women turned and looked at me, both together. There were a series of Indian dolls standing on the shelf in the family room. They looked down, too, with large, incredulous mat-painted eyes.

'My poor child,' Gita said, suddenly breaking into syncopated sobs. 'She has no idea what she is up against. These Australian men can be so cruel.'

'Oh my God,' said my father-in-law. 'Why get so upset? Everything will be fine. Who cares if she's left her boyfriend?'

He sucked on his pipe furiously.

'Bill was always very jealous,' said Jyoti. 'I think he suspected she was seeing someone else. She told me once that he wouldn't let her look sideways at anyone. You can't be too careful. Temptation is always around the corner.'

'How do you know it wasn't Bill who was having the affair?' said Milan.

There is another silence.

'He probably was,' said Jyoti. 'That's what men do if you are careless and let them out of your sight.'

She looked straight at me as she said this and smiled.

'Don't you agree, Tilly?'

I looked back at her, amazed. What was I supposed to say?

BURIED ALIVE

Later that night, after Milan and I had returned home, the telephone rang. It was Gita.

Milan looked irritated. He turned on the telephone speaker so I could listen.

'Whatever has happened,' Gita said to Milan, 'we must not give up. You must go around to Bill's house tonight and see what you can find.'

'There is nothing to find, Ma,' he said. 'What do you expect me to do? What is it that you are actually looking for there?'

'I think he has done something to her,' she said. 'It would be so easy for him. She may be lying murdered under the floorboards of the house or buried in a shallow grave in the garden.'

The thought of Priya's corpse lying under the

rotting floorboards of Bill's bedroom, in a dank and closed space, never to escape, returns to me now as we sit in the cave. Then I remember Milan clutching the telephone, trying to communicate with his distraught parent.

'What do you want me to say to Bill? Excuse me but my mother thinks that you have kidnapped our sister and murdered her. She believes her remains lie under the very boards that we stand on, so would you mind terribly if I just pull some up and take a look?'

'At least speak to Bill,' she said. 'Find out what he knows.'

Milan gave a long sigh. Gita began to cry.

'The least your sister deserves is a proper end. Only a proper Hindu cremation can purify her soul. Please, son, don't leave her lying in some foreign grave under the house, don't let this terrible thing happen, I implore you.'

Milan got off the telephone, his hands shaking.

'My mother has gone mad, completely stark raving mad,' he said quietly.

THE GLASS FACTORY

Sometimes we hope against all odds that everything will be all right. Sometimes it is. What seems impossible can come true. I remind myself of this as I sit in the dark.

In Venice, on a visit to a glass factory, we were taken into a room containing a small kiln and a glass-blower at work. The glass-blower picked up a rod and dipped it into a ball of molten glass.

The air in the little room was scorching and there was a smell of heat. Milan and I sat next to each other but we did not touch. I could see the sweat on his shirt. The fine hair on the back of his neck was matted into curls.

The glass-blower twirled the ball of glass in one hand, then he removed it from the rod and pulled out a long cane of molten glass from the ball. He blew down the tube and the ball expanded into a thin crystalline sphere pregnant with possibilities but as yet forming nothing. In a moment the sphere had been twirled and prodded until suddenly he placed on the ground before us a perfect miniature horse.

Milan put his arm around me.

We clapped and then we went into the shop next to the workroom. The shop sold goblets of green, blue and red Venetian glass. Some of them were decorated with gold. They all looked delicate and fragile. The salesman behind the counter was anxious to calm our fears.

'This glass is as tough as plastic,' he said to the assembled group.

He picked up a large green goblet and let it fall from his hand to the floor. It lay there perfect and intact. The crowd sighed.

SEVEN

THE ROCK CAVES OF ELEPHANTA

The island of Elephanta owes its name to the large elephant statue that the Portuguese found on its foreshore when they first visited the island in the sixteenth century. The rock caves are temples hewn out of large pieces of basalt in the cliff face of the island. One of the art books I bought at Chuckles shows a picture of the giant elephant that once stood on the foreshore. Now it is in the Victoria Gardens in Mumbai where it was reconstructed after it collapsed on Elephanta. Many years ago there was a smaller elephant which rode upon the back of the colossus but, over time, this has completely disappeared, worn away by the elements and the touch of humans.

My desire to go to Elephanta has grown so much that the day before we are to leave for Shundarpur

I go to the foyer of the Imperial Hotel to speak to the travel agent who has a small booth there. There is a sign on an archway that leads into a small arcade with some shops. *Mercury Travel* the sign says in large black letters. As I walk over I ponder why they would choose the name of a Greek god with winged feet. There must be Hindu gods that would be more appropriate. I am trying to think of one when the woman behind the counter sees me.

'Good morning, madam, my name is Shruti. How may I help you? You want to book a trip, yes?'

I assure her I do. I tell her I would like to book a trip for two to Elephanta. She seems delighted, as though I have just told her she has won the lottery. Shruti has a large smile with bright red lipstick and very white teeth. She asks how I would like to pay and I take out a credit card.

'There is a ferry leaving this afternoon from the Gateway of India,' she says. 'I am making the booking for you now.'

I thank her and walk out of Mercury Travel clutching a small travel brochure on Elephanta.

As I make my way back to our hotel room I open the brochure and begin to read:

Day Trips from Mumbai

Elephanta Caves

The rock caves of Elephanta are a short trip by ferry

from the Gateway of India at Apollo Bund and give the visitor a unique experience.

Although damaged by the Portuguese, who used them for target practice, the statues of Lord Shiva in the temple caves still delight and fascinate.

The visitor must traverse a steep flight of stairs to reach the caves, which cover a large area. The climb up to the cave mouth, which can be done by chair, ushers the onlooker into another place, the magical world of the god's mountain dwelling. On the temple walls the story of Lord Shiva is shown in panels. The magnificent Maheshamurthi, the three-headed statue of Shiva, rivals the Taj Mahal itself in beauty and awe inspiring magnificence. Onlookers often remark how the appearance of each face changes due to the play of light that is cleverly admitted through several openings in the cave walls.

The best time to visit is from November to March. The festival of Elephanta takes place in February during which many famous artists can be seen performing in this wonderful setting. Regular launch services from the Gateway of India take tourists to the Caves throughout the year, except during the monsoon season.

I see myself walking up the steep steps of the entrance to the main cave, stopping at the black mouth to peer around for a moment before stepping inside.

I am back in our room when the telephone rings. It is Shruti.

'Hello, madam,' she says. 'I have made your booking.'

'That's great,' I say. 'Thank you.'

'And I have just cancelled it.'

'I beg your pardon?'

'I am having to cancel your booking owing to a large Japanese party.'

'You can't do that,' I say. 'Mine was made first.'

'I am very sorry,' she says. 'I have made you a refund. Japanese take priority because there is a very large number. Very sorry.'

And she hangs up.

I sit there for a moment, looking at Milan. I had been hoping to walk inside the cave and look at the ancient statues. I had thought I would be able to examine the walls of the cave to see the layers of rock laid down over time with all the minerals and fossils captured in each band indicating what kind of geological event had occurred in that period to put them there. I may even have seen a piece of precious metal or stone caught there in the rock. Now I would see nothing.

THE SHEESHAM TABLE

The next day we prepare to set off for Shundarpur. We have presents for the family that Ranjit has piled up in the front seat of the Contessa. There are packages of Toblerone chocolate and English soap.

Amongst the requests for gifts we have been asked to buy during our trip there is one from Jyoti who wants a wooden table. She asked me for this when she rang me up just before we left. But first she had an offer for me.

'Oh, Tilly, do you want Indy's old baby clothes?'

I wasn't sure what to say. I did not see the trap, like an elephant pit with steep sides that plunged into a deep ravine before me.

Shortly after we were married Gita began to make inquiries about my health. Whenever we visited her I would see her staring at my stomach.

'Is Tilly pregnant?'

Sometimes she would take Milan aside and ask him this question. I knew what she really meant. Would I give birth to a male child, would I give the family an heir? Would the grandfather live to see his face? But I was not ready to become pregnant. I was still traversing that narrow-ledge of land between two worlds. How could I carry a child across such a dangerous isthmus with me?

Jyoti went on, 'If you want the clothes, I can give them to you now. Otherwise I'll give them to Shanti.'

'Oh, don't keep them on my account,' I said. 'I don't know when I'll use them. By all means give them to Shanti.'

There was a silence at the other end of the phone.

Then Jyoti said, 'If you are thinking of having a baby, it probably would be a good idea to have one in about three years. Then my children would have grown.'

'Oh,' I said.

'Yes, don't have one now. It's not a good idea. I need Ma to help me with my children.'

I didn't say anything. I was not sure how to take what she had said. Was it a threat?

Milan tells the story of King Kans who, in ancient times, in the kingdom of Mathura, put to death every newborn male child because he feared the birth of the god Krishna. When Krishna's parents fled with him to another kingdom, Kans sent the demon Pootana to kill the child with milk from her poisoned breasts.

'It's really difficult,' Jyoti said, 'bringing up two children in this country. I don't know how I would manage without help. Before you were married, Milan was wonderful. Such a tremendous brother he's been. After I had my first child he came over and helped with the cooking. Kishore couldn't do it. He was too busy. Now wasn't that thoughtful!'

There was a strange hiccupping noise at the other end of the phone and I realised that she was weeping.

'Yes,' I said. 'It certainly was.'

'And the children can be quite unmanageable at times. They don't get on with each other. If I were you I wouldn't have a child at all.'

She gave an embarrassed little laugh.

'Why not just help me with mine? Perhaps you could look after Cherie for me tomorrow. I can't manage her. I think if I don't get help soon I will have to call in a social worker.'

She began to weep again.

'At least girls are easier to control than boys. Pray God you don't have a boy.'

King Kans was afraid of a boy also. Like Herod, he was told that he would die at the hand of a first-born boy who was allowed to grow up and become a man.

'I'm afraid I can't look after Cherie tomorrow,' I said.

'Oh.'

The sound had a petulant ring to it. There was another silence.

'Well, I'll tell Ma,' she said finally. 'I'll tell her that I can't get any help from you and perhaps she will be able to take her tomorrow.'

'Fine, you'd better ask your mother.'

'By the way, I might ask you to get me a little carved table made of sheesham wood when you go to India. Shanti brought one back last time she went. It is really lovely.'

'I don't know if we are going to be able to,' I said. 'I don't think we'll be able to carry it with us but I'll have a look for you.'

'Oh, they're very light. I'm sure you'll manage,' she said. 'Such lovely things you can get in India. But the really good things are expensive. I suppose if you've decided not to have children then you can afford them,' she added archly.

'I haven't decided,' I said. 'In fact we may decide to get pregnant very soon. Who knows, we may be parents by Christmas.'

Jyoti made an abrupt sound as though something had just given her a shock.

When King Kans sent Pootana to kill the child Krishna, the demon changed her shape and took the job of a nurse in the exiled family's home. One day when Krishna's mother was too ill to feed the baby, Pootana offered.

'I have plenty of milk in my breasts,' she said. 'Let me do it'.

She smeared poison on her nipples and put the child to the breast. But the child, being a god, did not die. He sucked until Pootana cried out in pain. And as she screamed he drained the life out of her and killed her.

'Well,' Jyoti said, obviously unsure what to say next, 'the first time you get pregnant people usually miscarry, so don't be upset if you do,' and then she hung up.

PHRENOLOGY

I am not sure what Priya would want us to bring her back. Ten days after her disappearance Bill rang my mother-in-law with news of a card he had received. It said very little other than the fact that she was well and was thinking of going to Gippsland to look for work. The front of the card showed a boat sailing on a lake with a small dog running along in the foreground. *Sail in Fine Waters*, the inscription on the card said.

'*Ki*? Does he honestly think that I am fooled by such a card?' said Gita. 'I am her mother. Do you really think,' she forced Milan to look at her as she said this, 'that a girl would buy a card like that?'

Milan looked at her mutely.

'No, she would not. This is a man's card. Anyone can see that. Men buy cards with dogs and boats. This card has been written by Bill himself to cover up what he has done to her.'

'It is probably not a good idea to make too many rash assumptions,' said Milan. 'We have no proof that there is anything wrong. We cannot accuse Bill without some evidence.'

'Evidence!' Gita almost dropped her cup of tea. 'There is too much evidence. And besides, I only have to look at Bill's face to know what is going on.'

'What do you mean?' asked Milan wearily.

'He has a mean nose, I can see it. A criminal nose. Your features always betray your character. You cannot hide it. A good person does not have a nose that pinches at the end.'

Milan looked at her.

'You know some people in the nineteenth century used to think you could read a person's character from the bumps on their head. They called it phrenology. Perhaps you'd like to examine his skull next time he is over.'

Gita said nothing. We were sitting at the dining table eating bitter gourd and rice. Gita had made a large plate of *luchis*, thin pockets of bread which swelled up with air when they were heated, to eat with the curry.

Eventually she said, 'I know you and your father think I am saying stupid things but you don't know what it is like to lose a child. For a mother it is a dreadful thing. You don't care. Soon you will leave for India and I will have to worry for you also.'

Her eyes were filling with tears as she said this.

'No, Ma, I do care,' Milan said, lowering his voice to a gentler tone, 'and I know how upsetting it must be for you but we must be careful not to get too worked up and start seeing things that are not there. I am sure that my sister will contact us soon. Let us give her some time.'

On top of the mantelpiece in the lounge room there was a statue of Lord Nataraj, the lord of dance. He was dancing in a frenzy, one hand beating on the drum of time, the other holding up the flame of destruction.

Jyoti had been listening to all this in silence. Now she said, 'Priya is so selfish, she thinks she can do anything she likes.'

'The trouble with this country is that no-one is really educated.' My father-in-law said as he balanced a large glass of beer on his stomach and sucked on his pipe furiously.

'If we had not come here,' said Gita, 'this would not have happened. My daughter has become a sacrifice to your whims. You brought us here. You wanted to go on this journey. I didn't. Now Australia has devoured our child.'

She began to weep profusely.

'It's not as though she has been gone for so very long,' said Jyoti.

'Exactly,' said Milan. 'Let's keep things in perspective. Our sister will return. Let's not get caught up in believing a story that no-one hopes will become true.'

PICTURES ON THE SARI

Seated in the back of the Hindustan Contessa I take out an album of photographs. Some of them are old and some are new. The new ones are still in their packets. I have not yet taken them out and placed them in their position in the album. This is probably because I do not know where they belong. They have not found their place in the narrative of pictures. On the front of one of the packets there is an inscription: *Dayal Nair's Bombay Pix. 24 Marine Drive. Mumbai.*

Underneath there is a photo of a happy Indian family, all wearing Western clothes except the mother, who wears a sari and has a speech bubble coming out of her mouth which says: *Capture your family on film Kodak for happy memories. Snap with Kodak—the Mahatma of film!*

I open up the packet and glance through it. They are snaps of Bombay.

I put this packet aside and open the album. These pictures are different. Some of them are old and yellowing, frayed at the edges. Others are glossy and new but they are not photographs of India. We have brought this album with us from Australia to show to relatives. At Milan's suggestion there are some early photographs of myself placed there as well.

Towards the end of the album there is a photograph of myself wearing a sari. I am wearing a purple Baluchari—an authentic hand-loomed sari from Bengal. The veil of the sari is splendid. In the picture I drape it around myself so it can be seen clearly. The veil is divided into embroidered segments which together form a story. Each box-like segment shows a scene of the story and the narrative, which is the tale of Ram and Sita, moves forward, like pictures in an album.

THE GOOD WIFE

The tall dacoit comes over to me. He stands near the cot and slowly strokes his chin. It is a deliberate movement carried out as though it has great significance. Perhaps it does.

'What kind of wife are you?' he says, putting great emphasis on the word 'wife' as if it is a foreign word that he has only just learnt. 'An obedient wife, a traditional wife, do you know how to make *paan*?

Do you lay your husband's clothes out on the bed for him in the morning and do you massage his feet when he comes home? Can you sing a *ghazal*? Play the *veena*? Would I like to eat your *masala*?'

He moves closer. When he opens his mouth I can see his red-coloured teeth all stained with the betel nut that he chews constantly. His clothes smell slightly rancid as though he hasn't changed them for several days. Then he laughs.

'No need to feel frightened,' he says. 'We are not rapists. It is your white men that sleep with women and take their honour. They are the ones who leave their families.'

Eight

VISHNU AND LAKSHMI

Vishnu and Lakshmi on their mount Garuda.—an opaque watercolour on cloth.

A god and goddess seated together on a giant bird which is flying towards the sunset. The god is blue and his consort is alabaster. She wears gold jewellery and a red Banarasi sari. Above and below them white cranes fly and their movement is mimicked by the great speed of the bird which is carrying the pair over the Indian countryside.

LEAVING THE CITY
In the early morning we drive through the streets of Mumbai. A brown dog with a curly tail roams the street, marauding. On the sidewalks people are

cooking. Women squat, saris over their heads, by a burning brazier and turn chapattis. From a window high up a song floats down to the street.

I sit in the back of the car wearing the *patola* sari, dyed by hand with saffron, madder and the juice of the rind of the pomegranate. Around my neck is the antique silver necklace and the antique fish bracelets are on my wrists They must have made other journeys before this. The five metres of sari material are suffocating and the blouse is so tight it stops my movements. As the car jolts along, I catch a glimpse of myself in the rear vision mirror: an Indian girl being taken to the house of her in-laws by her husband for the first time.

A FAMOUS MAGICIAN

Ranjit drives at a dangerous speed over the Indian road which is strewn with large gaping holes and small stones and boulders. He seems to be in a pensive mood. Perhaps it is because we did not buy enough goods from his cousins. What are the family implications here? Has Ranjit lost face? Will his in-laws take it out on him because he did not deliver?

'Are you knowing that I am a famous magician?' Ranjit says suddenly as we drive along. He looks at me sideways as he says it, a look of pride on his face.

'No, I was not aware that you were a magician. Do you know many magic tricks?' I say, quite taken aback.

I look at Milan, who grins silently in the back of the car.

'Oh, yes, many,' he says. 'Walking matchsticks, lying on sword tips, bottomless pot of water, swallowing unending ribbon.'

'What made you decide to become a magician?' I ask.

'From my father when he was a child,' Ranjit says. 'He taught me many things. He was the village magician.'

'Then why did you become a driver?' asks Milan.

'Very hard life, sir,' Ranjit replies. 'Very hard life. And my wife. She objects.'

'Is your wife in Bombay?' I ask.

'Not at all. She is in Nagapur, the town of my in-laws, with my children. My wife says she does not want our children to become sorcerers. My wife, you see, is a child of a dhobi. She is used to family having full enterprise. When my marriage was arranged my father did not tell her family that I had magical aspirations. Otherwise they would have objected. So in their eyes I am driver. I must pretend but that is not my big ambition.'

'You still want to become a professional magician?' I ask incredulously.

'Of course,' he says. 'Such a beautiful life. The life of an artist. You have heard of course of M.T. Bali?'

I have to admit that I have not.

'He is the king of magicians.'

Ranjit's face has taken on a kind of glow and his voice has dropped several notes as though he is in a sacred place.

'When he was alive there was nothing that M.T. Bali could not do. Ride bicycle on the water, fill magic pot, make things disappear. He prayed to Maya Devi, goddess of magic.'

THE INDIAN ROPE TRICK

'Would you like me to show you a trick?' Ranjit asks.

'What can you show us?' Milan says.

'Anything you like, sahib. I am full of variety.'

'Can you do the Indian rope trick? Can you climb up a rope and disappear?'

Ranjit looks perplexed.

'I could, sahib, but I do not have the equipment. It is necessary to have a special kind of rope. If sahib would like to invest in such a rope I would be very obliged and then I will show you a magnificent trick.'

'And where does one buy such a rope?' asks Milan.

'At Tanjore's, but that is in Mumbai. A great shop, sir, worthy of a visit. I can personally take you there when we return. I know the manager.'

Milan smiles.

'Magic has a very long history in India,' says Ranjit. 'You have heard, no doubt, of *The Mahabharata*?'

I nod.

'Then you will have heard the story of Abimanyu, the son of Arjuna?'

'No,' I confess. 'I have not.'

'The story goes,' says Ranjit, 'that when the Pandavas fought their enemy, the Kauravas, they found their enemy had built up a wall of shields that kept them safe as though it were a shell. The shell was protected by a special mantra. Only someone who knew the words could pass inside it. The only person who knew these words was the warrior Arjuna, but he was not there. As the warriors were discussing what to do, Abimanyu, the son of Arjuna, said: "I can help you because I know the entry code to the wall of shields. I heard my father tell my mother when I was in her womb".

'"Then open up the wall for us", the soldiers said, "and we will penetrate the magic phalanx".

'"I will", said Abimanyu, "but there is one problem. I do not know the exit code. Once I am in, I will not be able to get out".

'"Do not worry", the warriors said. "We will follow you in and force a way out. We will be right behind you".

'So upon their instructions Abimanyu approached the wall of shields and uttered the magic words he had learned. As predicted the shields opened and Abimanyu was able to enter the shell. However, as soon as he had penetrated, and before the other warriors could follow him, the shields closed up again. The warriors tried to find an opening but the shell was locked tight and they did not know the entry code. They were left standing there only able to hear the cries of Arjuna's son as he was killed by the Pandavas without their protection.'

'How dreadful,' I say. 'What a terrible story. How can that be of interest to a magician? Surely you can't open up a magical shield with a mantra like that. For one thing there are no magic shields. They do not exist now, if they ever did.'

'How do you know?' says Ranjit. 'Just because you think you have not seen a magic wall does not mean it is not there. And I believe magical words can unlock magical doors. When a magician is saying *abracadabra*, what is he saying if not a magical mantra, an entry code, if you will? I see only a small skip and a jump between *abracadabra* and *om nama shivaya* or *om mane padme hum*. The *Rg Veda* tells us that the vibration of certain words caused the cosmos to take form. We must respect that.'

'But it's a bit of a long shot with *abracadabra*, don't you think?' Milan interrupts. 'Next you'll be telling us that the phalanx of shields was actually a computer and that Abimanyu typed in his father's password after he saw *Welcome to Windows XP*.'

There is a silence as Ranjit considers this. 'I

know nothing about computers, sahib, but I'm not ruling out any computer significance,' he says finally. There is a hurt note in his voice. Clearly he is not sure if Milan is making fun of him.

NINE

M.T. BALI JUNIOR

We drive along in silence for some time until finally Ranjit says: 'You have heard, I suppose, of M.T. Bali Junior?'

My blank stare in his rear vision mirror shows that I have not.

'He is the elder son of M.T. Bali, who took over when his father died. He has also done many great things. Bicycling on the water, death defying escape from road roller, riding a bike without seeing, but the greatest of all is his disappearing act.'

'Oh?' I say. 'And how does that work?'

'No-one knows how he achieves these miracles, but I have personally seen him on live television make a whole train disappear. An entire locomotive with passengers was seen to disappear in broad daylight. It was shown all around the world. How could you have missed it?'

'I really don't know,' I say.

'Last month there was another miraculous sight. It took place at the Taj Mahal. A magical occurrence.'

'What happened?' I ask.

'Mr Bali made the Taj Mahal disappear—for two whole minutes. He performed a magical illusion while standing on the banks of the river Yamuna. None of the people watching could see the celebrated monument for that time. I heard one man fainted. The shock for him must have been so great. We Indians do not believe anything can ever happen to the Taj. Someone suggested that Mr Bali had simply hypnotised the crowd, but in the newspaper he has denied this. "I hid the Taj away from your eyes", he said. "It was a faultless illusion". It was in all the news. I am wishing very much that I had been there.'

'Perhaps he will do it again,' I say.

'I am very much hoping so,' says Ranjit. 'It was a disappearance of the first class.'

VANISHING POINTS

When light enters a gemstone it is slowed down, bent from its original path and split into two rays which travel along different paths at different speeds through the gem. When the refraction is great an object viewed through the gem can show a double image.

When Milan and I visited the Taj it was fully visible under a cloudless sky. We stood at the gateway looking down the corridor of water which leads up to the marble edifice.

'It seems so far away,' I told Milan.

'It is a trick,' he said. 'The minarets at the back are actually different in height from those in front: they give a false vanishing point. It's an optical illusion.'

The minarets tapered off in the distance. Behind them the river Yamuna flowed. Shimmering in the heat, the Taj seemed to be hovering in the air over the water garden.

'This is the tomb of Mumtaz Mahal, the wife of Shah Jehan. Her name means the Chosen One of the Palace. She was his favourite wife and she died giving birth to their fifteenth child,' Milan said.

The marble on the outside walls of the Taj was inlaid with garlands of fuchsias, tulips and jasmine, all created by inlays of red carnelian, green malachite, blue lapis lazuli and other precious stones whose names I did not know, each one chosen for its colour or iridescence. The detail was astonishing. Here and there, however, there was a gap, a hole where a flower had lost its stamen or its bud. Some of the walls were pitted with holes. It seemed like a great loss.

We took off our shoes at the entrance to the tomb and walked into a room shielded from the outside heat by walls of yellow marble veined with white. The quiet gave a feeling of a kind of absence. In the centre of the room a fretted screen of marble with lozenge cut-outs created small jewels of light on the floor.

Beyond the screen there were the two crypts. According to our guidebook they were empty. Beneath them, apparently in the vaults below, were the real remains of the Emperor and his favourite wife or, perhaps, as the book suggested, they were not there at all but cunningly concealed in one of the many secret underground passages.

'It really is difficult to believe everything you read,' said Milan. 'For instance, according to legend, Shah Jehan meant to build his own tomb on the opposite bank of the Yamuna in black marble but there really is no evidence to support this and, in fact, the way the crypt of Mumtaz is positioned, so off-centre, indicates that her husband expected to be laid in the centre on her right-hand side, his heart next to her: the traditional place for the husband to be laid in the Muslim faith.'

The tourist book I was carrying also claimed that at its completion, Shah Jehan had the artisans' hands cut off to prevent the reproduction of any other similar work.

'A terrible beauty,' I said. 'A monument to cruelty.'

'But once again, probably not true,' said Milan. 'Another one of the myths surrounding the Taj.'

Outside we reclaimed our shoes from the attendant and walked around the side of the building to look at the immense Yamuna river which flowed past.

As we were admiring the view a hawker came up.

'Ma'am, sir, you want to see Baby Taj? You want to buy marbles boxes?'

I said to Milan, 'I'd like to buy a souvenir to take back.'

'They'll take your money,' Milan said. 'Be careful. Buy something from the tourist shop instead.'

I went in search of the shop, leaving Milan to admire the river. As I passed the lotus pool, I saw, standing in front of the Taj, a little boy with one hand held up in the air. From a distance as his father photographed him it appeared as though he was holding up the dome of the Taj. In the developed photograph the most famous tomb in the world would, no doubt, appear like an exotic bauble dangling precariously from his tiny fingers.

I watched him for a moment. The late afternoon heat was still shimmering on the tomb's giant double reflecting in the water, which seemed almost more beautiful than the real monument. The Taj itself was glowing. The pale milky stone was beginning to turn orchid pink in the rays of the dying sun.

A girl with a cap of blonde hair was sitting on one of the stone benches in front of the Taj. She was very pretty.

I looked at her. She stared back at me and then smiled as though she knew me.

People say the Taj is slowly dissolving in acid rain. According to *The Handbook of Gems,* precious gems should be *unchanged by the temperatures, dust, abrasions and chemicals that they encounter daily.* But I wondered if they really were.

The shop sold goods from Agra and Jaipur.

'You're coming here a bit late, I think,' the shopkeeper said when he saw my camera.

'Oh?' I said. 'Why is that?'

'Why, last month there were a lot of foreign visitors here, taking photographs. For the eclipse.'

'What eclipse was that?' I asked.

'Complete eclipse of the sun, ma'am,' he said deferentially. 'A great sight. Seen best from the vantage point at Fatehpur Sikri. The sun went black and it was surrounded by a halo of light. Then there was a great orb of light at one end—just like a ring with a large diamond. The astrologers here said it was very auspicious. I am thinking that it was very lucky.'

I agreed with him that it was, then I bought an enormous marble elephant. It weighed several kilos. I would probably never be able to get it home. The belly of the elephant was hollow. Inside there was a baby elephant. It was a grey-green colour, like a pumice stone.

Milan and I paid a small boy to take a photograph of us sitting together on the bench with the backdrop of the Taj behind us and at our feet we placed the elephant.

That evening at our hotel I wrote a description of the girl at the Taj in my Book of Travel. Perhaps I thought that in this way she would become nothing more than just another part of the journey.

VULTURES NEAR THE TAJ

Our hotel, The Mogul Palace in Agra, was set in twenty acres of garden. The garden was surrounded by a high concrete wall along the top of which there were shards of glass embedded in the bricks, pointing upwards like knives. They had been put there to catch a small brown wrist or foot as it tried to enter paradise.

The hotel had mounted a powerful telescope in an outdoor observation tower in the pleasure garden. Through the telescope you could also see the Taj Mahal. On our second morning there Milan and I woke up early and climbed up the observation tower to see the Taj at sunrise. Through the telescope we could see the Taj turning pearly iridescent white in the first light.

Beyond the hotel there was a cluster of mud-brick houses. In front of the houses some children were playing. The lens of the telescope was so strong that I could even see into the courtyards of the houses. A woman came out of one with an urn on her head, her sari knotted round her waist so she could work. Her long brown arms clasped the urn. She squatted down and drew her veil over her head. As she adjusted the veil she looked up for a moment straight into the lens of the telescope. I felt ashamed, like a voyeur. I moved the lens off her face to a group of small boys playing cricket in front of the houses. Several local dogs were also chasing after the ball. At the edge of the game I noticed two other dark shapes. When I adjusted the focus I saw that the dark shapes were two vultures sitting watching the cricket game. Their long protruding necks were tucked into their powerful shoulders which were hunched up like American football players. Occasionally the ball rolled near them or a dog scuttled by in the dust and they lifted their heads just slightly. The boys were quite undisturbed by their presence. They might as well have been fieldsmen standing in the slips.

THE EVENING WITH STEPHANIE

The night after we went to the planetarium, Milan came home very late. I was lying in bed when I heard the front door latch click back in place. I heard him take off his shoes at the door and walk silently down the hallway like a phantom. His shadow appeared in the frame of the door. I lay very still. I could hear him breathing, trying in his clumsy male way not to disturb me.

As he lay down beside me I could smell the fruitiness of his breath, the proof of some bacchanalian festival that had taken place at The Spotted Dog after work that evening. He slid over in the bed and put his arm around my waist.

For some reason I am not even sure of now, I recoiled. He could not have known why because I did not tell him. All I could think of was Stephanie's face, her olive cream skin and her cap of perfect blonde hair.

I felt that if we were not careful, something could break. I felt it was a warning of what might be to come.

RAHU AND KETU

In the foyer of the Mogul Palace, in a room with a lattice window that looked out over the lobby, there was an astrologer. His name was Hari Gopal. Milan wanted to consult him before we left Agra.

I was suspicious. Most of these soothsayers, I felt, were just good psychologists.

'He probably analyses people as they sit there,' I said.

'But it will be fun, and something we can talk about when we get home,' Milan said.

Hari Gopal was a short man with a round Buddha-like face. He sat cross-legged on the divan in front of us. We sat in silence in his room while he did calculations and looked up ancient texts. Through the lattice window I could see the passers-by, who looked in curiously as they went. Occasionally Hari Gopal looked up and smiled and nodded his head from side to side as though he had suddenly discovered something important.

He filled in a sheet of information with my date

and country of birth. On the bottom of the sheet there were two squares with a grid of squares within them, drawn in pink ink. One said *Birth Chart*, the other *Moon Chart*. Each of the small squares had the name of a planet in it.

'Your father died very young. Your mother has restless thoughts,' the astrologer said to me.

I turned my face away from him and looked out of the window. How could he possibly know about my father?

'You were under the influence of the cusp,' he went on. 'You balance on the bridge. Things could go either way.'

When he had completed my horoscope he drew up Milan's details.

'Fear of abandonment,' said Hari Gopal when he looked at Milan's chart. 'Fear of trusting another. Saturn has brought misfortune to you. He has left you in the middle of a strange land from which you cannot escape.'

As he said this he fixed his large cow-like eyes rimmed with kohl upon us.

'You were taken from your home at an early age,' he said. 'The ruling constellation is *Hasta*, which means The Hand. In this case the Hand has lost its grip and has had to let go of something dear to it.

'The sixth bright moon in Gemini was present at your birth,' he told Milan. 'You will meet some-one from far away.'

My cynicism returned. Surely this was obvious? I was sitting next to Milan.

'They will abandon you,' the astrologer said with an impassive face. 'Ketu is in the ascendant.'

I felt a jolt of incredulity and anger. The astrologer was obviously a charlatan.

'This person will come back to their own country after a long time. They left someone there and then came back.'

The last sentence struck me as unusual. I suddenly realised that Hari Gopal was careless with his tenses. Time, my sense of time, the time of linear progressions, did not seem so important to him.

Grammatically, he was living in the past and present together. This did not seem to be a problem for him. So, the event could have already taken place. When had a foreigner abandoned Milan? I thought of the mother he did not recognise leaving him in India and then coming back to collect him so many years later.

'You understand,' Hari Gopal went on, 'the concept of Rahu and Ketu in the North and South Nodes of the Moon? This is the influence of Ketu. The Dragon's Tail or what some call the South Node of the Moon. Ketu is a malevolent force.'

I could see Milan was visibly shaken. He pressed his lips together until they were almost a thin line. He jutted his chin as though to defy this invasion into his secret life. I wondered if he was putting the interpretation on it that I was, or had he found another meaning?

I said nothing. I looked around the walls of the room we were seated in. They were covered with framed letters that the astrologer had received from faraway places such as Tampa, Florida, USA, or Balwyn, Melbourne, Australia. The letters praised the astrologer for predicting the circumstances of the letter-writers.

One writer was a woman from Melbourne. This woman wrote:

Dear Mr Gopal,

Since I visited you in 1999 many of the things that you told me have come true. I have recommended you to my friends and they will certainly consult you when they come to visit Agra.

Underneath the woman's letter there was a photograph of her. She had pale skin and black hair.

What was this girl doing in India, visiting an astrologer, I wondered. In the photograph she had the startled look that people sometimes get when the flash goes off in their eyes. Her disembodied head on the wall looked out of place amidst the Indian decor. As I stared at her I had an odd detached sense of my own identity. I saw myself seated on the edge of the astrologer's divan next to Milan: a girl with white skin and red hair dressed in a *salwar kameez* with a *doupatta* scarf draped around her neck and it seemed equally strange.

At the end of the session the astrologer gathered up our individual charts and made some final annotations. Then he turned to us both and said: 'Beware of unforeseen accidents. Make attempts to be on time.'

He gave us each a pink envelope with our charts inside. On the top of each chart his name was written: *H. Gopal. Astrological bureau.*

On the front of the pink envelope there was an astrological wheel and on the circumference of the wheel the words: *Your Destiny and the Stars—Astrology is the Eye of Fate.*

THE ENVELOPES

As Jesus goes through our belongings he comes across two pink envelopes.

'What are these?' he asks.

We do not answer. We are no longer in the mood to reply to every question. It has begun to occur to us that we are not as much use to them dead as we are alive.

On the front of each envelope there is a drawing of a chakra—the stylised Indian wheel of life. Jesus slits open one of the envelopes and reads: *Astrology is the Eye of Fate.* He laughs. 'Once your fate is sealed there is nothing you can do to change it. The stars only tell you what is ordained. Thinking that you can avoid what is inevitable by acting according to the stars is foolish. It is an illusion.'

TEN

THE MOONLIGHT GARDEN

'How were you finding the Taj when you were there?' asks Ranjit, as we drive along.

'It was very beautiful,' I say.

'They tell tourists lots of stories but most not true. Do you believe in the black Taj?'

'According to Milan it is just a story,' I say.

'A true story is the moonlight garden,' our driver says.

'What is that?' Milan asks.

'A garden for the middle of the night, sahib. It is opposite the Taj on the other side of the river. They have just found it.'

'You mean the garden is still there?' I ask.

Ranjit laughs. He has a mischievous laugh.

'No, madam, not there any longer. But they have found the remains. It is called Mahtab Bagh. The

Archaeological Survey of India have dug it up. It is a garden built by Shah Jehan to sit in at night and look at the Taj. The ASI say the black Taj was not a real place.'

'How do you know so much about the Archaeological Survey?' says Milan, suspiciously.

'I have previous clients, sahib, they have been to the Mahtab Bagh.'

'What is a moonlight garden?' I ask.

'A garden planted with all flowers and trees that show up well in the moon's light,' says Ranjit. 'The paths are all painted white so they can be seen at night. It is a beautiful Hindu garden with *champa*, *jujube* and *chirungi*.'

We sit in the car and imagine ourselves, not in the heat of the day, but walking along silver paths to the centre of a cool and fragrant world pale like a ghost beneath the moon. Amongst pools of sacred lotus and trees of fragrant large magnolias, small night birds fly to eat the fruits of the *jujube* and the sweets seeds of the *chirungi*.

I wonder what sort of clandestine meetings, reunions or betrayals, took place in night gardens such as these. They were, no doubt, a refuge for women who could not appear outside alone in the sunlit world. How many desperate liaisons and pleas for help were made beneath the white flowering *champa* with the moon's watery double as their witness?

◆

A NIGHT MESSAGE

It was in the middle of the night, before we left for India, that we received the telephone call from Priya. It was long distance and her voice had a weird echo to it as though she was speaking from inside a diving bell under the sea.

'Hello? Hello? Babu is that you?'

'It's Tilly,' I said. 'Milan is asleep. Shall I wake him?'

'Yes,' she said. There was an urgent note in her voice. 'Hurry, I've only got enough coins for three minutes.'

I watched Milan struggling with the receiver as he tried to wake up and comprehend what she was saying.

'You're *where*?' he said. 'Canada? What in God's name are you doing in Canada, Priya?'

According to Milan's account, there was a pause in the conversation, then Priya said, 'I've been mugged.'

The expression on Milan's face changed from surprise to absolute incredulity.

'Mugged? Mugged?'

I strained to listen.

'I've been in Canada with Roger for a week, but he had to go back to France so I am here on my own now and I am calling you from the Vancouver police station because last night a man jumped on me and took all my cash and credit cards. So what I need now is some money because I would like to come home. Do you think you could send me some?'

There was another pause. I think if Priya had told her brother that she had just taken a rocket to the moon and was calling him from a space station situated on one of the moon's seas of dust, he could not have been more shocked.

'Ma is very worried about you. She thinks you have been kidnapped and murdered. Do you think you could possibly give her a call and reassure her?'

He stopped for a moment and listened.

'Yes, first thing in the morning, I'll wire it to you.'

I could see he was irritated. He was drumming his fingers on the table that held the telephone.

'OK, OK, take care.'

He hung up the telephone and then, turning to me, said, 'My sister, the goddess, has been robbed.'

ENGLISH BAZAAR

'English Bazaar is a town in Bihar,' says Ranjit suddenly. As he speaks, he looks at me in the rear-vision mirror of the car. 'I am always wanting to go there.'

'It's an interesting name,' I say. 'Is that why you want to go there?'

'No, I am wanting to go there very much because of my grandmother. She used to live there.'

'Well, that's a good reason to want to visit, to see your family.'

'*Acha*, that is why I am taking you to see Devinagar.'

'What do you mean?' I ask.

'Just beyond this bend is my mother's village. None of her family live there now but the people still remember us. You don't mind if we stop?'

There is a silence in the car. I can tell that Milan minds very much but Ranjit now has the upper hand. We are in the middle of nowhere in a hired car and without his help we will not reach Shundarpur.

'Only for a very short time,' he says. 'We don't want to lose too much time.'

'*Tik ache.*' Ranjit accelerates enthusiastically and we hurtle around the bend in the road as if we are on the Grand Prix.

RANJIT VISITS A VILLAGE

The village is a collection of low mud-brick buildings. There is a large tree with enormous spreading branches in a central area and near this is a pump well and a shrine with a clay figure of a goddess with a garland of flowers around her neck and a tattered shawl of sari material tied around her shoulders. A small brown dog with a curly tail lies in the dust and jumps up when we drive past it. As we come to a standstill I see a young girl in a skirt and a buttoned-up *choli* blouse standing shyly watching us. She has large black eyes rimmed with kohl. They are fish-shaped.

Ranjit gets out of the Contessa and looks around proudly. He seems to be waiting for someone. Eventually an elderly man wearing a white dhoti and a brown waistcoat hobbles over. He has a stick and what seems like impossibly bandy legs. When he sees us he puts his hands together in the traditional greeting.

'*Ram, ram*,' he says to Ranjit, who reciprocates with the same words. It seems to be a customary way of invoking the hero Ram and at the same time making a salutation.

'My passengers,' says Ranjit proudly. 'Very VIP people. From Australia.'

The old man regards us for a moment and there is a look in his eye I cannot describe. Is it curiosity? Contempt? Or expectation? Then he nods his head. I glance at Milan. He seems uneasy. The old man begins talking to Ranjit very quickly in Hindi. Ranjit keeps on smiling and shaking his head in agreement. The old man seems very pleased.

'He is saying that he has been expecting me for this past week,' Ranjit says. 'Everyone is very excited.'

'Excited about what?' I ask.

'My magic show,' says Ranjit. 'They have been waiting a long time for me to return.'

'You mean to say we have stopped so that you can put on a magic show today?' I say.

'Oh no,' says Ranjit. 'Tomorrow is the auspicious day. The magic show is tomorrow.'

Milan looks thunderous.

'We are not staying here until tomorrow,' he

says. 'We are driving on to Shundarpur. That is
what you have been hired to do and I will not pay
you if you do not.'

Ranjit looks horrified.

'But, sahib, the company with whom the
Contessa is belonging, specifically,' he says the word
specifically with great emphasis on the exploding
vowels, 'specifically said that I am to stop in my
own village for one day. That is one of the require-
ments of my service. I am asking you only because
you are VIP people and I very much respect you.
They have already agreed. You must be knowing
this.'

'I know nothing like this,' Milan says, all the
while trying to avoid the gaze of the old man who
is now smiling and putting his hands together again
in greeting. 'For one thing, where are we to stay?
There is no accommodation for us here.'

'All is arranged, sahib, do not worry,' says Ranjit
triumphantly. 'The family of the Shakespeare
Bungalow Hotel is honoured to have you as guests.
They are used to foreign visitors. You will have a
very nice accommodation.'

Even as he says this Ranjit is taking our bags
from the car and placing them on the ground ready
to be carried off. A small boy appears as if from
nowhere and begins struggling with the larger of
our suitcases.

I get out of the car clumsily and look around. I
am feeling numb from the ride. The Contessa does

not seem to have very good suspension. I can hardly feel my legs.

'Does the bungalow have air conditioning?' I ask somewhat petulantly. 'Do they have double beds?'

THE SHAKESPEARE BUNGALOW

At the Shakespeare Bungalow Hotel we are shown into a room with an ancient slate-lined bathroom and a separate sitting room with windows overlooking the lake. A man with flat opaque eyes comes with us. He looks Tibetan. Once inside the room the Tibetan rushes excitedly over to a large television set in the corner of the room and with a flourish turns it on and begins to tune it in. After some minutes he stands back, obviously satisfied and apparently quite excited.

'Colour television, madam.'

These are the only words he speaks. Later that day when I turn on the set I watch a Marathi program which shows two men seated on a rug apparently conversing in Marathi about a potato which is placed on the rug between them.

The hotel is the former home of the English tax collector. As we walk down the passage to the dining room his picture can be seen hanging on the wall. Although once a grand place it is now looking old and dingy. The carpet is dark and threadbare in places; our room, although palatial in size, lacks hot water after eleven in the morning and the only means of heating is through hot water pipe heaters that cover the walls.

The dining room is furnished with old-fashioned rattan chairs and tables. We find we are the only guests. Despite this the chef has prepared a gigantic feast. He stands in a menacing fashion at the end of a table groaning with copper *bains-marie*, his arms crossed over his considerable belly, and watches us as we make our way down the line of dishes in frightened silence.

'What are they going to do with all this leftover food?' I ask Milan. 'There's no-one else here to eat it.'

'That's where you're wrong,' he says. 'Don't imagine for one minute that this is for us. There is an entire kitchen full of staff and other helpers who will be taking home what's left tonight. Don't look at it from our point of view. If you do you will be mistaken.'

WATCHING TELEVISION

We eat a lunch of *muttar panir*, curried fish and an interesting cousin of the zucchini which Milan calls *potol*. The chef scrutinises our every mouthful. I have the feeling that our choice of menu will have circulated the entire village by the time we have finished. No doubt next week the fried and stuffed zucchini will have changed its name to *potol VIP*.

After lunch we take a stroll in the English gardens surrounding the bungalow. Against the daub walls of the house there are hollyhocks and stock struggling in the heat. I take out my camera and try to insert a film. The spindle does not take up the film properly and, by accident, I wind it back too far. The end of the film disappears inside the spool. I am unable to retrieve it and do not have a spare film. The nearest shop that sells any kind of film is probably in Bombay or Shundarpur.

'I've wrecked the film,' I tell Milan. He looks at me.

'Don't worry about pictures.'

But I do. I prise open the end of the film spool with my keys and pull the dark unexposed film out into the daylight. Then I wind it back onto the spool. I am not sure how much of it has been exposed.

'Perhaps there is more film in your bag in the room,' I say to Milan. 'I'll go and check.'

I go up to our room to look. As I turn the key in the lock I feel it stop. I turn again and feel the same resistance. I reinsert the key and try again. Somewhere in the pit of my stomach a wave of fear is beginning to surge. What can possibly be stopping the key from turning? Suddenly the door swings open. Standing in the door frame is the Tibetan. He looks at me for a moment.

'Hello, madam,' he says.

I am at a loss to understand why he is here and why the security lock has been fastened from the inside. He leans over very close to me. I can feel his body heat. He observes me. Behind him in the room I can see that the television has been turned on. The Tibetan smiles. Has he simply been watching television?

The Tibetan gestures for me to enter. Ridiculously, I thank him and walk inside. I stand in the centre of the room and look around. I realise in that split second that I am actually too scared to question this man further. I should report the incident to the manager but it would be far easier just to accept it on face value.

I go into the bedroom and cast a cursory glance over my jewellery wrapped up inside the cupboard. I cannot immediately find anything missing. I go over to the door to ask him to leave but when I get there I discover that he is already gone.

THE OFF-SEASON

That night in Devinagar the heating in our room is so suffocating that Milan suggests we open the windows. The windows of our room have no screens and open up like French doors. If you stand at them you can see an enormous plane tree spreading its arms across the lawn below. In its branches I can just see the black silhouettes of some giant birds with powerful shoulders and drooping necks.

'Lots of eagles in Maharashtra,' Milan says.

Despite the cool breeze I sleep fitfully and not deeply. I dream I am in a shipwreck. Suddenly I am awake and see on the sill of the window a large dark shape. It looks like a demon or a succubus. Staring at it for a longer period does not change its shape. It spreads out two large wings like a satanic angel and lifts itself into the air. My heart pumps.

'Wake up,' I say to Milan. 'Wake up.'

He turns to me sleepily.

'What is it?'

I point wordlessly to the disappearing form.

'It's only a vulture,' he says. He puts his arm around me. 'Lots more things to worry about in India than birds,' he says. 'It's probably more distressed at finding us here than we are at seeing it. After all, this is the off-season.'

The next morning the young man who has been our servant for our overnight stay comes in carrying a flask of fresh drinking water. He is dressed in black pants and a white shirt and carries over his shoulder a red checked tea towel. He is a pleasant and polite young man. As part of his eccentric program of charity, Milan takes out one thousand rupees and hands them to him. The young man looks at the money silently with an expression of abject terror.

'This is your tip,' says Milan.

It is the equivalent of about forty Australian dollars. In India it is equivalent to about three months salary. The young man does not seem to know what to do.

'Put it away. It is for you to keep,' says Milan.

He looks at Milan in disbelief then he throws himself full length on the floor at Milan's feet.

'Sri, sri,' the young man says. When he stands up there are tears in his eyes.

Later I ask Milan why he gave such a large tip.

'For us,' he says, 'it just seems like a large tip. For someone like that it is enough to change their life. There are no social services here. Life can change dramatically if one has or has not. I can give out five rupees to every beggar I see or I can make a decision to do a few good acts. That is what I have decided to do. Besides,' he adds with a smile, 'wait until the Tibetan hears he has missed out.'

RANJIT PERFORMS A MAGIC TRICK

Magic develops in the hearts of the audience. When the audience cannot find a rational explanation for its hidden power, they give in to the world of illusion.

M. T. Bali Junior

Having read this piece of philosophy to a bemused crowd, Ranjit arranges a large piece of cotton material with appliqué work on the ground under the peepul tree. He seats himself cross-legged in the middle of this makeshift rug. In the centre of the rug he has placed a small skull of an animal whose origin we are not sure of. Milan comments that it looks as though it may be that of a mongoose. We

hear our driver begin to address the skull as though
it were a ventriloquist's dummy.

'Here's Rikkitikkitavi,' he says. 'Speak up, Rikki!
Should we take care? What will Ranjit the sorcerer
do that the eye cannot see?'

After this stirring speech he beams at us. Then
he leaves off speaking in English as though the
introduction was solely for our benefit and continues on in Marathi, so that the crowd of assembled
villagers can follow the proceedings. What happens
next needs no explanation in any language.

Ranjit takes a series of coins which were hidden
under Rikkitikkitavi's head. He places them in one
hand and holds each one up for the audience to
see. Then he puts them one by one into the other
hand and closes it tight in a fist. He beckons to a
young boy in the audience who comes up shyly
and, under Ranjit's direction, opens the closed fist
and examines the contents. Of course there is
nothing inside and when Ranjit holds up the
empty fist the crowd gasps. They gasp even more
when our magician plucks the missing coins from
behind the young boy's ears.

Next Ranjit does a trick which involves pulling
whole eggs and then a large rubber ball out of the
boy's mouth. It is all standard magicianship. Nothing
you would not see at any amateur magic show, but
the audience is entranced. Milan and I sit politely at
the back and clap and exclaim appropriately at the
right moments.

Then something changes. Looking back I realise now that the first tricks were just a way of warming up for our driver. They were not what the show was about at all. They were finger exercises. Suddenly Ranjit sits down alone in the centre of the cloth, places his hands on his knees and closes his eyes gently.

'*Ram, ram,*' he says, as though he is invoking the deity.

There is a hush in the crowd as if they were expecting this. When a little boy starts to cry his mother puts her hand over his mouth. Opening his eyes Ranjit takes the mongoose skull in both his hands and looks at it with great concentration. The crowd waits.

I find myself suddenly and inexplicably very tired. The air around us seems bright with sun and overhung with a fog of heat. As the atmosphere swirls there appears to be a density in the shimmer that parts momentarily around Ranjit's hands. I see a small head covered in what looks like fur and as I concentrate further it appears to move. It raises up and turns towards me and in the brightening haze gleam two black bead-like eyes.

THE WARRIOR GODDESS

> *. . . when the maiden Durga saw the buffalo demon coming at her to kill her, she took the unassailable form of fire.*

Milan has taught me that transformation is a common talent in India. The gods often assume different forms. The goddess on our lounge room wall is, he says, famous for her shifts in appearance. One of these occurred when she fought the buffalo demon. When the demon approached to attack her she took on the form of cosmic fire. She rode out of the fire on her lion in the form of a terrible warrior with many arms.

A copy of the *Vedas*, the ancient Indian texts, is one of the few books that I have with me in the cave. An English translation, purchased to read on the trip, has been left by the dacoits. Perhaps they feel that it will improve my Western mind to study it. I find it now oddly reassuring and exciting to read how a woman warrior once overcame her enemy:

> *Then Brahma and the gods came there and bowed to Durga, who had the form of the doomsday fire, and worshipped her by giving her all their own weapons . . . The magic Goddess, Durga, filled her many hands with blazing weapons, and she put on her armour and quickly mounted her lion. The terrible energy of Durga filled the very circumference of the skies, and when the buffalo saw it he fled, for he was unable to bear it.*

It is strange to me that I lie in a cave thousands of miles away from home thinking of a painting that hangs on the wall of our lounge room in Australia. It is stranger still that the painting depicts a woman one of whose forms the dacoits themselves worship. And that now I should be finding her image so comforting.

THE ATTEMPT TO STEAL THE GODDESS

Some of the walls of the village houses in Devinagar are decorated with paintings of the goddess. They have been whitewashed and the surfaces have been covered with two-dimensional figures in navy blue, dusty pink and black. The figures have aquiline profiles and large elongated eyes. I would like to ask about them but I am nervous in case it appears that I am one of those tourists whose sole interest is in acquiring the artefacts of the places they visit.

An attempt was made once to steal the goddess from my mother- and father-in-law. It was at a dinner party held by Gita to entertain several academics from the university where my father-in-law worked. One of them was a large American with a moustache. He admired my mother-in-law's cooking and the many art works my father-in-law had brought from India.

'Mighty fine meal, Gita,' he said. 'I guess Jiban is used to having such a fine cook at home but for me it is a real treat. Last time I was in India I ate myself silly.'

He went on: 'I hear that you have some

Shundarpur paintings. I sure would like to see those.'

My father-in-law puffed on his pipe.

'Actually we have several,' he said. 'Why don't we show you some while we have coffee?'

Jyoti was there with her two children. We sat down in the leather chairs in the lounge.

'I hate sitting on leather,' said Jyoti, smiling at the American. 'It just doesn't seem right. You know,' she looked at me, 'Brahmins don't sit in leather chairs.'

I looked at her Italian shoes.

My mother-in-law brought out three paintings. One was by Ratnamala Das, the other two were by Bimala Devi, her daughter. Two of the paintings represented moments in the marriage ceremony of Ram and Sita, the third, which was the painting now hanging on our lounge room wall, showed the goddess Durga riding on her lion. They had been stored under her house with some others, rolled up in pairs of pantyhose to protect them. The paper that they were done on was the coarse thick paper that was available to the artists at that time and the colours were from a limited palette of pink, red, indigo, ochre and black.

'*Bhalo chobi*,' my father-in-law said when he saw them. 'Beautiful pictures. They remind me of my childhood.'

'Let me tell you the story about these pictures,' he said to the American. 'Who would have thought that Shundarpuri pictures would become so famous? When we were children growing up we used to think of these pictures as just homemade decorations. Decorations put up on the walls for special occasions like a marriage or drawn on paper to use to wrap gifts.'

He paused to make sure that we were all listening. 'Then suddenly in the 1970s we find that an archaeologist has come here looking for the original art of the region.'

He stopped again and gave us a hard stare.

'Now this region, you understand, was there from the olden days. That means the days when the great epics were written, like *The Mahabharata*.'

I realised suddenly that the story had taken one of his unexpected twists, veering off at a tangent, to fill in some background information that the listener may not have been aware of, or giving another interpretation of the facts that they may not have thought of.

'Now *The Mahabharata,* you understand, was not set in this region. It took place in Mithila, which was an ancient kingdom. The plain of Kurukshetra, where the great battle between the Pandavas and the Kauravas took place, is there. That was where Arjuna took his chariot steered by Krishna through the battle and the god Krishna recited to him the Bhagavad Gita.'

My father-in-law went on but very few were listening to him with their undivided attention. In one corner of the lounge room there was a large

TV set. The set was on and you could see a succession of images dancing across the wide screen. The film on the television was *Interview with the Vampire*. The picture on the screen showed a young man with blond hair sucking the blood from someone.

Jyoti was talking in a very loud voice about the latest achievements of her son, Indy.

'Actually, he's very good at computers. His teacher has entered his project in the Victorian Schools competition.'

There was a scream as one of the vampires found a victim.

'If you have any problems with your computer I'm sure Indy would be happy to sort them out for you. He's going to start a little business as a kind of hobby. I'm encouraging him. Please encourage him too. He'll give you a discount.'

'Thanks, but I don't have any problems,' I said.

Jyoti raised one long slender arm and shook down a cascade of gold and glass bangles. She always wore a sari at family dinners. The millefiori brooch was pinned on the shoulder to keep the veil in place.

'Kishore likes to see me in a sari,' she told me. 'He says what's the point of my marrying an Indian woman if she can't dress to please me?'

There was a sudden pause in the conversation.

'I sure would like to get hold of one of those paintings,' said the American.

A group of vampires were walking down a darkened street.

My father-in-law looked blankly at him for a moment.

'In 1986,' he said, 'I visited India. The purpose of the visit was to do a *pindi* for my dead father. So naturally I had to go to Shundarpur. When I got there I saw that these women had started to sell pictures to tourists. And there were art collectors coming to buy them. I couldn't believe it! Even my own mother was doing paintings at that time. So I thought, well, I'd better purchase some paintings. Now there was an old woman there whose name was Ratnamala Das and that is her picture there. It seemed that her work was very highly sought after, so I went to her house. Her daughter, Bimala, came out and I said: "Can you get Ma to paint me a picture?"

'"Oh no", she said. "Ma doesn't paint anymore. She's too old".

'Well, what to do?

'"I can paint you a picture", Bimala said.

'"Just tell your mother to come out here", I said. "I want to speak with her".

'The old woman came out. She must have been at least ninety-five. She looked at me.

'"Don't you recognise me?" I said. "I am Chotu".

'"Of course", she said. "I remember you when you were little. You used to come to our house".

'So I asked her if she would paint me a picture and she agreed.

'"What subject should I paint?" she asked. "A Ganesha, a cosmic mandala, Baba with his trident?"

'But I asked her to paint me a marriage scene and a picture of Devi, which is what you see here. Her daughter did some pictures too and when she was finished she signed them in Hindi: *Bimala Devi*. So I asked the old woman to sign her name as well.

'"*Likiche na*", she said. Which means "I can't write".

'"I'll sign them for her", said Bimala.

'"Don't touch them", I said. "I want an authentic painting signed by Ratnamala herself".

'Then I got a pen and I wrote *Ratnamala Das* in Hindi on a piece of paper and gave it to the old woman.

'"Here", I said. "You're an artist. Copy this".

'So she did. With a ballpoint pen at the bottom of the picture she signed it. You see, you can just make it out, it's a bit faint, in the left-hand corner.'

We all looked. The American drew his finger lovingly across the name.

'So,' he said, 'I reckon this would be the only painting by her that has ever been signed. What a catch,' he said softly under his breath.

I looked at the painting and I saw the thin spidery blue lines of the words in Hindi. Then I looked at the painting. It showed the goddess with her head in profile like an Egyptian figure. The mouth of the goddess was bright red and the outline was painted in with a trembling hand that could not keep within the border of the sketch.

'What happened to Ratnamala?' I asked.

'She died a little while later, I believe,' said Baba.

'And Bimala?'

'Ah, Bimala, she's most likely still there. Yes, I believe she would be.'

'You don't reckon, Jiban, that you could spare this one, do you? I sure would like to hang it. It's a real piece of history.'

The American was cradling the canvas on his lap as he began to roll it up to replace it in the pantyhose. It did not look as if he was going to put it back in the pile of other nylon rolls on the coffee table. Gita stopped pouring coffee and looked at him.

'What do you know about the goddess?' she asked.

The American prided himself on his knowledge of India.

'I wrote a paper once, if I recall, about the phenomenon of this art. I am acquainted with Le Couvert, the author of the book. He's the archaeologist you are referring to, I believe. Hot dang! I'd really like it,' he said.

'This is not about papers,' my mother-in-law replied. 'The painting is not available. But you may like to buy yourself one next time you go to India.'

On the television the vampires had disappeared into the night.

'Sure, I reckon I will,' he said looking crestfallen. 'Reckon I will.'

When the painting arrived at our house from the framer, Milan hung it on a white wall so, at a distance, if you narrowed your eyes, you could, for a moment, imagine that it was a fresco painted on the whitewashed internal wall of a house in Shundarpur.

RESCUE

'Perhaps you are hoping that someone will rescue you? Or that you might escape?'

The tall dacoit says this. He seems to have a sneer on his face.

'Because if you are hoping that, you will be sorry. We will not be taken by surprise and when we decide to set you free, if we ever do, it will only be after we have been paid a proper amount.'

'And what will you do with this amount?' the aunt asks.

'We will put it to good use, sister,' he says. 'We will liberate our brethren from the yoke of the oppressor.'

'Oh,' I say, 'who are your brethren?'

'You would not know of them,' the dacoit says. 'Our people suffer. We will not be conquered.'

'We're sorry for your grief,' I say, 'but we are not to blame. We are not your oppressors.'

'Ah, but you are,' says Jesus. 'The West stood by and did nothing. They always do nothing.'

He looks at me sideways through his cat eyes. Green slits for eyes.

ESCAPE

Escape is a word that we all use a lot at the moment.

'Do you think that we can escape?' the aunt asks.

'If only there was a way out of here, a back entrance to the cave, perhaps, through which we could escape,' I say.

'The great Houdini could escape from any-where. No box, chains or locks could restrain him. If only we had that power,' Ranjit says wistfully.

Milan is the only one who does not believe we can get out.

'Escape is too dangerous. We are better off in here. At least inside we know what we are up against. Outside we have no idea where we are. You don't understand the concept of how these dacoits operate. Sometimes there are whole villages where the entire population is supported or run by the dacoits. At least whilst we are here we are protected from the rest of them.'

But escape is all some of us can think of.

SORCERERS

As Milan pays our bill at the Shakespeare Bungalow I sit on a chair near the entrance with our suitcases. I am wearing a hat with a wide brim which comes down over my eyes. As footsteps approach I look up. My eyes meet the face of the Tibetan, who bends down and looks up at me, sharing the space with me under the brim of my own hat.

'Hello, madam,' he says.

His voice is low.

I do not know what to say. I turn my face away and look out of the door. Surely a greeting cannot be a threat? When Milan returns I tell him.

'Get in the car quickly,' he says. 'Ranjit is waiting just outside the front door.'

He follows me, puts our cases in the car boot and then leaps into the back seat with me.

'Lock your doors,' he says. He winds down the car window next to him and, leaning out, yells to the doorman and the porter who are waiting expectantly to see us off: 'This is for you. Share it among yourselves.'

Then he thrusts a handful of notes into their hands. Standing a little way apart on the steps is the Tibetan. His face is contorted with rage. It looks like the hideous mask of some demon in an Indian dance.

'We'll never be able to go back there,' I say as we drive down the hill, laughing. 'If we do he'll cut our throats.'

'No, he'll just spread the rumour that we are evil sorcerers who came to the local village and enchanted the people,' Milan says. 'The next bad thing that happens hereabouts will be blamed on us. He'll say that Ranjit was just our familiar who did party tricks while we did our real work. Indians like magic because they believe in illusion and trickery. That's how they view the world.'

Eleven

TRUST

'If you think that you can trust my brother, then you are wrong,' Jesus says to me out of the blue. 'If he says he will not harm you, do not believe him. His mood changes with the weather. I believe that he does mean to abuse you if you do not cooperate.'

He is smiling. I am not sure if he is giving me advice or threatening me. Does he support his brother's changeability? Is he telling me this because he wants to protect me from an errant colleague who is quite obviously not his brother? Or is this pressure being brought to bear to make me more malleable?

'You must be careful of my friend. He is not at all stable. He would like to shoot you. He hates Westerners,' Jesus says.

He is squatting down surveying us all as though

we were his protégés. He smiles. He has a sensitive well-drawn mouth.

'I can protect you,' he goes on. 'But only if you do what I say.'

DEAD FLESH

There is someone else in the cave. We can hear his voice. He is talking in a low voice. I am trying to catch the sound of the language he is speaking. Suddenly Muni comes in. He places on the ground before us a large plate with some pieces of chicken on them. But it is not exactly a plate, rather a large leaf, a makeshift serving dish.

'Big surprise,' he says, eyeing me. 'Grand meal.'

He gestures at the food with the air of someone who has taken full credit for what has just been produced. I am sure Muni has not cooked it. The only stove is in the corner near our beds. We would have seen him, so it has been brought in from outside. Someone else knows we are here.

'Eat,' says the Kashmiri.

I pick up a piece of chicken leg and sink my teeth into it. It is good. Succulent, aromatic, just lightly spiced.

'Why are you not eating?' Muni asks Milan.

There is a silence in the cave.

'I am a vegetarian,' says Milan. 'I don't eat dead flesh.'

The dacoit's eyes widen in disbelief.

'You are a vegetarian?'

'Yes,' says Milan.

'What sort of joke is this?' the dacoit says. 'You are not religious. You are not even a proper Indian. You have no beliefs that prevent you eating this. Don't tell me inside that Western dress there is an orthodox sadhu. I will really laugh.'

Milan says nothing. What is a proper Indian? I have often wondered what would make me one.

DIWALI

The previous year Gita had arranged a party at her home to celebrate Diwali, the festival of lights. An old friend of the family, Mrs Fernandez, was there with her husband and son.

'Tilly, you look just like an Indian girl. I wouldn't have believed it. You look so authentic,' she called out when she first saw me.

I was wearing a *salwar kameez* that Milan had bought me in a sale at Taj Bazaar in Carlton. It had green pyjama pants, a tunic with green and orange checks and a long scarf made of green silk threaded with gold. I felt like a character out of a pantomime.

Outside on the patio Gita had arranged some long candles on a table and around them some plates of *samosas* and *pakhoras*. I had brought with me a gift of a 'tea light tray'. It was an aluminium tray with round holes in it which were supposed to hold small flat candles. When I gave Gita the tea light tray she exclaimed: 'How thoughtful! How wonderful. It's just what we need.'

The tray was placed with great ceremony on the table and filled with tiny lights which were then lit. The electric lights were turned off and the children and the adults were given unlit sparklers. The table looked like a sea of light floating in the dark. We leant forward and placed the long thin wands of the sparklers in the little fires. For a moment as you held the grey stick in the flickering flame it seemed as though nothing would happen then, suddenly, there would be a splutter of silver snowflakes and the dead stick would erupt in a cascade of sparks. The children shrieked and ran around the back yard making circles of sparks in the warm night air.

Mrs Fernandez came and stood beside me. In the dark all I could see was a shadowy version of her face like a waxwork.

'Tilly,' she said, 'such a lovely *kameez*. You look so pretty. Just like a Kashmiri girl,' she laughed. 'You know, Tilly, I have just seen such a film. It was such a story. I felt when I had seen it like I had eaten a piece of chilli. When I saw you looking like that, it immediately made me think of it.'

'What was the film about, Auntie?' I asked.

'Terrorists,' she said. 'It was about the assassination of Rajiv Gandhi. A great and wonderful film,' she said. 'It made me think of you because Milan always reminds me so much of Rajiv. The resemblance is quite strong, I believe.'

When Mrs Fernandez said the word *terrorists*,

she rolled the r's in such a way that it made the word sound more frightening than it already was.

'You must see it,' she said. 'When I saw you dressed up like that immediately I thought how much you would enjoy it.'

She gave me a shrewd look.

'Australian men are such rapists. I never would feel comfortable if any of my girls went out with one. But it seems that Australian girls are different. An Australian girl can take on the views of her husband. Just look at you, a real Kashmiri girl.'

Something similar was said to me once in the Shalimar Gardens in Kashmir by a photographer, a small man in a waistcoat and embroidered hat who held up a cardboard album of photographs.

'Madam, have your photo taken as a Kashmiri girl!'

He opened the album and I saw photo upon photo of foreign women dressed in traditional Kashmiri wedding dress.

'*Nahi,*' I said. 'No photo, thank you.'

'But, madam, you are looking so much the part. I am thinking you must be Kashmiri. A beautiful Kashmiri girl. You have the look.' He proceeded to take out from a suitcase by his side the props for the photograph: a long chiffon headscarf and a coin necklace.

It was not unusual in Kashmir to see a woman with white skin and blue eyes, even red hair. He was right. I could belong.

'No thank you,' I said. 'I am not Kashmiri.'

I was not sure what Mrs Fernandez expected me to say. Did she want me to tell her that I had become an Indian girl and that was why I was dressed up like one? How could I tell her that I felt I had nothing in common with a girl who had been brought up in a valley of Kashmir cut off from the rest of the world by the Himalayas? How could I tell her this without being rude?

KASHMIR

I want to ask Jesus if he comes from Kashmir but I don't dare. Conversing, setting up a dialogue with your captors, is surely the course recommended by the experts. I have been to Kashmir. It is a topic we could share but one look at the dacoit's eyes makes me stop. His narrow green eyes shine unnaturally when they meet mine. It is as though there is a reflection between us that stops us both seeing the real person.

I could tell him that Milan and I travelled to Kashmir, arriving there on a snow-cold day and that, as our plane circled down over the airport, we saw a grey-coloured landscape dotted with silver birch trees. I could also describe the shock of the change from Agra, which was extreme. The flight had crossed over the Himalayas. But even before it had left Agra we noticed how different our adventure was becoming.

WALKING THE TIGHTROPE

At the airport a young man in front of us at the luggage check-in wanted to carry a transistor radio on board, but the officer on duty said: 'No! It is expressly forbidden. The taking of electrical equipment is not allowed. There will be no exceptions. I am telling you this but you are not listening.'

The passenger kept on smiling. He was one of those people who felt that no harm could ever come to themselves from a terrorist bomb in a plane. He did not realise how easy it was to be killed in Kashmir.

Once on the plane Milan and I found ourselves seated opposite one of the main doors. An air hostess approached the open door and began to close it. She was a slight girl and her arms were impossibly slender. As she strained to close the door another hostess came up to help her. Together they pulled the large circular hatch until it was brought into line with the oval piece of sky in the doorway and clamped shut.

We flew north from Agra across Madhya Pradesh, the middle ground, as the name meant, towards the roof of the world, the home of Mount Kailash, and Mount Meru, the magic mountain, the home of the gods.

'It's wonderful,' said Milan, gesturing towards the window. 'Just look.'

Outside our window I could see several snow-covered peaks coming up through the clouds. The pilot appeared to be threading his way through the maze of peaks as though he were weaving a cloth. I looked down into the abyss below and I imagined us suddenly losing our upward thrust and catapulting into the depths.

'I can't,' I said. 'I can't look down.'

'You can't afford to miss this,' Milan said. 'It's the opportunity of a lifetime.'

His eyes deepened with excitement. I felt like a tightrope walker who could only continue along the narrow thread in front of them as long as they did not look back or down.

As we approached Srinagar and the plane began to descend in a spiral towards the valley of Kashmir, two airline officers came down the aisle and stood in front of the door opposite us. They began a charade of nodding and shaking their heads, occasionally bending down to inspect the seal around the locked hatch.

'Look,' I said to Milan. 'There's something wrong with the door.'

'Nonsense,' he said. 'There's nothing wrong. They're just inspecting it.'

'No', I said. 'There must be something wrong. Those girls didn't shut it properly.'

Sometimes in your life you can develop a way of thinking that makes you see everything through a veil of impending disaster. You become, in fact, a human seismograph, a needle on a scroll of paper waiting for the first tremor to send you quivering over the page. Several people within earshot of our seat turned and looked at us as they heard me speak. I felt embarrassed. Surely they realised how tenuous life was, that even the smallest crack in a door's rubber seal could, over a period of time, lead to our disintegration?

According to Milan, many Indians still believe that the world is held up by four cosmic elephants. When one of the elephants moves, this produces an earthquake. This is a Vedic view of the cosmology. Most Westerners believe that the Earth's surface is made up of fragmented plates which fit together. When two plates collide or move apart, this causes an earthquake—this is the theory of Plate Tectonics. Neither system of beliefs, however, can accurately predict when a disaster such as a plane crash or an earthquake or tidal wave will actually occur.

My father-in-law will tell you that the dangerous places for people to live are the areas that lie along boundaries or edges.

YOUR GOOD NAME

The interior of Srinagar airport was lined with wood and was heated. As we were leaving the terminal a man wearing a small fur hat stopped us.

'Excuse me, sir, may I know your good name?' he addressed Milan.

It was an archaic form of address. Elsewhere in India, when foreigners leave an airport, an army officer at the exit booth yells: 'Name and destination?' in a practice designed to protect travellers from unscrupulous drivers who might take them off to the hills, cut their throats and steal their valuables. But in Kashmir, where time has stood still, people still spoke about your *good name* as though it mattered who you were.

'And may I know where you are destined?' the gentleman continued.

After Milan gave him our particulars, he said, 'May I welcome you both to Srinagar and wish you both a very pleasant stay in Kashmir.'

He said nothing about how foolhardy we were to be travelling to an area where tourists were now warned not to go, an area of civil strife and frequent hostage-taking. But perhaps he believed that we would be safe because one of us was obviously an Indian. As he walked away I looked at this gatekeeper from another world. He had a long narrow face with heavily lidded eyes. The face of a poet, I thought. But who could tell?

PAHALGAM

In Srinagar a local guide took us on a sightseeing tour. His name was Rijul Singh. Looking back, now, with hindsight, I fervently hope he was not one of Ranjit's cousins. We asked Rijul where we could go that would be of interest. We asked him to show us the real Kashmir.

'I can take you to Pahalgam, madam,' he said.

The drive up to Pahalgam was mountainous and cold. The car's engine spluttered in the thin air. We could hear the revolutions increasing as the car attempted to climb into the foothills of the Himalayas.

'What type of car is this?' I asked.

'This is a Premier Padmini, an Indian make of car, madam,' our guide said. 'It is named after one of our folk heroes: Padmini, the Rajput queen of Dewar.'

'Why is she a hero?' I asked.

'She walked into the fire with her handmaidens, madam.'

'Why did she do that?' I asked.

'To avoid being captured and raped by the invaders, of course.'

We stopped by the road and looked down at the winding rapids fresh from the snow churning over the black mountain rocks surrounded by pines. Milan took my arm and stood with me on the crest of the road looking down at the scenery.

'Is everything going according to plan, Tilly?' he asked.

'What do you mean?' I said.

'Are we OK?'

'Yes,' I said.

'Because you don't seem to be OK.'

'No, I am,' I said.

'It's difficult, you know, to travel in India if you are a foreigner.'

'Well, I am not being greeted everywhere with open arms but I can understand that. After all, my ancestors pillaged their land.'

He sighed.

'You know, whatever happens, that you are my

life. If all this is too much we can leave. I'm only here for you—because you wanted to come.'

It was a very steep drop down the mountainside from Pahalgam. And it would have been easy to slip from the edge over into the abyss. I looked into his large eyes.

We hung in each other's arms over the precipice, feeling the other's heartbeat against our own. Breathing in short sharp gasps of desire.

THE SHIKARA RIDE

From Pahalgam we drove down roads lined with poplars and houses with steep wooden roofs. When the car slowed down we saw to our right an endless expanse of blue dotted here and there with an early lotus. The water's edge came right up to where the footpath began. There was a sign erected on the path: *Keep Dal Lake Beautiful.* The car stopped and we sat for a moment in silence.

'Dal Lake,' Rijul said, as though we were not able to understand this for ourselves. 'All the celebrities that I drive like to stop here,' he said. 'Some like to picnic as well, and of course they all take a *shikara* ride.'

I had seen large billboards in Mumbai advertising the fact that the actress, Dimple Kapadia, spent her summer every year in Kashmir. According to Milan, during the high season in Srinagar, before the political unrest had begun, the town used to be thronged with Indian film stars and politicians.

By the side of the lake there was a cohort of *shikaras*, long boats which looked like gondolas, moored together. There was also a gathering crowd of locals who all looked like they could steer a boat.

After one of the boatmen had drawn his boat up to the jetty, we boarded and sat in the stern as he moved the *shikara* off with a long wooden pole. Our vessel glided effortlessly down one of the canals. Beyond the main body of the lake there were countless small waterways that led through the vegetation. The water was like blue agate.

'Are there many flowers here in spring?' I asked the boatman.

It was a stupid question to which even a blind man could possibly know the answer, but I felt I must engage. Otherwise what was I but another tourist, another impostor?

As we floated over the lake the boatman began to sing. It was apparently a package deal. Much like the gondoliers in Venice who serenade lovers as they travel the waterways. He did not have a good voice but the intensity of the rendition made it seem musical.

'What are you singing?' I eventually asked him.

He looked at me intently, as though gauging how deeply he might respond.

A knife at the throat is preferable to the sorrow
Of lovers who cannot touch.

'It is a song of love,' he continued. 'You cannot know what it is like to be losing your beloved.'

THE VOYEUR

But how would he know what a memsahib thought? How would he know how hard I tried, sitting there in his *shikara,* not to think about Milan and Stephanie?

As we drifted through the carpet of water plants, a scene arranged itself in my imagination. I saw Milan and Stephanie in her flat. There was a Japanese paper lantern hanging from the ceiling visible through the lounge room window. There was a small alcove in one corner of the bedroom with an arched window where Stephanie used to sit in the late evening reading by the light of a metal lamp.

But now, in this reverie, she was not there. She was seated in a white bathrobe on the floor of the lounge room watching television. A tall figure came up behind her and placed his arms around her. Then both she and Milan got up and I saw them walking through the length of the apartment until they reached the farthest room at the end where he stood up for a moment at the window and lowered the Roman blinds slowly, section by section.

TWELVE

THE PENITENT

'*Acha*,' says Ranjit suddenly. 'Shundarpur.'

The news takes me by surprise because I can see no sign of the town. Apparently there is some indefinable way of understanding that we are near the metropolis and only Ranjit knows this.

Soon, however, I realise that he is right. The occasional house and people travelling on foot reveal that a town cannot be far off. As we drive along the landscape begins to take on a familiar look. I wonder how this could be because I have never been here before. Then I remember the photographs in Milan's family album. I see the dry river bed with the palms growing up around it and the women in their saris tied in the local style, and I know that we are returning to the landscape of Milan's childhood.

An old woman is walking along the side of the road. She is not walking normally but hopping on one leg then the other. As she does this she flails her arms from side to side as though she is whipping herself. When I see this I realise what she is. She is a penitent. Someone who has made a pact with the gods that she will perform some act of self-mutilation or sacrifice if they will forgive some indiscretion or grant a boon. I hope it is worth it.

The depth of the obsession that people like this have in India has already shocked me. Whether it is to pay for something or to subjugate the flesh in some bizarre ritual to obtain something, there is always an example of it not far away: men who refuse to cut their fingernails on one hand until they are five metres long, others who bury themselves up to the neck in sand or who make long pilgrimages on only their hands and knees.

Before we came here I would have been more critical but, as my own drama with Stephanie unfolds in my mind, I have begun to realise how much something can imprison you.

SHUNDARPUR

'What will you do while we are at Takuma's?' I ask Ranjit.

'I'm visiting my family also,' says Ranjit.

'Oh?' I say. 'Do you have relatives in Shundarpur?'

'*Ha*, naturally,' says Ranjit. 'My sister's husband's

aunt, his *pishima*, is living in Shundarpur. Also my mother's brother's wife's nephew. He is also there.'

In an Indian family, the links between its members that would seem tenuous in my family are like pieces in an indestructible web that spread further and further out but never break away from the centre that holds them.

'Where does your family come from originally?' I ask Ranjit.

He looks at me seriously.

'Actually,' he says, 'on my father's side we are coming from Durgapur. But none of us are living there now, except one of my uncles.'

So this was the centre of the web—the ancestral village. In travelling back to Shundarpur we are going back to such a place. A place that resides in the thoughts of the whole family even if, scattered all over the globe, they have never been able to go there. *Shundarpur*, meaning Beautiful City—how the name must linger in their minds.

We are travelling by this time along a narrow dirt road that winds through the outskirts of Shundarpur. Occasionally a truck or a bullock cart passes us. Ranjit begins to hum a popular song. Then, as the approach grows nearer, he drums his fingers on the dashboard in an accompaniment. As he does so a large dilapidated old bus rounds the corner. Its bonnet is decorated with two large eyes, no doubt to help it see. As it makes the turn, however, the eyes seem to blink, because it veers off-centre. At the same time Ranjit, caught in an ecstasy of song, takes his hands off the wheel, momentarily.

We hit the bus on the corner of its front bumper. The shock of the collision reverberates through the whole of the Contessa. I am thrown over on the back seat. Milan falls on top of me, Ranjit hits the dashboard. Miraculously no-one is hurt. But for a moment it seems that our whole world has been thrown upside down.

'Son of a pig!' Ranjit yells out the window at the driver. 'Look at my car! I am carrying VIP passengers. How dare you hit the vehicle of such persons.'

The bus is taking local villagers to another neighbouring town. Now they put their heads out the window and stare down at us in the car. I look up and see a pair of eyes studying me intently from the vantage point of a bus seat several feet above me. A large fat man with a bald head and crooked teeth leers down at me, sitting there, resplendent in my sari.

Suddenly, from out of nowhere, people begin to congregate to see what has happened. Some hawkers begin to peddle green coconuts. We get out of the car while Ranjit and the bus driver argue vociferously in Hindi.

I am still sitting in the car when an old man comes up. He jigs up and down in front of me, excitedly, brandishing an object in his hand.

'Ma'am!' he shrieks, proffering the goods for me to see. 'Ma'am! Very old.'

He waves in front of my eyes a silver bracelet so encrusted with verdigris it appears to be almost black. I shake my head. The hand continues dancing about in the frame of the window.

'No,' I say. 'Thank you. *Nahi*.'

I look at the silver bracelet. It is probably tin and rolled in the dirt that morning to make it look old.

'*Bhago*,' I say. 'Go away. I don't want it. It's dirty.'

He reaches out and tugs at my sleeve while still dangling the bangle in front of my nose.

'How dare you,' I say, turning and looking him in the face. 'How dare you touch me. Leave me alone. I don't want your bracelet. Go away.'

But as I say this I hear my voice trailing off into the dry dusty air around us. It does not sound like my own. I see the astonished look on his face as he understands that I am angry and I realise that the voice I am using is my grandmother's.

SANDESH

Ranjit takes the wheel of the Contessa again, which is remarkably undamaged despite its ordeal. I look out of the window. Far away in the distance I can hear a faint rumble like the sound of gathering rain clouds.

'What do you think is making that noise?' I ask Milan.

He shrugs. 'Perhaps a storm is brewing.'

The storm continues to gather as the car drives along the road to Takuma's house. People are beginning to come out of their houses and shops to fasten down shutters and awnings. As we pass the owner of a small roadside stall tying down his rattan sun blinds I look up and see a sign which says *Turmeric Vanishing Cream* hanging over the shop. *For a natural complexion, to add lustre to your skin,* the sign says. Underneath this is another skin care product: *Lakshmi Soap—for the perfect countenance, reach the sublime, look like a goddess with this pure Ayurvedic soap.*

In the next shop a table is covered in doll-like statues of gods, goddesses and saints to put on the household altar. The clay figures are painted in brilliant colours. The goddess wears a red sari decorated with gold and has an ivory face above which there sits a golden crown. Her dark eyes are painted in, large and almond shaped, and her mouth is red and curved. Next to her is a statue of Krishna with brilliant blue skin, playing the flute.

We stop at a small sweet shop outside the town and Milan goes in to buy some *sandesh*. He comes out empty-handed.

'There's none left,' he says. 'He's already sold it.'

He looks at me.

'How dreadful to arrive without any *sandesh*.'

THIRTEEN

THE FAMILY HOME

The Chaudhari family home is a brick house with two storeys; the top storey belongs to Takuma, who has her own kitchen and servant so she can follow the dietary laws and restrictions placed upon a widow. According to Milan, who gives me a short lecture as we drive along the winding dirt road up to the house, she does not eat with the rest of the family and she does not allow anyone who is not of the Brahmin caste to set foot on her level. In general, I am told, Takuma does not like non-Brahmins to visit the house at all, and the rumour has spread in the family that Takuma refused to receive her granddaughter and her husband because the girl had married a man of a caste below her.

'Really?' I say. 'Will she receive me then? I have no caste at all.'

Milan looks perplexed. 'I don't know,' he says. 'We will see. Just remember, if she refuses to touch you she is not being rude; she has no choice.'

When the Contessa stops in front of the house and I climb out of the car, my legs are numb from the bumpy ride. When I put my feet on the ground it is as though there is no ground beneath them at all.

Milan's eldest paternal uncle and his wife, his Borojatha and Borojathima, or Big Uncle and Big Auntie, come to meet us at the door. I see the look in their eyes immediately. What is a real memsahib doing dressed in a sari? It is almost a look of disillusion. Where is my printed English dress and straw hat? I take off my shoes at the entrance to the house as the others do, but the Big Auntie insists that I put them back on again.

'You do not have to do these things,' she says. 'It is not expected.'

Once inside, however, I fervently wish I had removed them because I am the only person in the house with shoes on. The others are walking barefoot on the floor.

We are taken into a bedroom on the first floor where we sit awkwardly on a small sofa, our hands folded, and after a moment's silence Big Auntie says, 'Would you like some *sandesh*?'

Ten *sandesh* come on a large plate with one spoon. They are put in the centre of the table in front of us.

'Eat,' says Big Auntie, smiling. 'Eat.'

I look at the ten white balls glistening on a large metal plate. I don't know how to eat them. I look at Milan.

'What do I do?' I ask.

He shrugs. I had expected the *sandesh* to come in individual sweet dishes with small spoons, as Gita usually served it. I expected to be able to pick up one of the spoons and delicately eat one or two balls of the white curd. This plate is so large it is overwhelming. I look at Milan.

'What do I do here?' I whisper. 'I have no idea of how to behave.'

He looks at me.

'I don't know either,' he says. 'This isn't my home now, you know.'

I look at the plate. The white balls sit there, coarsely granular and untouched, each one studded with a blot of pink food colouring.

'*Kau*,' says Big Auntie.

I know this means 'eat' but I pretend I cannot hear. Perhaps the locals will say in years to come: 'Remember the year the memsahib came dressed in a *patola*? And she refused to eat the *sandesh*? *Sandesh*, you see,' they will say wisely, 'is not something a memsahib eats.'

THE MESSENGER
Ranjit has gone to visit his relatives in Shundarpur. Before he left I asked him how we could contact him when we were ready to leave.

'There is no need, madam,' he said. 'I will know. Just tell the *wallah* at your Boropishi's house. I will get the message.'

'Who are your relatives?' I asked.

He looked sideways at me. Clearly this was something he did not want to tell me.

'They are not VIP people, madam, so your uncle will not know them.'

THE QAWWALI SINGER

After the *sandesh*, people start to arrive from the neighbourhood to see the overseas visitors at the Chaudharis'. Takuma is still at the temple, which apparently she now visits five times a day. A widow, it seems, has very little to do but prepare for her eventual union with her dead husband in paradise.

'This is our friend, Mrs Sen,' Big Auntie explains, presenting a lean middle-aged woman in a cotton sari who smiles and nods. Mrs Sen only speaks Bengali, so we have to make do with sign language and use the aunt as an interpreter, but Mrs Sen does not seem inclined to talk anyway. She simply smiles and observes us.

'We have prepared some entertainment,' says Big Auntie proudly. 'We thought you would like to hear some music so Hamid, our qawwali singer, is coming to give a performance. He will be here shortly.'

A young servant girl had been standing by the

doorway dressed in a short skirt and pink blouse. Having disappeared for a moment, she suddenly reappears in another outfit, this time a different coloured skirt and a peacock green blouse. Her face is flushed and she looks up at us shyly as though to gauge our response.

'We gave her some new clothes, for the occasion of your visit,' Big Auntie says softly. 'She is giving you a fashion show.'

As we wait for Takuma, Big Auntie takes me up to the second storey where there is a bathroom with a Western style toilet. As I am descending the stairway again, after I have left the bathroom, I trip on a corner of the sari. I feel my feet miss the next step and I almost fall down the spiral staircase. I stand on the landing about to go down the next flight, trembling uncontrollably. What if I had gone head over heels down the steep spiral and fallen dead on the hard concrete at the bottom? That would be the making of another legend. I think of the old crones of Shundarpur sitting outside their front doors gossiping.

'It is Mother's will,' they will say. 'She was supposed to die. It was the wrath of Durga.'

MIDDLE AUNTIE

Milan's other aunt, his Mejopishi or Middle Auntie, has come from a nearby town to see us and to hear the qawwali singer. She will be returning to Bombay in the car with us to see her son. She has brought an album of photographs to show us. One of them is of her house. It shows an entrance hall which is paved in bubblegum pink and green marble.

'We have just had the house redecorated,' Middle Auntie says. 'We went on vacation while it was being done and the *wallah* chose the colours. Doesn't it look pretty?'

The servant is giving us tea and *nimki* which we eat in the bedroom adjoining the kitchen.

'What happened to all your old furniture?' asks Milan. 'The beautifully carved chairs and table?'

'Oh those things,' his aunt says. 'They were chopped up for firewood ages ago. They were terrible dust catchers. We have gone all modern. It's so much more convenient.' The photograph shows some vinyl chairs at a laminex table covered with a plastic embroidered tablecloth.

There is silence. We sit in the damp still air of the room—Middle Auntie in a printed cotton sari, myself in the *patola*. Occasionally she glances at me when she thinks I am not looking. She must find me peculiar, a paradox. The foreigner dressed as an Indian bride.

'I am admiring your bracelet,' Big Auntie says eventually. 'Very authentic. Where did you get it?'

'In Mumbai,' I say.

'Your mother-in-law had such a one,' she goes on. 'I remember her wearing it to Shundarpur.'

'Really?' I say. 'I've never seen it.'

I try to think back to all the jewellery I had seen

Gita wearing in the past. I cannot place a kissing fish bracelet on her.

'No, well, you wouldn't,' says Middle Auntie. 'I believe she sold all her jewellery—including the gold wedding jewellery—just before they left for Britain.'

'Why did she do that?' I ask.

'I suppose she was helping to meet the expenses,' Middle Auntie says. 'They were going overseas.'

She gives a large sigh.

'We have suffered so much. It is so hard, you know, living in India.'

I think of Gita, thirty years before, a shy thin girl with large fish-shaped eyes standing in the market-place while the jeweller weighed her gold bracelets on a pair of scales. Clunk, clunk, the weights went as the jeweller carefully let one drop upon the other. Measuring out her worth in gold. There would have been no precious gems amongst them. Just plain twenty-two carat gold. The price of a bride.

Then finally when the gold was weighed and the price was still not enough, the girl put her hand down to her wrist and pulled out the pin that held the two halves of the kissing fish bracelet together. The fish parted, their mouths open, deprived of each other.

Middle Auntie brings out another large photograph album with a picture on the front of a Dutch windmill. She hands the album to Milan.

'You must show Tilly some family snaps,' she says.

Milan opens the album and puts it in front of me. The first half of the album is in black and white and the second half is in colour. Middle Auntie turns to the colour section and begins to show me the photos.

'This is Hemanto and I and Lalita and her daughter, Queenie, in Nepal last year. This is one of Hemanto at Gandhi's memorial. This is Arjuna's school class. This is our Queenie's birthday party.'

She prattles on, almost oblivious to what effect the pictures might or might not be having on me. When she comes to the black and white section she riffles quickly through it.

'Very old,' she says in an embarrassed tone, as though anything not modern could not be of interest to me, a memsahib.

'No, show them to them,' Big Auntie insists. 'They can see how we used to live.'

The photos in this section have a strange, timeless quality. Some of them are actually daguerreotype. They all have an intensity of contrast in the central area of the image which fades out gradually into a white oblivion towards the corners. The effect of all this is to focus the attention of the viewers on the main subject and to give an immediacy which is disconcerting and compelling. I stop the aunt when she comes to a photograph of a young moustached man dressed in a dhoti with a blanket, folded in a bundle, balanced on his head. In one hand he holds a hurricane lamp and in the other a walking stick.

'Can't you recognise who this is?' she says.

'I have no idea,' I say.

'Why, it's your *shoshur*, your father-in-law,' she says. 'Going on a pilgrimage to Bodhgaya.'

When I look again I realise she is right. It must have been taken about forty years before. He is standing on the brow of a hill against a misty sky-line. In the foreground there is an enormous tree with spreading branches and further back a large shrub. It is an antique landscape. I wonder if my father-in-law ever imagined that, forty years later, a memsahib who marries his son would come to India and look upon him. Could the storyteller ever foresee that one day he would become the story?

'You're right,' I say. 'It is Baba.'

'*Tik ache*,' she says. 'He is dressed like a pilgrim, you understand.' She says this in an apologetic manner, as though she is ashamed of the way he looks.

I turn over the page of the album. Looking back at me are a group of children. There is a little boy seated in the foreground of the photo. He has an unhappy look on his face. On his lap is a small suitcase.

'And who is this?' I ask.

'Why, it's Milan, of course,' she says. 'Isn't he so cute? Sitting there with his suitcase. He carried that case everywhere with him. It was full of stones. People used to say to him, "Hey, Babu, what have you stolen? You look like a gangster in one of the movies walking around with that case".

'You know what children are like. They'll collect anything. Your mother-in-law wanted to throw the stones away but he wouldn't let her. I remember the fight they had. It was just after his parents came back from Britain and we were all staying in Shundarpur. Gita said she didn't want her son to go around with a suitcase full of rocks like a common stonecutter. "Next he'll be sitting at the side of the road breaking them up to sell", she said. But the description of her son as a gangster made her very unhappy.

'"What are you saying?" she shouted. "My son is not a thief. Who are you calling a thief?"

'"No one is talking about thieving", Takuma said. "It's a joke. Like in the movies".

'"That's right", said your father-in-law, "the littlest outlaw. Al Capone. To catch a thief—Cary Grant and Grace Kelly, very nice movie".'

Milan is listening to her story with a blank, unmoved expression. He does not smile.

THIS IS YOUR WIFE

At that moment an old woman in a white sari appears at the door for a moment then shuffles in. Milan bends down and touches the ground at her feet and then his forehead in a gesture of respect.

When I do this I feel ridiculous, as though I am trying to curtsy. A servant woman follows the old woman into the room. The woman stands looking at me. Takuma sits down in a chair and I take the opportunity to look at her more closely.

She is an old woman in a white widow's sari with white hair scraped up into a bun. As she speaks her head nods up and down. She sits next to Milan on the chair. I am on the small sofa. Between us is the table with the plate of *nimki*. There is a silence. It is Takuma who breaks the silence. She speaks slowly in English with a strong accent.

'This is your wife,' she says. 'Can she speak Bengali? What will I do if she doesn't understand my English?'

'Your English will suffice, Takuma, and where it does not I will translate,' says Milan.

'There is a memsahib living down the road,' Takuma goes on, as though his approval has given her the idea to tell a story. 'She has some English cows. The English cows give three times as much milk, and what's more, they have skin like velvet.'

We sit there silently thinking of the cows, imagining their warm flanks moving in and out as we stroke them.

'You came here in a car,' Takuma goes on. 'When I was married I travelled to the house of my in-laws in a sedan chair. That's how a bride went in those days. Halfway there the chair broke. What was I to do? I was only twelve years old. I jumped out, hitched up my sari and ran through the fields until I reached the next village where my husband waited. I was terrified that someone would see. My family would have been ashamed of me.'

She looks at me.

'I had red henna flowers on my hands and, on my wrists, gold bracelets. On my head I wore, because I was a Bengali girl, a gold tiara. And there I was racing through the paddy like a goddess in a story. When I reached my mother-in-law's house she was furious.

'"You foolish girl", she said. "What if you had been robbed all decked up like that? Where's your common sense?"

'And then she beat me. Later on I heard an old man in the fields had seen me and the story started that the goddess Lakshmi had come to bless his crops, after which he saw her fly off into the sky on her mount Garuda.'

As I listen to Takuma I have a vision of the eagle taking off with the girl on its back. As the eagle rises it turns its head and I see its dark round eye shining at me.

I look at Takuma. She is staring at me. Her mouth moves up and down as though she is chewing on some invisible food.

'Say something to her in Bengali,' Milan says.

'What will I say?' I ask.

'Ask her how she is.'

I dredge up one of the few lines I know from my memory:

'*Namashkar, Takuma,*' I say. '*Apni kamon achen?*'

Greetings, Takuma. How are you?

She turns and smiles at me as though she has just seen me for the first time. Suddenly she holds out her hand toward me. I am frozen, transfixed. A non-Brahmin may not touch a Brahmin widow. It will pollute her. I am not sure what I am supposed to do. Perhaps she does not want me to take the hand? Is it just a mime? *I would touch you if I could?* I ignore the proffered hand and pretend it is not there. She puts it down and does nothing for a few minutes. Then, as if it is an action controlled by some external timer, she does it again. I look at the gnarled, trembling hand wavering in the air in front of me. It is simply the hand of an old woman looking for another. I take it.

We sit in the bedroom and listen to stories of the past. Occasionally Takuma turns and speaks to Milan in Bengali.

'What is she saying?' I ask Milan.

'*Ki sunder meye.*'

'What does that mean?' I ask

'What a beautiful girl,' he replies, and smiles at me.

LUNCH

Big Auntie has prepared a lunch of curry. Lunch is served in the small room next to the kitchen which is dark and cool and opens out into the courtyard where there is the family well.

'The well is very deep,' says the uncle, 'so deep, if you look down you can never see the water. And the water from this well is pure. It tastes like snow from the Himalayas.'

A copper beaker is brought and taken to the well where the uncle lets down the bucket into the black depths and brings it up again full of clear sparkling water. He dips the beaker into the wooden bucket and gives it to me and I drink.

A separate collection of china bowls filled with food is set at my place and a knife and fork. As I sit down to eat there is a silence. I see the servant girl seated on the floor in the corner, watching me with her mouth open. I pick up the bread and begin to eat with the fork in my left hand, Western style.

THE PERFECT MAN AND WIFE

After lunch we sit on the couch in the bedroom and Milan takes our photograph. Takuma sits next to me and holds my hand. I see the look of shock on the faces of the others that she is allowing a foreigner to touch her. There is a white mark of devotion on her forehead. She has just come from the temple. After I have left she will have to go back to the temple and ask God's forgiveness for allowing herself to touch me.

'Smile,' says Milan.

We smile at the camera as we sit, ramrod stiff in a studio pose, and blink as the flash goes off in our eyes, blinding us for a second.

When I open my eyes I see that on the wall of the bedroom there is a Shundarpur painting similar to our painting at home. The painting shows a god and a goddess seated together on a giant bird which is flying towards the sunset. The god is blue and his consort is alabaster. She wears gold jewellery and a red embroidered sari. Above and below them white cranes fly and their movement mimics the great speed of the bird which is carrying the pair over the Indian countryside.

The uncle sees me looking at the painting and says, 'Vishnu and Lakshmi on their vehicle Garuda. The eternal couple. The perfect man and wife.'

A DIFFERENT VERSION

'We have a Shundarpur painting on our wall at home,' I say. 'It shows Durga holding her weapons. Ma and Baba gave it to us. It is by Ratnamala Das.'

'Ah, Ratnamala,' says Takuma. 'I knew her well. She died just recently. She was one of our first painters.'

'Do you paint, Takuma?' I ask.

'Not now,' she says. 'My hand is weak. But I did once. I used to paint when Milan was a little boy. I have some old paintings still. Would you like to see?'

Big Uncle goes to an ancient-looking *almarah*

that stands in the sitting room adjoining the kitchen and comes back with a bundle wrapped up in a faded silk sari. He unwraps it and lays the paintings out on the table. They are the familiar indigo and pink paintings of the goddess showing her in her many different forms.

'Take as many as you like,' says Takuma, 'they are no use to me now. I am an old woman. Take them back and hang them up if you like.'

'These are genuine Shundarpur paintings,' Big Uncle says.

'What is a genuine Shundarpur painting?' Takuma says. 'Some professor comes here and suddenly what we have been doing for years becomes something special. When I was a young girl we used to do these pictures on the walls just to make them look beautiful, *shundar*. But now it seems that we didn't know what we were doing. Perhaps I should repaint the bedrooms and then we can ask him to come and look at them.'

'Takuma doesn't like the fuss,' says Big Auntie. 'She just wants to have a quiet time. Who can blame her?'

'Quiet time? Quiet time? What would I know about quiet times?' the old woman continues. 'I've had nothing but worry all my life. Nothing but suffering. I just want it to end. Every morning I wake up and ask *Bhogoban*, I ask God, why hasn't he taken me yet.'

'Perhaps you should give him a hand,' says Big

Auntie gently. 'Why not hang yourself from the ceiling fan? I'm sure he'd be grateful for the trouble you've saved him.' She has an amused but long-suffering smile on her face.

'Let me tell you about some of the catastrophes I have seen. Let me tell you about the big earthquake,' says Takuma.

She begins to tell a story and it is only then that I realise that she is the original storyteller: the one who taught her son, my father-in-law, how to spin a tale and it is the same earthquake.

'There are many signs for earthquakes,' Takuma goes on. 'Cows mooing, snakes moving, fish jumping about in ponds. The water in the well drops so that you cannot see it.

'You can't imagine what the big earthquake was like. I was only a young woman. People will tell you that the quake was not big—but that is only because there were no telephones, no television, and it did not happen in an important place like Britain. They were supposed to be in charge here but they did nothing to help us. And so now in their history books it did not happen.'

As she says this I recall my father-in-law's description of that fateful day. The physical details of how he fell into the crevice in the ground and later the embellishments he made to the story.

'People forget,' says his mother, 'when they talk about the quake what it was really like. I dare say some clever scientist somewhere will tell you that the quake was caused by the movement of the earth. For us, living in Shundarpur, this was not so. We knew what had caused it.'

'Oh?' I say.

'Yes, it was the shaking of Airavata, the cosmic elephant. He was unhappy with us for some reason. Perhaps we did not worship Baba enough, perhaps we did not do the sacrifice properly. Who knows? Anyway, it was not the quake itself that was terrible. It was what happened afterwards.'

'Oh?' I say. 'What happened?'

'We could not stay in the village anymore. It was too dangerous. So we moved out onto the plain near the forest and put up tents. Even the houses in Shundarpur that were left were not safe to live in. You can imagine how hard life in the tents was. There was no running water and food was scarce. I had three children. The youngest was only two months and all the servants had gone home to help their own families. I was only nineteen.'

Nineteen. Suddenly the old woman in the white sari transforms before my eyes into a young girl. She is lithe and small and she wears a red cotton sari knotted at the waist. Her eyes are large, dark and frightened. Her arms are thin and brown and on one of them there is a silver bracelet on which two fish kiss.

'The worst part of it,' says Takuma, 'was not knowing if anyone knew we were there. We thought that the outside world might have forgotten us or

not heard that our village had been destroyed. For all
we knew the whole world had been destroyed and
we were the only ones left alive, like in the story of
Noah's ark. Perhaps, we thought, Shundarpur had
been chosen as the place of our salvation. In which
case, as some pointed out, it would not have been
Baba's curse that was visited upon us but rather his
blessing.'

This sudden turnaround strikes me as incon-
gruous but at the same time quite probable.

'How long did you stay in the tents?' I ask her.

'Eight months,' says Takuma, registering the
shock on my face and smiling. 'Eight months of
wondering if help would come before the rainy
season arrived and our tents were washed away.
Every night the women would light the lamps and
stand at the front of the tents sounding the
conches: to ward off the evil spirits and to welcome
in the gods.'

As she says this I see the women, hundreds of
them, standing at dusk in a surreal tent city, their
hands held up to the half-light of the heavens, with
the white spiral shells between them. *Bhaaaoom*,
wail the conches out across the bowl of the sky.
Bhaaaoom, the sound comes back to them, echoing
along the rim. This is certainly a different story
from my father-in-law's story.

'What happened then?' I ask.

'Oh,' says Takuma, almost as though she has lost
interest at this point, 'we were saved. Tipu Babu went

for help. Then it was all over.' She says this almost as if she is reluctant to mention Tipu Babu's name in case he should replace the real heroes of the story.

I know something about Tipu Babu from my father-in-law's story.

'Tipu Babu,' he once said, 'was our neighbour and had a cousin in the Red Cross. When it looked like all was lost he decided to walk out of Shundarpur to the next valley to try and put a call to his cousin. It was a two hundred kilometre walk. We saw him go and we didn't know if we would see him again. Four weeks later we looked down the road and saw a convoy of jeeps coming towards the village. On the side of the jeeps was a big red cross. And sitting in the first jeep was the man who had saved us, Tipu Babu.'

He gave us all a look of pride. 'Everyone came out of the tents and started to cheer. The women were going "la-la-la-la". The conches were blown: *bhaaaoom, bhaaoom*. It was like a *mela*, a fair.'

'But you know,' Takuma says, 'I thought we would be rescued. I had prayed to Kali. I made a pact with her. She promised me that we would be saved. There is a very special ritual that you can perform if you want to conquer death. If you like, I will tell you about it.'

THE OMEN

I am very tired. The heavy lunch and the long journey in the car are beginning to take their toll. Whilst the family continues to talk and reminisce, I feel my head growing heavy and my eyelids drooping.

'Jathima wants you to know that she has prepared a bed where you can lie down in the guest room,' Milan comes over and whispers to me. 'She can see that you are exhausted.'

'I'm fine, really I am,' I say. 'I'll just sit here and listen.'

'Also, she wants to know if you would like a hot bath. One of the servants has been boiling water all morning so that they can fill up the cast iron tub in the upstairs bathroom.'

'Oh no,' I say, quite horrified at all these arrangements just for myself. 'I can't. I don't want a bath. I'm a guest. I would be too embarrassed. Tell her that I don't need it.'

He smiles again. 'OK, I'll tell her, but she'll keep on insisting. She wants you to be one of the family. Until you sleep and bathe here she won't feel that has been accomplished.'

I listen to the family conversing in Bengali. They are no longer speaking in English for my benefit because I am not participating in the conversation. My head swims.

As I feel myself beginning to lose consciousness, I hear a noise in the outer courtyard. The qawwali singer has arrived. Dimly through a veil of exhaustion I see him come into the family room and set up on a cotton *dhurrie* at the end of the room. There is a young boy with him who carries a *tabla*.

He puts the drum down and begins to check its resonance with the help of a small hammer, tapping on the drum skin. Tap, tap, tap. I hear the soft concussion of the hammer on the hide. Then, as I finally sink beneath the waves of sleep, the qawwali singer begins his recital.

I am suffering from the pain of separation. Oh Ma, why are my thoughts a prisoner here in this cave of pain?

OVERNIGHT
After the performance, against our better judgement, we are persuaded to stay overnight.

'You're not leaving,' says the uncle. 'Your visit has just begun.'

It is a difficult decision to make because it means that we will have very little time when we get back to Mumbai.

A message is sent out to Ranjit that the return journey will be delayed. The messenger who comes back seems concerned. Apparently a local soothsayer has predicted an earthquake. Several townspeople have already, on the basis of this prediction, left the area. The messenger shakes his head ominously and says in hushed tones to Milan: 'Sahib, there have been signs. People say it is just talk but it may happen very soon.'

The signs, in this case, apparently, amount to a local sighting of a band of *dhora kraits*, a deadly but playful crossbreed of black snakes which inhabit the rice fields in this area. In several cases the snakes had been seen in places other than their usual habitat and were last seen curled up in the back seat of a Premier Padmini belonging to the local judge.

Big Auntie, when she hears of this warning, however, is dismissive.

'This is just a rumour,' she says. 'You can't believe these types of predictions. If you ask me they just cause trouble. It's perfectly safe for you to stay.'

In any case our room has already been prepared on the first floor. It is a large room with an enormous bed covered in an old paisley silk spread. There is an overhead fan but it is not working and the room is stiflingly hot. Milan and I lie on the top of the spread, naked, sweltering in the terrible heat. There is an old-fashioned lock on the door which looks fragile but we have secured it nevertheless. I turn to look at Milan.

'How did you find Takuma?' I ask.

He gazes for a moment at the fan which does not turn.

'OK,' he says.

Outside the noise of a distressed koel pierces the air.

He gets up from the bed. The old bed frame rocks on its uneven legs. He turns around, eyelids lowered, and makes a sound which I cannot recognise. In the distance the Indian cuckoo makes its long plaintive cry again.

'I did not realise how I would feel coming back

here after all this time,' he says haltingly. 'I thought I would feel detached, like an observer, but instead the pain is too great.'

He sits down on a wicker cot by the window. I put my hand on his shoulder. His whole body heaves with an eruption of sadness. I do not know what to say.

His dark naked body is a black shadow against the white wall. Through the open window I can see the sky, punctured with early stars. The stars have known the past; they must have seen incidents that have shaped the present we are now in.

'Even if you feel abandoned,' I say softly, 'that is in the past. You are here now with Takuma and I am here. I will not leave.'

We sit there in the room which has gradually grown dark. Long shadows are cast across the room. On the *almarah* a small bronze figure of Lord Vishnu is seated on Ananta, the cosmic serpent, dreaming the universe into existence.

'Uckoo, uckoo.'

The koel, having taken over the nest of another bird and killed its young, proclaims its dominion at dusk. I can hear Milan breathing. His breath comes slowly now, more even and regular. My broken lover shivers in the rapidly cooling night air. I get up from the bed and place the paisley quilt over his shoulders. He turns suddenly, mutely, and, placing his head in my lap, begins to weep uncontrollably. I hold him. As the night wears on I sit with him by the open window and watch the stars sending us their secrets.

THE BATH

The next morning when I get up and look out the window I see the mountains of the Western Ghats, purple on top with the deep rich brown of the foothills descending to the flats. The early morning air is so crisp and clear it gives everything a closeness and immediacy. I feel as though I could reach out my hand and touch them.

As I watch one of the slopes I see high up on it a small winding road. A man is walking up the road. He carries a staff and on his head is a large turban. In front of him there is a herd of goats. They have bells around their necks and as they walk the bells tinkle. The sun shines across the hills and glints occasionally on the metal bells. On the slopes there are purple flowers growing in profusion.

While Milan sleeps coiled up in the bedspread on the edge of the bed, I go up to the second level of the house to use the toilet. In the bathroom next door a servant girl is pouring hot water from a large urn into the bath. She looks at me.

After I come out of the toilet the girl gestures to me.

'Ma'am, ma'am,' she says.

I am not sure what she wants but I follow her to the room next door where she motions to the bath. Then she begins to assiduously wash down the floor of the bathroom with cold water and a small hand whisk. I understand at this point that the bath is for me.

After she leaves I lie in the bath in the little concrete room and let the hot water soothe me. Downstairs in the kitchen I can hear someone making breakfast for us. There is no-one else around.

THE STOLEN HEART

When I return from the second level Milan has left the bedroom. I continue until I reach the room in which we were first received, where, as I approach the doorway, I see the Indian grandmother and her grandson. Takuma sits in a high-backed wooden chair and at her feet kneels Milan.

I remember what Gita has told me about her mother-in-law—the *ojha,* the kidnapper of children, the demon. It is only when I enter the room that I realise this is not what this scene reveals. The two figures sit, frozen, clutching each other's hands. Tears flow from the old woman's eyes. In front of her Milan weeps.

I look at his grandmother. Surely this is not the aggressor, the perpetrator of crimes? Her hands shake as they grasp her grandson's hands, a look of desperation, of long-suppressed pain, on her face. Does the wicked fairy look like this?

Wordless, the pair sit, unaware of my presence. They remind me of the pictures you often see of survivors of a terrible calamity. I think of the photograph of the 'Unknown Family of East Bengal', the two daughters and their mother looking so lost and desolate, victims of some great calamity, clutching each other in despair. Here too, in front of me, are the victims of a great loss.

According to *The Handbook of Gems* there appears occasionally within a gem some element that was captured in the stone long ago. These are called inclusions. Inclusions can be liquid-filled cavities, salt crystals, gas bubbles, hollow tubes, needle-like crystals or fractures.

Inclusions can show the identity of a gem by revealing where and how it was formed. They can prove a gemstone's authenticity and natural origins. Most inclusions are best seen under a microscope where they often appear as features of startling curiosity and great beauty.

THE SUITCASE OF STONES

Big Uncle has found something he believes Milan may find amusing.

'Look,' he says. 'Here is something I found in the back cupboard. It belonged to you when you were a little boy.'

He is holding a small suitcase made of tin. Its dull metal-colour is worn smooth with age, although perhaps at one stage it was red because there are some faint russet patches.

'You may like to take it back with you as a memento. Hey, Al Capone, what've you got in that case? Bang, bang! Remember? We used to tease you about the stones you kept in the case. There's some still inside, I believe.'

He gives the case a shake which produces a jangling rattle.

Milan looks at him and then at the case.

His uncle puts the case down on the low table in the sitting room. It has two rusty latches on it. Milan prises first one lock and then the other open. Then he eases the lid up with both hands.

The bottom of the case is lined with newspaper. We can just see the headlines of an edition of the *Patna Telegraph*. It contains a number of small bundles wrapped up in the same edition. Tentatively Milan opens one. He lays its contents down on the table next to the case. It is a piece of quartz.

'Yes, that's right,' he says in an even voice. 'It is my suitcase. I will take it back with me. Thank you, thank you very much.'

GIFT GIVING

At Big Auntie's insistence there is a gift-giving ceremony. We all stand nervously in the sitting room while the family solemnly presents me with three pieces of gold jewellery—a ring, a pendant and a brooch.

'We would have given you earrings,' Big Auntie informs me sadly, 'which is the proper gift for a bride when she enters the house of her relatives for the first time, but we were told that a memsahib does not have pierced ears.'

As she says this she gives her husband an angry look and he appears embarrassed.

The ring and the brooch are made of gold and set with clear stones. The brooch is a special gift from Takuma. She pins it onto the shoulder of my sari to keep the veil in place.

THE MANY VERSIONS OF HER STORY

There are many versions of the goddess's story. In some she is a golden-skinned woman called Gauri, in others she is known as the Maiden with Excellent Hips. In others still she is Lakshmi or the black-skinned Kali. Followers of Kali believe that it is only through her that one can live life fully and face death. Takuma is a devotee of Kali. She goes every day to a shrine in Shundarpur to worship the black goddess.

'You cannot live properly until you have faced death,' she tells me. 'Mahakali will overcome you unless you face what she has to offer. People think that we Indians worship Kali because we have some strange desire to suffer and die, but it is just the exact opposite. We know that death is the ultimate expression of life.'

We are sitting by ourselves in the small bedroom when she says this. Milan is with his uncle. She leans over and looks at me, her eyes shining.

'There is a special ritual you can perform if you wish to get her help. I will tell you about it.'

The light in the room is growing dark. Outside the storm that has followed us to Shundarpur is gaining strength. Dark clouds are gathering around the sun.

'You must get the bones of someone who has died. Any person will do just as long as their skeleton is gathered at night and in secret. You lay the bones out in a room separate from the rooms of every day. This is the room where you will worship Kali.

'Then you must sit and pray to Devi. You must stay there all night. During the night the black goddess will come to you and she will try and overcome you. You must wrestle with her and gain the upper hand. This is a mental fight, you understand, not a physical one. She will enter your mind and try to dominate you. You must use all your willpower to prevent this and to show her that you are master of your own mind. If you succeed she will become your servant. You will have a power over her that others do not.'

As she finishes talking I can just hear the sound of rain beginning to drum against the outside walls. The rain is slow and its gentle fall can be heard as a barely discernible rhythm.

A GOOD BOY
In the early afternoon, at the gate, we say good-

bye. As we attempt to make our farewell I watch Milan.

'Are you OK?' I ask him.

I can tell from the way he is standing that he is not. He has his back to the rest of the family. His shoulders are taut and he is trembling as though he is cold. When I walk over to him I see that he is weeping, silently, convulsively, his mouth distorted into a grimace of pain.

'*Ki bhalo chele.*'

It is Big Auntie who is speaking. She is nodding her head in satisfaction. She obviously thinks he is crying because he must leave his grandmother. Such grief is respectful and admirable and that is why she is saying in Bengali, what a good boy. The rest of the family looks embarrassed but approving also, especially Takuma, who seems pleased. She stands by the gate, small and squat but dignified, all in white with a béatific expression. Everyone smiles and we climb wordlessly into the Contessa. Now there are four of us in the car. Milan sits in front with Ranjit. I sit in the back with Middle Auntie and an enormous handbag.

'I hope,' says Middle Auntie, 'this car is air conditioned. I can't take the heat anymore. My health is poor.'

'Don't worry, Auntie,' Milan says. 'We will get you there safely.'

A small boy comes out of one of the neighbouring houses to watch us go. As the car pulls out of the street, I look back through the glass of the rear window and wave. The boy sees me and waves back. I smile at him and he jumps up and down excitedly and lets out a whoop of joy.

Fourteen

TWO WHITE CRANES

The sky up ahead is glowing violet like the background on an Indian painting. At any minute two white cranes may fly across the lowering skies and a pair of lovers will appear to dance across the horizon. It is very hot and as we drive along, Middle Auntie fans herself. The air conditioning does not appear to be working.

'Can't you tell him to turn it on?' I ask Milan as his aunt leans her head against the seat and closes her eyes.

He whispers back to me, 'I think it's broken. Just pretend it is on. If she thinks it is on she will feel better.'

BEL FRUIT

From the car window I can see, on the side of the

road, myriad stones of all different colours and sizes. Beside us is a railway line. The track is laid on a built-up ridge. Women are walking along it scavenging for coal. They look up as we pass, curious but aloof. On the side of the track a woman is using a long stick to bring down a large green fruit which is hanging from a tree. As the fruit hits the ground it makes a smacking noise.

'*Bel* fruit,' says Milan and then, turning to me, asks, 'have you ever eaten *bel* fruit?'

'No, I've never heard of it,' I say. 'What is it?'

'I think in English it is called wood apple,' says the aunt.

'But what is it?' I ask.

'It's a kind of fruit,' she says helplessly. 'Very nice.'

'Ah, *bel* fruit,' says Ranjit, who has overheard us. 'You must know the story of the hare and the bel fruit.'

'Actually I don't,' I say.

'My mother always told me these stories as a child,' he says. 'It goes like this. There is a hare sitting under a *bel* fruit tree and the thought occurs to him: what if the ground should start shaking and the world should end? Just at that moment a *bel* fruit drops from the tree and lands on the ground with a thud. The hare gets such a fright. He is sure it is an earthquake. He gets up and runs for his life. Soon he meets a gazelle and he shouts to the gazelle: "Earthquake! Earthquake!"

'The gazelle is terrified and gets up and joins the

hare in his flight. Soon they meet an elephant who also takes flight, and then a monkey, and a python and a mongoose and a rhinoceros. Finally they come to a lion who roars at them: "Why are you all fleeing?"

'"Oh, sir, there is an earthquake".

'"Who told you so?"

'"The mongoose", says the rhinoceros.

'But the mongoose says, "The python said so".

'And the python says, "The monkey".

'Whereupon the monkey mentions the elephants.

'Who attribute it to the gazelles.

'But the gazelles say, "Sir, we know nothing about this. It is the hare who is the source of our knowledge".

'"Well then, Master Hare", says the lion, "tell us about the earthquake".

'"I was sitting under the *bel* tree", says the hare, "when it began. I was terrified for my life".

'"Really?" says the lion. "Let us go to the site where the catastrophe occurred and see what remains".

'He places the hare upon his back and gallops off in the direction of the fabled tree.

'When the hare and the lion arrive at the *bel* fruit tree there is no sign of devastation. No cracks have appeared on the ground. No trees have fallen and the *bel* fruit tree stands gently blowing in the wind. On the ground, at its feet, is a ripe fruit.

'"You see?" says the lion. "All remains as it was. No earthquake has occurred. No end is foreseen. All we have here is a fruit. Take it and show it to the other animals whom you have scared".'

'I think,' the aunt says to me after Ranjit has finished, 'you have stories like this too. "The lady who swallowed a fly", I remember. This type of story is very popular here.'

'The story has a meaning,' says Ranjit.

'What does it mean?' I ask.

'It means that one thing leads to another. Everything is connected,' says Middle Auntie.

'It has another meaning also,' says Ranjit. 'It warns you not to believe the stories of others but to check facts for yourself.'

MARUTI

A bright blue smudge at the end of the road ahead of us takes form and solidifies as we approach it. It is a small Indian car, a Maruti; a modern car named after the storm gods, the Maruts. At its wheel is a young woman. She is no doubt wealthy, wearing make-up—perhaps *Lakme*, for the modern girl. But it is her expression that captures me. It is cool, aloof, superior. The world outside her Maruti does not exist. She has a disdain for it. She reminds me of my grandmother.

I remember a photograph I once saw of my grandmother in a popular magazine standing beside a motorcar.

Mrs G.C. Smythe is shown beside her ten horse-power Standard Saloon in the grounds of her lovely home in Bevan Street, Balwyn. The magnificent tree gives an English atmosphere in keeping with the English car. Mrs Smythe is a keen golfer and a member of the Eastern Club. This is her second Standard car.

The article was entitled 'Women Drivers with their Cars in Charming Home Settings', and it went on:

Surely no other car has made such a strong appeal to a woman's love of beauty and her desire for simplicity as the smart English 'Standard' cars shown with their proud owners in these Table Talk photographs.

Behind the wheel of one of these cars one steers through traffic as easily as walking in a crowded street. One flips the synchromesh gears up or down without a sound and with scarcely a thought. One looks at those superior men drivers with disdain and yearns to show how well a woman can drive, because with a Standard everything is so unbelievably easy.

I try to remember when I last saw my grandmother in a car. When she was seventy-six she drove a green Vauxhall. It was a large car, almost too large for a small woman. My grandmother's carefully made-up face could just be seen above the rim of the steering wheel. She wore 'Milk of

Roses' on her white skin and her hair was dyed purple.

Once, in the Vauxhall, my grandmother hit a tram. The accident occurred at the corner of Johnston and Nicholson Streets, Fitzroy. According to her own account, my grandmother got out of the Vauxhall and went up to the tram driver, who had just alighted, and asked him why he had hit her. Before the tram driver could reply, she pointed out the large dent in the front of her car and informed him that he had no right to go around running into other people's cars like hers. The tram driver swore at her, got into his tram and drove off.

HAPPY TRAVELLERS REFRESH HERE

Government of India Guesthouse, the sign says. *Happy travellers refresh here.*

'Oh Ma,' cries the aunt. 'Perhaps we will stop.'

Milan and I look at each other. We have scarcely begun.

'Stop here,' Milan says to Ranjit. 'We will use the toilets. And have some tea.'

Inside there is a counter where we buy some tea and sit down at a long table. When Middle Auntie leaves for the bathroom, Milan leans over and holds out his hand to me. I look at his open palm with the thin sepia network of lines crisscrossing it like a web.

'Thank you,' he says, 'for coming with me to visit Takuma and for playing the part.'

'What do you mean?' I ask.

'The perfect Indian wife is not an easy role to play.'

'I don't think I have played it,' I say. 'And I am confused as to why Takuma allowed me to touch her. What happened to her fear of pollution?'

'She has conveniently put it aside for my wife,' he says. 'She told Big Auntie that for a child brought up in India like her granddaughter, it is important that caste lines are followed, but not where I am concerned. "How many Brahmin girls do you think are walking down the streets in Australia?" is what she actually said.'

'Is she allowed to break the rules just like that?' I ask.

'Rules can be reinterpreted and seen from different angles. In Takuma's mind everything coexists with everything else quite nicely.'

He picks up a spoon and begins to stir his tea.

'It's that simple. It's like the story of the anthropologist who visits a Bengali village and asks a Brahmin, "How many people are living in this village?" and the Brahmin says "Fifty-six".

'Then the anthropologist takes a census and counts two thousand people. He goes back to the man and says, "Look, you told me there were only fifty-six but I've counted two thousand".

'"That may be", said the man, "but only fifty-six of them are Brahmins".'

At that moment an Indian girl sitting at the end of the table leans over.

'Excuse me, but I couldn't help noticing you are Australians. We're from Australia too.'

She motions to a blond man beside her. 'Hello,' I say, and we all shake hands. They are on their honeymoon. They come from Melbourne, not far from Dight's Falls. We drink some tea with them and talk about their trip. Then the blond man and Milan go inside to look for the toilets.

'Don't you find it difficult being married to an Indian?' the Indian girl asks suddenly.

I don't know what to say.

'Not really,' I reply, 'but at times I find it difficult to know who I am married to.'

She looks at me.

'What I mean is that I find sometimes in Milan there are warring parts. I'm not sure if there is an Indian part and an Australian part, but sometimes I feel I'm dealing with the part that is not appropriate for that moment.'

She smiles.

'Of course, an Indian girl always adjusts her behaviour to her husband's.'

When she says this I think of a painting I saw in Mumbai. It showed the milkmaid Radha prostrating herself at the feet of Krishna, the dark blue god. She was holding Krishna's dark blue feet in her pale red-tipped hands while her forehead touched them. Underneath there was a caption which read: *Krishna and Radha dallying in the Grove.*

I look at the Indian girl from Melbourne. Her

hands are covered in silver rings and her nails are painted crimson.

'That must be hard for the Indian girl,' I say.

She gives me a sidelong glance.

'I don't think I could put up with a relationship like that,' I say. 'I see us as two equal people making up a couple.'

The Indian girl says nothing, then smiles again.

'Well, I wish you well,' she says. 'We might run into you again sometime.'

She gets up from the table and follows her husband inside the guesthouse.

BHAGOBAN

A red clay statue roughly in the shape of an elephant on the side of the road stares back at us with large white eyes as we drive past. Amongst the offerings at his feet there is a mound of peanuts.

'You are seeing Ganesh, I am thinking,' says Ranjit, turning slightly in the driver's seat. 'He is the god of all good fortune.'

'*Ha*,' says Middle Auntie. 'He protects us from ignorance. He liberates us from all obstacles and removes them from our path.'

'But only God protects him,' says Ranjit.

'What do you mean?' I ask.

'Bhagoban, God, is above all,' says Ranjit.

'But you believe in many gods,' I say. 'Surely that is what Hinduism teaches?'

'*Tik*,' says Ranjit. 'We do. The gods created the

earth and they protect it and they destroy it but who created the gods?'

'I don't know,' I say. 'I have never thought of that.'

'And it is quite obvious,' says Ranjit, warming to his topic, 'that you cannot have a model without a plan, a blueprint, if you like, from which to make the model. How can the earth have been made if there was no-one to write the plan? How could it have appeared out of nowhere without an original to copy? God must have given the gods that copy. And with each new age they make the model again. Surely you cannot believe that they could do this without some original to follow?'

I am astonished. I turn to Milan for advice but he just smiles. Middle Auntie is shaking her head in agreement, as though this is common knowledge.

'It says in the *Veda* itself,' says Ranjit.

'And every villager in every village, including the lower castes, believes this?' I ask.

'Every villager,' says Ranjit.

I am dumbfounded. I sit in the car chastised like a child. Up until that moment I had not known at all what Hindus believed. I believed what I had read in Western books. And, as Ranjit had previously said, I was married to a Hindi-speaking kind of person.

THE LIFE OF BRAHMA

I cannot remember now how long we have been in the cave. Have our captors had us here now for three days or three weeks?

The book of *Vedas* says that twenty-four hours in the life of Brahma, the god of creation, is equal to one year in a human life and that one year of his life will take one thousand years of our own. The *Vedas* do not seem to believe in time as we know it. They go on to describe the god with long tendrils of hair and on the end of each hair there hangs a world. These worlds, they say, will continue to be dissolved and changed by Brahma until this whole universe is brought to an end and a new one is created.

MAYA

'Your magic act in the village,' I ask Ranjit in the cave. 'How did you do it?'

Ranjit looks at me as though he is not sure how to proceed. He leans towards me in the dark as though he is telling a secret.

'People believe what they think they see,' he says. 'But you know everything that you see in this world is an illusion. All is *maya*—that is the Hindu view of the world. The world is not really there. We just imagine it is.'

'Is that how you think magicians do their tricks? By making the audience believe that something is there when it is not?'

'*Acha*,' Ranjit says solemnly. 'In my case I am trying to bring into their minds the apparition of Nakul, the cosmic mongoose. He is the vehicle of Lord Kubera, the god of wealth. When the god puts his hand on his stomach, Nakul vomits jewels for his master. I am thinking that would be a very fine thing to see.'

'We could benefit from some tricks like that now,' says Middle Auntie sourly. 'Why don't you conjure up a king's ransom for us, or at the very least a taxi?'

As she says this I think of our holiday in Venice. There are no ordinary taxis in Venice. Venice has no cars. Everything goes on the water, just like it was a main road. To get to the airport the quickest method is to take a water taxi. The water taxi will pick you up outside the front door or jetty of your hotel and take you through the Grand Canal onto the open sea.

Then I think of the girl with green eyes. Her memory is always at the back of my mind, lying there in the coiled seahorse brain that records everything. I no longer feel that I can dismiss her but if I allow her to capture me completely she may poison my mind. Perhaps now it is only by thinking about her that I will be able to dominate her. I must lay her skeleton out in my thoughts and by examining it bring her under my will.

FIFTEEN

GIRL IN A CAR

It is now late afternoon and the light is beginning to fade. Suddenly there is a noise like water gushing up from a pipe. The Contessa gives a lurch.

'Oh Ma,' cries Middle Auntie, clutching on to the back of the passenger seat.

The car gives out a loud drumming noise, the engine splutters and then quite suddenly it dies. There is perfect silence. I look out of the window. Ranjit gets out and lifts up the bonnet of the car.

'Kaput,' he says, and scratches his head. He touches a part of the engine tentatively with one finger. '*Garam*,' he says finally. 'Overboiling the radiator. I am getting some water from the field.'

I look out of the window. We are in the middle of nowhere. I watch Ranjit go down an incline from the road to a pond below and dip a tin into the murky pond water. He returns with it full of stagnant water which he wrinkles his nose at. I wonder what is in the water and how long it will be before it fouls the car's engine completely. He tries the engine again but still it will not turn over.

THE COUNTERFEITERS' MUSEUM

One by one Milan, Middle Auntie and myself get out of the car and stand looking at it in disbelief. The Contessa has not proved to be reliable at all. In my heart I blame Uncle Pralad. After all, he arranged its hire. Did he think he could dazzle us with a car that looked like an imported model when all the time it was only a badly made copy?

The authentic articles shown here are deliberately placed next to the counterfeit items so that the visitor is better able to compare them. If some of the copies seem too obviously to be poor imitations, please remember that in everyday life the risk to the consumer is much greater because the consumer is not able to compare them side by side in this manner.

Our risk of being cheated by a member of Milan's family did not seem to exist at all when I read this pamphlet at the Counterfeiters' Museum in Venice on our honeymoon. Il Museo della Contraffazione had several rooms showing objects that had been copied: children's toys, perfumes, credit cards, watches, art posters, even Roman coins and amphoras. There were Barbie dolls with badly painted faces next to real Barbie dolls, real French perfumes next to fakes, and bottles of imitation liqueurs. In every case the copy was of inferior quality while masquerading as an object of genuine worth.

Looking at the Contessa now, it seems to me that we have been naive.

Before we left the Counterfeiters' Museum I collected a bumper sticker to take home written in the passionate language of the trade union: *La contrafazzione, io dico NO:* 'I say NO to counterfeiting'.

STRANDED

Middle Auntie sits down on a grassy embankment by the roadside and fans herself with the veil of her sari.

'Pray God,' she says, 'that we are able to reach Dolali. There is a stall there where they sell petrol. They will have a mechanic.'

'What'll we do if we can't get going?' I ask Milan as we walk away from the edge of the road to find a place on the grass to sit.

'I guess we could try and hitch a ride or find a village around here and see if there is a telephone,' he says. He glances over at Middle Auntie, who is languishing on the grass oblivious to our conversation.

I look at the surrounding scenery. For miles there is nothing except the road and cultivated land with the occasional small field shrine. The pond where Ranjit collected the water is set in a small field. A network of streams cross it leading into a large lake: its silver surface shines like a mirror.

'Tilly, I have to tell you something.'

I look at Milan. A bulbul shrieks in a tree nearby.

'I have read some of your travel diary.'

'Really?' I laugh. 'And did it make a good read? "Today we ate *masala dosa* and saw the Taj"?'

'Yes it did,' he pauses. 'Why can't you believe me?'

'What do you mean?'

'What my mother implied about Stephanie was purely fantasy.'

There is a pause.

'I know that,' I say. 'It's just that I can't get the fantasy out of my mind.'

'It's true that we went out once or twice before I met you but I never slept with her. Once I met you, nothing else mattered.'

He stares at me mutely, expectantly. I don't know what to say.

'When did you read it?' I ask.

'Just before we left Shundarpur.'

GREEN INK

He does not have to tell me how it happened. I can see it in my mind's eye. He is standing by the bedroom window of the house in Shundarpur. His head is bent and he holds something carefully in both hands. It is my travel diary which is open at a page with green handwriting on it.

He stares out the window through which you can just see a ravine. All around the town there are deep gorges. When the British were here they built hill stations to come and admire the local terrain. He walks over and places the diary down on the table. Jewels of light from the window fall on it. He stares at the words on the page for a moment: *Today I saw a woman who looked like Stephanie.*

He stops for a moment and puts his head in his hands. He twists his hair around his fingers into a tight knot. He hears me at the door. He blinks and holds his mouth set in a straight line. He walks up to me and pushes past, refusing to look at me. Then he is gone. Out the door, into the landscape, trying to escape.

THE SHRINE

Close to where we are standing there is a small roadside shrine. It is a beehive-like structure made of white stone. A niche has been carved out of it for the deity. The god is a large black boulder covered in silver paper and decorated with a garland of flowers.

Milan walks away from me and stands next to the shrine. He gives me a look of despair.

'Tilly.' His voice is restrained.

I do not know what to say.

'I'm so sorry,' he says. 'I'm sorry about my

mother's and my sister's behaviour. I'd do anything to change what has happened but I can't and you hate me for it.'

'I don't hate you,' I say.

He closes his eyes for a moment.

'You do,' he says. 'But you can't admit it. It's too painful.'

I say nothing. I am trying to control myself.

'But you've got to give it up,' he says. 'We can't go on if you don't. It controls you.'

Sometimes you find yourself looking back at the past and you are not sure what has happened. The view you had that seemed so clear and transparent seems suddenly to be only a peephole. You are no longer the informed observer but the ashamed voyeur.

I look down. The dust of the road and the grass next to it is scattered with petals from a nearby *palash* tree. They look like smudges of blood. I sink to my knees in the bleeding leaves and weep uncontrollably.

DROWNING THE GODDESS

'Oh Ma,' cries Middle Auntie suddenly awake. 'Durga protect us. We're going to die. This is a place for dacoits.'

She apparently does not notice that Milan is kneeling beside me on the grass like a priest kneels before an effigy.

'Cover your head,' she says. 'If they see you we're

gone. What a dreadful thing if they see us and you sitting here looking like a bride.'

Ranjit is trying to resuscitate the Contessa. Repeated administrations of water have not filled the radiator with life-giving fluid. As he stands perplexed in front of the leaking cooling system, we hear the sound of bells. Looking over the hillside we see a small procession of villagers making their way along the terrain to the lake in the distance. They appear to be carrying something aloft in their hands which looks like a person.

'Vijaya Darshami,' says Ranjit. 'It is the ninth day. The coming of spring.'

Every year in India during Durga Puja the statue of the goddess is carried in triumph through the streets of villages and towns. The statue is made of clay and painted to represent the goddess who is seated on her lion. Her large fish-shaped eyes stare out from her clay head and the faithful see in them the spirit of the deity and worship her presence.

The final day of the celebration is called Vijaya Darshami. In the evening the spirit of the goddess departs and with the clay vessel's use at an end, the worshippers immerse the idol in a river, pond or the sea.

THE GIRL IN THE AMBULANCE

The last time I saw the girl with green eyes in Venice we were walking up the canal near Ferrovia. When we came to the railway terminus of Santa

Lucia, we found a strange scene was unfolding on its steps. A girl had been in an accident and an ambulance had been called.

It was the green-eyed girl from the square.

The ambulance was a small speedboat. It had just moored on the jetty outside the station and two paramedics carrying cases had jumped out. Another carried what looked like a collapsible stretcher but which subsequently unfolded into a kind of deck chair. They put the girl into the deck chair and carried her like an unconscious bride in a sedan chair down to the water.

A small crowd of tourists and passers-by had gathered on the terrace to watch. They were silent and attentive. We stood by the canal and looked out over the water to where the girl in the deck chair was being borne away in the small boat.

Sixteen

THE DACOITS

The dacoits come up to the car one by one. Just as though they are fellow travellers also on the road. As though they are going to ask us the way. Anything is possible. One waves his hand. He has a strange smile on his face. I do not immediately see the danger. Dacoits are supposed to swoop down upon you with scarves over their faces and knives in their belts. These robbers are too urbane. But I cannot see Ranjit's face. Perhaps that would have told me everything.

They look with interest at my jewellery. But not too much interest. That would have been too crass. Too country bumpkinish—and they are not country folk. Two of them speak English. They have been to school. They have learnt the ways of the oppressor.

We are trapped.

SEVENTEEN

LIFE IN THE CAVE

There are several famous cave complexes near Shundarpur. Two of the caves house ancient Buddhist relics and in the hillsides around them there are many abandoned cells where hermits used to pray. Milan and Ranjit talk about these caves often and where they would be in relation to the place we now find ourselves in.

'I am thinking that this is on the northern side of the Vajra cave. I am thinking also that the sun penetrates the Vajra cave at sunrise from the east. There is a window in the roof of the cave and the light comes through the sun window and blesses the Buddha.'

'Perhaps you are right,' says Milan, 'but the sun does not seem to be rising on our left when we face the cave mouth. I do not think we are northeast of Vajra.'

'Does it matter where we are?' says Middle Auntie. 'We were in the car, now we are captives. We are somewhere between Shundarpur and Mumbai, but we are not going anywhere now. Save us the geography lesson.'

She is seated on the floor of the cave, her sari veil pulled over her head to keep out the cold. The cave air is musty and damp and there is moisture on the walls when you run your hand over the surface. The walls are a dull grey colour and covered in small lichens and dirt. I wonder if a hermit ever lived in this space and if there are any remnants of his life left here. When I rub away the dirt on the walls I can see the rock strata like layers of a cake, some pink, some yellow, some white.

Since entering the cave I have lost my sense of place as well as time. I am often somewhere else in my mind than the present moment. My mind wanders. I thought a person went through life in a straight line. Now I realise that this is an illusion. At any point in your life you can be in several places and times in your mind and what may seem real or the right point of view in one may not be so in another. Everything is relative to where you feel you are at the present.

As I run my hands over the coloured strata I think about how long it must have taken for these layers to form. Each one is itself a world which has ripened then perished. Our whole lives are made up of worlds which coexist, some flourishing, some dying.

'You Westerners,' Ranjit says with a new bold-
ness brought about by our forced intimacy, 'think
that you know how the world works. One thing
causes another in one world. But the gods show us
that there are many worlds. And what may seem
one way in one world may look different in
another. And we believe that these worlds can be
talking to each other. One of our famous scientists
says that actually there are more than three dimensions. He has counted thirty-nine.'

THE GREAT EXHIBITION

*Diamonds were worn in India for many centuries but
Indians did not cut them for fear of damaging the
magic of the stones.*

Muni comes and stands in front of me, grinning.

'Please disrobe yourself of your personal jewellery,'
he says.

I look into his face. He has already been through
most of our belongings and taken many things.

Milan is angry. But I can see that he is trying
hard to hide his outrage, perhaps because he feels it
is not safe to show it.

'This jewellery is a present from my Takuma,'
he says evenly. 'Surely you have some respect for
that. My paternal grandmother. Don't you have a
grandmother?'

The Muni narrows his eyes and looks at my

husband. His almond-shaped eyes are dark and opaque. Then he laughs.

'We're not interested in grandmothers,' he says. 'Grandmothers are not part of our plan.'

'What is your plan?' asks Milan.

'You wouldn't be understanding any of this,' the dacoit says. 'Our plan is far more important than you can possibly realise. Why do you think we want these trinkets? Do you imagine we want to give them to our wives? We know what to do with gemstones. We don't cut them up into stupid shapes.'

The Handbook of Gems has a sketch of the Koh-i-noor diamond when it was brought from India to England for Queen Victoria. The *Illustrated London News* wrote of the gem:

A diamond is generally colourless and the finest are quite free from any speck or flaw of any kind, resembling a drop of the purest water. The Koh-i-noor is not cut in the best form for exhibiting its purity and lustre, and will therefore disappoint many, if not all, of those who so anxiously press forward to see it.

The magazine went on to say:

The shape of the Koh-i-noor is that of a pear, or rather more oblong; and it would be much reduced in size if cut by a European diamond merchant. Its marketable value would however be increased. It would probably become, if properly treated, one of the finest diamonds now in Europe.

The Koh-i-noor or The Mountain of Light, as it came to be known, was first put on display at the Crystal Palace. In the centre of the palace there was a fountain made of crystal. Many people who visited initially thought that this magnificent fountain was the mysterious jewel that they had come to see and were quite disappointed when they realised their mistake. Many stories had been told about the stone's beauty and size that had raised people's expectations. Rumours abounded that the gem would bring misfortune to whoever wore it. Another rumour, however, claimed that the ultimate value of the diamond was the value of the good fortune it brought the wearer.

For the duration of the exhibition the diamond was kept inside a special diamond case made by Chubb; it looked like a large birdcage made of iron. Inside the birdcage the diamond was imprisoned within a small glass dome. Any attempt made to steal it would be met with the glass dome descending immediately below the cage into a closed wooden base. In front of the cage there was a sign informing the onlookers that they were viewing this invention for the first time.

The *Handbook of Gems* also shows a picture of the stone following the exhibition, after it had been rose cut and reduced in size by eighty carats.

While its size was valued in the East, the Victorian jewellers were anxious to render it more brilliant by cutting the facets of the crystal so that they better reflected the light and gave off more lustre. The loss of its size in this manner must have been devastating for its previous Indian custodians. They must have wondered at the loss of power that the jewel would suffer with its reduction in size.

'At the Queen's coronation in 1953,' my grandmother once said, 'I saw the Queen Mother wearing the state crown with the Koh-i-noor set in the front. She looked so regal. I can never forget it. A crown or a tiara looks so well on a woman when she is in a long dress.'

In a chest of drawers in her bedroom my grandmother kept a circlet of gold decorated with four-leaf clovers. She wore this at her coming-out ball in 1903. At Milan's and my wedding, my mother was annoyed when she saw my mother-in-law's crown on my head.

'If we had known that you were interested in wearing a tiara, I would have given you your poor grandmother's,' she said pointedly.

WRITING THE RANSOM NOTE

Another of my possessions that the dacoits have taken is the Sheaffer pen that I bought at Chuckles. I have described every place we have visited in India in my black book: time, place, interesting features, and always in green ink, the ink the owl-like man sold me that afternoon in Mumbai. Now I must use an old pencil stub to write this account: that is all the dacoits have left me with. When he took my Sheaffer the Kashmiri held it up admiringly and turned it deliberately to see if it was still in good condition.

'Ah, Sheaffer,' he said, as though he was intimately acquainted with the brand. Perhaps he was. He took the pen and wrapped it up in a piece of cloth. I never saw it again.

Now, a piece of paper and a biro with a chewed end have been placed on the ground in front of me. The Kashmiri brings along a wad of newspapers to put under the paper like a low table. His attention is almost solicitous.

'Now you will write,' he says.

'What is it I am supposed to write?' I ask.

'How much you want to go home,' he says. 'What will happen if they do not help you.'

'Who are they?' I ask.

'Your parents, of course.' The Kashmiri looks at me scornfully as though to say, surely you Westerners have parents who care? 'Your Ma and Baba.'

'But I have no Baba,' I say. 'My Baba died many years ago.'

The Kashmiri looks taken aback for a moment.

'All the more reason then that your Ma would want to have you back by her side,' he says.

'But she doesn't want me by her side,' I say. 'She

married my stepfather and went to live in Portsea. She has no reason to miss me.'

The Kashmiri looks as though he will hit me.

PASSPORTS

My passport is open on the ground beside me. The Kashmiri has thrown it there in a pile with the others. He has been scrutinising our details. *Matilda Chaudhari* it says under the picture. I did not want to change my name when we were married. But when it came time to renew my passport I thought about the difficulties of travelling in India with Milan under different names. We would have to produce a copy of our marriage certificate. I imagined a weedy looking clerk at the hotel, staring suspiciously at me over the reception desk. I saw him thumbing his way through the passport, silently, trying to find some proof that we were truly married before he gave us a room, whilst I, self-consciously, played with the gold band on my left hand in front of him.

Perhaps even then the piece of paper signed by Vera Da Cruz, the cabaret singer cum marriage consultant, would not be convincing. What did an Indian marriage certificate look like? I had seen a birth certificate. It belonged to Milan. It was not an official birth certificate but a form designed by his father and signed by a local official. It was typed on a yellowing piece of flimsy paper with a very faint ribbon. In the bottom left-hand corner there was an official stamp in watery purple ink in the centre of which was just visible the outline of Asoka's pillar.

Unfortunately my father-in-law had forgotten to include Milan's intended middle name on the form so the traditional name, *kumar*, meaning prince, was lost to him forever. Only this piece of paper, it seemed, obtained by his father when his son was five, stood between Milan and non-existence. In a country like Australia, not being able to prove who you are on paper was almost the same as having no identity at all.

It was in order to prove to strangers in a foreign country who I was that I decided to have my name entered in my passport as Matilda Chaudhari. But when I saw the name typed neatly next to the photograph, I felt a sense of the unreal. Who was this girl? She didn't seem to be someone I knew.

When I first met my mother-in-law she exclaimed over my first name.

'Matilda,' she said. 'Such a pretty name. Do you have any other names?'

I told her that my middle name was Sara.

'Sara,' she said. 'It comes from Saraswati, the goddess of wisdom, whom we call the "white goddess" because she is so fair. In India it is considered to be a great asset to be fair. When you go there you will be thought of as a great beauty.'

♦

THE RANSOM

'How much do you think you will fetch?' Muni is enquiring with a smile.

I try and ignore any questions the dacoits put to me now. I do not want to be pulled into their conversation anymore.

'Most likely hard labour for twenty years if you don't set us free soon,' says Milan.

Muni laughs. He throws back his head and we can see his square, even white teeth. All the jewellery has been placed in a wooden box on the floor next to the rolled-up bedding where the dacoits take turns to sleep. Next to the box of jewellery there is Milan's child-sized suitcase.

'And how much will we be getting for these, do you think?'

Muni opens the box of jewellery and holds up the necklace that the aunt and uncle had given me. I stare at him. If they are anxious to make money out of us, why don't they sell the jewellery now? Why are they delaying? Unless, of course, all this is a cruel game—the play before the kill.

As Muni takes the jewellery out of the box, the star ruby that Milan and I bought in Mumbai rolls onto the floor. The tall dacoit picks it up and grins. He comes over and grabs my hand. I try to pull back but he has me in a vice-like grip. In a mock gesture he takes the ring and deftly places it upon my finger.

I wear this ring, he sings, *as a sign of my devotion.*

He is laughing but I am frozen to the spot where I stand. I look down at the purple dome of the ruby to see the star, but the stone appears so darkened that I can see nothing.

THE ILLUSION OF THE STONES

Milan's stones are still wrapped up in their cocoons of newspaper inside the little tin suitcase. Muni examines the suitcase and prises open the lid with a penknife.

'So what have we here?' he says.

'Something precious,' says Ranjit suddenly. 'Surely something a man of discretion will want to keep.'

'*Ki?*' the dacoit says. 'It is not anything of value if it is kept in this child's case.'

As he says this he picks up one of the bundles and tosses it gently in his hand to feel the weight. Then he slowly unwraps the paper. It is a piece of granite.

'A stone!' he says. 'A common stone.'

He unwraps the rest of the bundles and places the contents in a casual arrangement on the ground. There are pink, grey and white stones.

'You think that is all they are?' says Ranjit.

'What do you mean?'

The tall dacoit shows him his even white teeth in a smile that turns into a sneer.

'I mean,' says Ranjit, 'that I can show you something about these stones. I have magic powers that can show what lies beneath. The secrets in these stones will yield up to my powers.'

The dacoit looks at him sideways.

'We don't believe in party tricks,' he says.

'It is the way the light reflects on a stone,' Ranjit continues, 'that makes it beautiful. The light makes it have a certain colour, or shine, or even shape. Let us look at the way the light touches these stones.'

With this he walks over to where the suitcase is and places the unwrapped stones back inside it. Then, picking up the suitcase in his arms, he walks over to the door of the cave. The dacoits do not stop him but they are wary. Our driver begins to rearrange the stones on the ground near the entrance. He picks one up and turns it over in his hand. It is a piece of rutilated quartz with golden needle-like inclusions. He sits down cross-legged on the ground in front of the stone and begins to chant. I cannot understand what the words of the chant are but as the light catches the quartz the gold threads seem to melt and seep into the surrounding rock.

As this happens Ranjit picks up another stone and places it alongside it. It is a piece of bloodstone. Against the green of the host rock the veins of red jasper are clear.

'*Ram, Ram,*' Ranjit intones.

Motes of dust in the light eddy around the stones. The veins of jasper in the bloodstone begin to glow and darken. Then they seem to move as though animated by a pulse. The green heart of the stone palpitates as the blood flows dark and strong through its veins. Then the entire stone fluoresces brilliant green as though it were an emerald.

The golden stone and the emerald stone light up in the sunlit haze and give off a brilliant lustre and feeling of weight and substance. I try hard to concentrate on them to find out what sleight of hand Ranjit has performed to create this effect, but as I do I feel suddenly tired and, straining to see through the dust, I find myself unable to find a focus.

One of the dacoits, although I am not sure which one, lets out a cry, 'Oh Baba!', then there is silence.

THE HIJACKED CAR

Through the mouth of the cave I can just distinguish the front fender of the Hindustan Contessa. Somehow the dacoits have managed to get it going and have brought it here. Another part of their booty. I feel emotional looking at it. Had it not broken down we would not have been captured. Ranjit, however, has a more professional interest.

'The company will not be pleased that the car has absconded. But perhaps they will attempt to retrieve it,' he says.

'But that will be a good thing,' I say excitedly. 'Then they will know that we are here.'

'I'm not so sure,' says Ranjit gloomily. 'They are not into people rescue. Cars are their speciality.'

Eighteen

THE DREAM OF THE GRANDMOTHER

One night whilst asleep in the cave I have a dream. In the dream I see my grandmother. She is standing at the entrance to a door, surrounded by a bright light but behind her the door is dark. As I move closer I realise that she is crying. In the morning I tell Milan about it.

'Really?' he says. 'My mother believes that when one of her parents or grandparents comes to her in a dream, someone in her family will die.'

'Do you?' I ask.

'Well, I have never had a dream like that so it's hard to tell. It's true that when an aunt or uncle has died Ma has said that she knew it would happen because of one of these visitations, but it may be simply that, when someone becomes sick, Ma becomes anxious and in that state she often dreams about her mother or father.'

'What do you think my dream means?'

'That you miss your family and wish you were home.'

But I am not so sure. I feel that my grandmother foretells an end, of what I do not know.

THE OJHA'S BROOCH

There is one piece of jewellery that the dacoits have not taken from me yet. It is the brooch of clear stones that Takuma gave me. Pinned on my sari veil the folds of the sari have fallen over it and hidden it from view, and so it has escaped their attention. When I realise this I unpin it, when the dacoits are not looking, and refasten it underneath the sari blouse on the inside lining.

But it is to no avail. As I am bending forward to take a beaker of water, the material strains against it and the tall dacoit sees the shape of the bulge.

'*Kia hai*?' he shouts. 'What is this? What are you hiding?'

He walks over and grabs me around the waist.

'See?' he shouts. 'We treat you well and this is what happens.'

He puts his hand under the waist of the *choli* and yanks the brooch free. The curve of the metal grazes my skin and draws blood. Milan stands up to stop him but the other dacoit pushes him away roughly.

'You're not to touch her!' he yells, but Muni

ignores him and runs a hand teasingly, provocatively, over my breast. There is a silence. Time stops. I stand motionless in the centre of the cave like a figure in a stone temple frieze.

'This is the brooch of an *ojha*,' Milan suddenly says very quietly. 'You are a brave man. It was pinned on the *achol* of my wife's sari by my Takuma herself. She is an *ojha* who has the power of *ananku*. I wish you good luck. If you take it she will cast the evil eye upon you. And if you continue to imprison us she will be angry. Why at this very moment my grandmother is no doubt casting a spell for our release. She has the power of the Great One on her side. And you know that when Her loved ones are threatened, Her wrath is terrible.'

For a moment the Kashmiri seems frightened. He scratches his head and looks perplexed. Even if one does not believe, surely it is not wise to unnecessarily provoke the deities?

'Furthermore, you must know that coming by such jewels through theft can only reap destruction on the thief,' says Milan.

Muni tips back his head and laughs. He walks over to Milan and shrugs.

'Then keep the brooch,' he says, throwing it on the ground. 'I will take the wearer instead.'

With that he grabs my arm in a vice-like grip and pulls me roughly towards the entrance of the cave.

A sudden burst of light blinds me for a moment, and then we are outside.

FEAR

The dacoit drags me to where the Hindustan Contessa is standing. He opens the back door of the car and pushes me inside. Through the window I can see our prison. We have emerged from a deep orifice in a massive rock. The entrance is much narrower than the inside would suggest and apart from the car there is nothing to alert anyone that within its womb there are people being held against their will. I feel disorientated and find it hard to hear what the dacoit is saying. Eventually he yells at me and I realise that he is standing over me and that I am lying on the back seat of the car.

'Why has your family not tried to claim you?' he asks. 'Where are your relatives? Why has our ransom not been paid?'

I look at him.

'I don't know,' I say. 'Perhaps they think you are asking too much. How much are you asking for us?'

I lean back against the vinyl of the car seat. It seems so strange to feel something so modern and man-made after the primitive conditions of the cave. I sink my cheek into the upholstery. The dacoit is angry. I know I am in danger. I watch his hand as it flutters near the band of his trousers. I wait. Perhaps the gesture is subconscious, because he does nothing.

He leans further over me and I can smell his breath full of the scent of cardamom and *methi*. For one awful moment as I lie there I look at the strong line of his mouth and I wonder what it would be like to feel its pressure. Even as the thought occurs to me I retreat from it in my mind, horrified. How can I accuse Milan of unfaithfulness, even in spirit, if I am able to entertain such thoughts?

The dacoit must feel some of my confusion because he straightens up and explodes into a loud and satirical laugh.

'Frightened, memsahib?' he says. 'You don't know what frightened is. I'll tell you about frightened: frightened is what my little sister felt when she watched the soldiers in my country slit my father's throat in front of her. That is fear. You wouldn't know about fear because you come from a country where there is none. You look surprised. You don't imagine for a minute, do you, that if I was a real dacoit I would be able to speak to you like this? I am no more an Indian than you are. I have come here to hide.'

INTERRUPTED

Suddenly, inexplicably, in my mind I am somewhere else. One morning in Agra we made love in our hotel room. I was standing at our window looking down into the garden when Milan came up behind me and held me.

As we lay together on the bed there was a knock at the door. We tensed and stayed very still.

'It's all right,' I said. 'I've put out the *Do Not Disturb* sign. Just ignore it.'

The knock came again. We froze. Surely the maid could see the sign?

As the key turned in the lock Milan leapt from the bed.

'Damn,' he cried.

'Oh Baba,' the maid said.

THE SOUND

Muni is still standing over me when we hear the first sound. The noise of thunder rumbling across the sky. Or perhaps the sound of someone blowing a giant conch: *BAOOM, BAOOM* across the sky. Muni straightens up and listens.

It comes again. And then the first wave like a ripple of water under the ground: a ground that has suddenly become soft and malleable like *kheer*.

'Get inside,' he orders me. 'In the cave at once.'

And he pushes me once again roughly through the door.

NINETEEN

THE EARTHQUAKE

The walls of the cave shudder as though they are alive. We are all silent. I wait to see the ground open up in front of us into a deep and terrifying abyss. If the cosmic elephants are restless, impatient with the burden that the world makes upon their backs, what is there that we can do?

The floor of the cave heaves and small sections of the walls crumble. Milan moves next to me. I hear his breathing.

'Tilly.'

I lie where I have fallen, frozen with fear.

'Are you OK?'

He throws his arms around me. I look down. My hands are cut and my arms are covered in blood.

Middle Auntie is lying motionless several feet away from us. Ranjit is sitting, his head in his hands, muttering to himself. There is a strong smell of earth. Every time I shift my weight even slightly, I feel the soil beneath me move. The cave is pitch black because part of the walls has fallen in and blocked the entrance. We are entombed. I can feel the reverberation long after the earth has stopped moving. The dacoits are nowhere to be seen.

'O Lord of elephants,' I hear Ranjit intone, 'help us. Stay upright and firm. Hold the Earth on your back and protect us.'

Milan crawls over to where his aunt is lying.

'She's unconscious,' he says. 'I think she's in a bad way.'

Ranjit finishes chanting and turns to us.

'Oh Ma,' he says. 'We are going to die. They will leave us here to die.'

'They have to help us,' says Milan. 'They can't just leave us here. We are too precious to them. We still have immense value for them.'

GRAVES

'Hey, *Bhogaban.*'

The sound startles us.

Middle Auntie sits up slowly as though she is risen from the dead. She looks around and then begins to rock back and forth, wailing softly, like some kind of Indian banshee.

'We will not get out of here,' she says. 'They will leave us to die, I know they will. It is what they do.'

'*Nahi*, Auntie,' says Ranjit. 'They will get us out. Just you see.'

'Perhaps you should lie down,' says Milan, putting his arm solicitously around her shoulder. 'You have had a shock. And there is not much air. We should try not to use it all up at once.'

We are all attempting to look composed, to look as though our fate is not in someone else's hands. Milan finds a torch which the dacoits had been using occasionally at night, and he tests it. A small beam of light lands on the wall of the cave. When he turns it on us we appear like shadows, with ghostly surreal faces: serene polished ceramic masks with black holes for eyes. Only if someone sees our faces, suddenly, in the outside light, will they realise that we are frightened.

We could die here, buried under the rubble of the cave, asphyxiated eventually by the lack of air or perishing from lack of water and food. Just like people who were buried alive in crypts in years gone by.

But I have no death wish. I want to survive. I must root myself in the present and in this place. My feelings towards the dacoits grow from moment to moment more full of hate.

Ancient jewels were first discovered in graves many thousands of years old.

In the dark this one line from *The Handbook of Gems* comes to me.

TWENTY

STORIES

On every page of my travel diary I have begun a
description of a new experience. I have been conscious, as the terror in the cave increases, that my
mind digresses and that I begin to tell a story like
my father-in-law. I build the story up, layer upon
layer. I find some small detail, like a flaw in a gemstone, that I fasten onto. I travel through events that
spiral down and back, each to a new beginning.
Each part of the journey is a small episode that will
one day bear witness to what has happened to us
and how we came to be here.

Milan says that a traditional Indian story is deliv-
ered by a storyteller who embellishes to suit the
times. Contemporary references are often made to
the narrative. I cannot do this. These acts that have
occurred to us seem to me to be unique to us. But

I am sure that somewhere there will be people who have had a similar experience.

Milan also tells me that, if during the narrative the storyteller describes a special occasion, such as a birth or a wedding, the storyteller may celebrate the event with his audience. They may give him gifts to commemorate the occasion. The storyteller himself may hand out tokens of the happy event such as sweetmeats. If a tragedy occurs, he weeps with them.

Is it the time for sweetmeats or the time for weeping?

THE TRAJECTORY

'You can't change some things but you can change how you react to them.'

Milan is trying to comfort us.

'The trajectory, how things proceed along the path of life, cannot be changed. If something happens, it happens. Because of this you know you cannot change the event but you can change the way you react to it. So, by our way of thinking, we can change what is happening to us,' he says.

Ranjit is looking at him intently.

'*Acha,*' he says. 'That is what I believe. I am always changing how I think. A good magician must be ready to do this.'

'I am thinking,' Middle Auntie says, 'that we will never get out of here and even if we do the dacoits will eventually kill us because, you know, we have seen their faces.'

Ranjit looks at her gloomily. 'Auntie is right, we have. I have just changed my thoughts completely. We are going to die.'

'That is not how we should be thinking,' says Milan. 'We must not see ourselves as doomed.'

I look at his determined profile in the dark. I have always liked his chiselled mouth and chin.

'You have very good bones,' I once said to him.

'Are you referring to my face cut?' he asked.

'Face cut?' I said. 'I have never heard it called that before.'

As though it were carved out of a block of stone.

As we sit here I can see, under his chin, the scar where he fell from the railway embankment near Shundarpur when he was a child.

THE ILLUSION OF IMPRISONMENT

A small lozenge of light at the entrance appears, then another. The sound of someone yelling and the scraping of an implement against the dirt. It takes us a few moments to realise that it is the voice of one of the dacoits.

'They are wanting their jewels,' says Ranjit.

Although I would like to think that the dacoits are trying to rescue us I know in my heart that our use for them is beginning to wane. If they have demanded a ransom, no-one has been able to pay it. More than likely the request for payment has not even made it out of India but is lying on the desk of some local sergeant after it has been intercepted at the post office by a prying clerk who thought that the envelope contained something of value.

The sound grows louder and the lozenge of light grows larger. The hole in the rubble expands gradually to allow more light inside the cave. Then suddenly a man's head appears in the hole. It is the Kashmiri. He looks down upon us for a moment, observing us like a voyeur, then he smiles.

'OK, OK,' he says. 'Our guests are here.'

It is the first time he has referred to us as guests. It is as though the dacoits are suddenly seeing us differently. I watch the Kashmiri moving away the last shovels of dirt to make a life-size opening in the cave's mouth once again. And all the time he watches us.

IRREGULAR SURFACES

The dacoits have taken us outside the cave. We are seated on the ground a little way from the Hindustan Contessa. Something has changed on the part of the dacoits. Their resolve has been broken, perhaps.

'It is six days that you have been with us,' Muni says.

His tone has changed. It seems gentler, more subdued.

'We have been pleased to have you here with us.'

This seems shocking and alarming. I look at Milan. He gestures quietly with his hand. Stay silent, his gesture says. Do not speak.

I am certain they are going to kill us.

'My brother is leaving soon,' says the Kashmiri. 'He will go back to our country. He will take your car and your driver with him. You do not mind. I will join him soon after.'

There is silence. How can we possibly mind? We are not in a position to object. And we are not sure, either, what we are objecting to.

'You will stay here until we have left. Then you may make your way to Dolali. It is not far off.'

It is Muni who is speaking again.

'We will take all that belongs to us now.'

There is another pause.

'Your uncut stones are very valuable. They will provide us with the money we need. We are not interested in waiting for a ransom. Your families are people of low morals. They do not care for their relatives. We had hoped but we are not surprised. The West does not care for its people. They are corrupt.'

'Then why take our Indian driver with you?' says Milan. 'He is not your enemy.'

'He will drive us to the mountains. Then he can return. The car will be of no use to us then.'

'You have no right to have imprisoned us like this,' says Middle Auntie suddenly. 'If I was your mother I would whip you.'

'Thankfully you are not,' says Muni coolly. 'And you are also mistaken. We have not imprisoned you. For some days you have been our guests. We have kept you safe. Now you must go. That is all.'

THE MONKEY STORY

My father-in-law tells a story of how he was captured and taken prisoner when he was travelling on the Shundarpur road in a rickshaw at nightfall. I call this The Monkey Story.

The story begins one dark night when, as a student learning Sanskrit from the local *pandit,* the young man, Jiban, hired a rickshaw to take him the twenty kilometres back to Shundarpur from his teacher's home.

'It was late,' my father-in-law said, 'and I was hungry, so I bought a bag of peanuts from a street vendor to eat along the way. I was sitting in the back of the rickshaw eating the peanuts when I heard a loud thump. Before I had a chance to look around to see what it might be I felt someone's hot breath beside me. It was very dark and I could, by turning sideways, just make out a figure as tall as myself, sitting beside me in the cart. I thought it was some brigand come to cut my throat. I thought I was dead.'

At this point he would pause a moment to make sure that the gravity of the situation had sufficiently affected his audience.

'You'll never believe what happened next.'

'What?' I asked.

'The person sitting beside me put his arm up and draped it over my shoulder as though we were old friends travelling along together. Then he reached over and put a hand in my bag of peanuts.

It was the hand in the peanuts that did it. When I saw it my blood ran cold.'

'Why?' I asked again.

'Because it was not a human hand. It was a monkey's hand.'

As he spoke I saw the leathery large-jointed fingers with blackened nails of horn delicately picking the round peanuts from the bag.

'I was really terrified for my life then,' my father-in-law said. 'The monkey was bigger than me and these kind of monkeys are very strong. It is known that they can kill a man with a single blow. It was a nightmare ride. For the rest of the journey I was the monkey's prisoner. He sat with me, his arm around my shoulder in a vice-like grip, pretending to be my friend, and ate my peanuts. He had a large grin on his face all the time. Anyone who saw us would have assumed, in the dark, that we were two friends. Only every now and then he would bare his teeth even more in a kind of grimace that seemed like a threat but it was never possible to be sure. I was worried sick what would happen when the peanuts ran out.'

'What happened when they did?' I asked.

'He simply jumped off the rickshaw and disappeared into the night again, as though none of it had happened. I knew it had, however, because I was left shaking like a leaf with an empty bag of peanuts.'

TWENTY-ONE

A PASSING BUS

We reach Dolali that afternoon. A passing bus
stops when we hail it and takes us to the Dolali
road stop. Perhaps it might not have picked us up
but it has two eyes painted on its side and is indeed
the bus that we collided with just outside
Shundarpur.

'I am knowing that you are VIP passengers and
that is why I am transporting you,' the driver says.

UNCLE PRALAD

At Dolali there is a public phone box, a general
store and two petrol bowsers. We call collect
through the operator. The phone line to Mumbai is
crackling and indistinct. Small Uncle is in his office.
At first he does not know who we are.

'Hello, hello? Who is this? What do you want? I

am Pralad Banerjee. Hello? This is Devadas Industries. How may I help you?'

'*Babu kotta bolche*,' Milan speaks to him first in Bengali and uses his family nickname, Babu, meaning Mister.

'We are near Khandala. On the main road. We are at Dolali. Can you send someone to pick us up?'

There is a short silence.

'What are you doing there? What is wrong with your car?'

Milan gives him a brief version of the events of our last week. He is particularly critical of the car that his uncle has rented to us. There is a further silence.

'The Contessa did not seem to have any air conditioning either,' says Milan. 'It was not in good repair.'

'Frightful, frightful,' his uncle mutters as he listens. 'I will certainly speak to the company and seek a refund on the expenses for the car.'

BACK IN MUMBAI

At the Imperial Hotel no-one appears to have missed us.

'You have been with your Takuma?' says the hotel clerk. 'We are holding the room for you.'

The fact that we are ten days late does not seem to have alarmed him at all. Nor the fact that we appear in such a dishevelled state. The sideways glance he gives me says it all: you memsahibs, it says, often look strange.

The local police seem nonplussed when we tell them of our ordeal.

'You are coming back without the car?' a young moustached constable says. 'No-one has reported it missing.'

We fill in several forms on yellowing pieces of paper. Each one that we fill out causes the constable to scratch his head.

'You have a proof of the jewellery?'

I shake my head.

THE MYTH OF THE OVERSEAS COUPLE

Our room in the Imperial looks smaller and shabbier than we had previously believed. After the confines of the cave it should look bigger and even luxurious, but paradoxically things do not always look as we imagine them.

Milan is lying on the bedspread looking up at the ceiling. I lie down next to him and place my hand on his chest. I feel the rise and fall of his breath and watch the curve beneath his ribs deepen and flatten. He puts his arms around me and strokes my hair.

'One of the things you realise when you think you are going to die is how precious the world is and how much the people you love mean to you.'

He puts his arm around my waist.

'You're my prisoner,' he says, laughing.

'It's not a joke,' I say. I think about the way Muni grabbed me. I am trying to erase his face from my mind. After all, perhaps we were not prisoners. Just guests of the dacoits. A euphemism for terror. I know this, Milan knows this, but the rest of the world seems indifferent.

Perhaps the locals will say in years to come, 'Remember the year the memsahib came dressed in a *patola*? And she said she'd been abducted? Abduction, you see,' they will say wisely, 'is something a memsahib always imagines will befall her.'

That would be the making of another legend. The myth of the overseas couple who came to Mumbai and disappeared into the countryside only to emerge a week later with wild stories like Forster's Adela.

I think of the clerks at the Imperial Hotel standing at the reception desk gossiping.

'We saw it all,' they will say. 'She was with a local boy, a son of India, come back from overseas. She was his fair dessert, but said they had been abducted. Of course they would say that— otherwise what would his father think? To lose a son like that to a Western woman. It would be a father's shame.'

THE CHINAR TREE RESTAURANT
Small Uncle meets us in the hotel restaurant. He has insisted on meeting us for dinner so that he can offer us his condolences for what has befallen us.

'Terrible, terrible,' he says, shaking his head from side to side.

At least I am relieved that someone believes we were taken hostage and that all our valuables were taken. How else can we explain the fact that we returned from Shundarpur with nothing but the brooch Takuma gave me and the star ruby, which is still on the finger where Muni so unwelcomingly placed it?

The Chinar Tree restaurant is an outdoor restaurant on a terrace of the hotel. With Small Uncle we are watching a young girl perform a classical dance on a stage lit by fire torches. The food is served under a brass canopy where it is laid out on a buffet. I am spooning a portion of the chicken curry onto a plate when Small Uncle joins me.

'A difficult matter of course, you understand, to know what to do in these circumstances,' he says.

I notice for the first time how well oiled his moustache is.

'Well, we still have the clothes we left in our suitcases back here and some of the things that we bought, but I was wearing the more expensive jewellery so that has gone along with most of the gifts from the family,' I replied.

'Yes, yes, I understand all that,' he says. 'Very sad, I'm sure, but the matter of the car is what I am proposing.'

'What do you mean?' I ask.

'You understand that the car was not covered for

theft. It was not supposed that while you were in the care of the driver that the car would be the subject of a larceny.'

The girl has stopped dancing for a moment and the stage has been taken by a young *tabla* player. The *tabla* player begins to test his drums with a little hammer.

'Does that matter?' I ask.

'Well, the company is not happy,' says Small Uncle. 'They may be asking for compensation. But there is no need to worry. I will attempt to deflect them. A small sum paid in the right place may suffice.'

I look at him. He beams back. The *tabla* player has begun a measured but rhythmic beat.

'There will of course be an investigation by the company. Did you, at any stage, see the identities of your captors?'

Takka dini, takka dini, tak, says the *tabla*.

I stop for a moment. Then I lie. I have no idea why.

'No, not at all. They wore balaclavas the whole time they were with us. We have no idea who they were.'

Small Uncle looks relieved. The *tabla* is speeding up.

'Excellent, excellent. Then everything is as it should be. If you can give me about two hundred in American dollars that will do nicely.'

The dancing girl begins again to the accompaniment of the drums. She is performing a dance drama depicting the forms of the god Vishnu. She enacts the scene where the child Krishna steals the butterfat and eats it with his fingers. Then she becomes Ram and takes up the classical pose of the archer. One hand holds the bow while the other draws the string taut. The audience claps enthusiastically.

'Actually I don't think we have that much money left, Chotopisho,' I say as pleasantly as I can. 'Perhaps you could inform the company of this and also let them know that we are considering asking for compensation ourselves for the providing of an unsafe car whose defects led us to be captured and appallingly mistreated.'

Ram's arrow has hit its mark. The dancer begins a Kuchipudi dance. Her feet follow the beat of the drum.

Small Uncle looks taken aback. The *tabla* player has worked himself up now into a frenzy. Small Uncle smooths his moustache.

'I am sure, I am sure the company will be dis-tressed and will do anything to help you in a non-monetary sense. But what you say cannot be right. I understood you were treated very well.'

'Really?' I say. 'I don't recall us communicating we were treated well at all. Who told you this? How would the company know how we had been treated? Perhaps there has been an assumption here. I have found you have to be very careful not to assume too much.'

I stop for a moment.

'But you are right in one thing. There has been a larceny: all my jewellery has been stolen. I may have to seek compensation for that as well. I would call that a grand larceny, wouldn't you?'

The Kuchipudi dancer has taken a large copper plate and, having placed it on the ground, is now dancing on its rim. As the plate turns she moves her bare feet dexterously while balancing on its metal edge.

FAREWELL

As we are boarding the plane from Mumbai to Singapore I see a sign at the airport which says:

> *Using the right name is courteous, using the wrong name is not Indian. Mumbai is not Bombay. Mumbai is the city of the future immersed in the past. Life's tapestry is here woven on the handloom of integration.*

I think of Ranjit when we first met him. And of his cheerful farewell when we left him with the dacoits.

'I knew they would release you,' he said to me, smiling.

'How did you know that?' I asked.

'Because of the ruby ring, madam,' he said. 'The robbers gave it back to you. That is very auspicious. A star ruby contains the three spirits of *Dharma, Asha, Karma*—Faith, Hope and Destiny, imprisoned within the stone. Those who wear such a stone are protected by the captured spirits from ill-doing. The dacoit knew he could not keep it. It would have brought him great misfortune. To steal such a stone would have been very dangerous.'

'Please be careful,' I said. 'The dacoits may harm you.'

'*Tik ach*e, there is no need to worry for me. I will be fine,' he said shyly.

TWENTY-TWO

THE WRONG PICTURE

On the Indian Airlines plane from Mumbai I read some magazines.

In one I see an article entitled 'Calcutta Beat'. It is a tribute to the Indian film-maker Satyajit Ray, who has recently died. Underneath the title there is a photograph of an Indian girl, three-quarters on to the camera, in a wedding sari, staring down with unhappy eyes. The picture was taken from one of Ray's films. The caption under the photo says that it is a picture of the heroine of the film, *The Goddess*, which was produced in 1960.

But after looking at the photograph for some time I realise that there is a problem.

It is not the delicate pattern of sandalwood traced on the girl's face, nor is it the diamond stud in her nose or the girl's *tikkli* which drapes over her forehead beneath the transparency of her chiffon veil, through which you can also see her elaborate earrings hanging down like miniature chandeliers. Nor does the problem lie in the obvious misery hidden behind the girl's dark eyes. It is just that it is the wrong heroine.

I know that this is not a picture of Doya, the heroine of the film *The Goddess*. It is Arpana, the heroine of another famous Ray film, *The World of Apu*. Perhaps, I ponder, the writer of the article has not seen many Ray films. Perhaps one looked the same as the other to him. But how could he mistake the humble Doya for the privileged Arpana?

And how could the character of Doya so quickly have left his memory? The Doya who was forced by her family to become a living goddess? The Doya who hanged herself finally in grief at the impossibility of her situation? The only thing the two girls had in common was that they were both brides and they were, apparently, played by the same actress, Sharmila Tagore. Otherwise, I conclude, it is a case of mistaken identity.

The Goddess was showing at the Astor when Milan and I went to the late session. It was an inside view of a hierarchical Bengali household where ghosts and deities held as much sway as humans. A film where emotions seesawed from joy to grief like a melodrama.

'I simply can't understand what this film is about,' I told Milan. We had only just met and perhaps it was not a good choice of film for either of us then. Now it seems to me, as we fly over the water, from the country where it all took place, the most significant film in the world, the quintessential drama of our lives.

During the film an elderly widower sees his daughter-in-law, Doya, in a dream and suddenly, superimposed on her image, is the terrible face of Kali—the black goddess.

'Oh Ma,' Doya's father-in-law cries out in ecstasy at the image of Kali.

'I'll call you Ma also,' he says to his newly wed daughter-in-law later, 'because you are the mother of the house now.'

The same word for deity and human—a case of shifting and reinterpreted identity; an ability to merge reality with illusion that I can understand only too well now.

IN THE COMPASS ROSE RESTAURANT

If at dusk you sit in the large circular room of the Compass Rose restaurant in Singapore you can see over the water to the lights of Malaysia and Indonesia. The sights from the highest restaurant in Southeast Asia are best seen on a clear night, and on such an evening Milan and I are sitting at a window table looking down.

Our table is next to the waiters' station. Our waiter is an Indian, a slight man of about fifty with quick movements. Each time he takes the coffee pot from its burner he flicks us a quick look. I wonder if he finds us unusual—an Indian and a white woman together. Then I realise that he is listening to snatches of our conversation and that he is trying to construct the story behind our words. When Milan puts his head in his hands he brings us another pot of tea.

All this is done deftly, politely, not once does his gaze flicker onto our faces as he places down on the table top the white china cup, the silver tea strainer, and a pot of Darjeeling tea.

'I'm sorry,' I say to Milan. 'It is, I believe, all wrong.'

'What do you mean?' he says softly.

'The thing with Stephanie,' I say.

He turns his face to the window and takes my hand. There are tears in his eyes. At this point the waiter arrives with a small pot of honey and a plate of cut lemons.

'For the tea, madam,' he murmurs, neatly rearranging the items on the table so everything would fit on it. I thank him. I avert my eyes. He is probably wondering if we have just received tragic news, a death, perhaps, has occurred. He casts Milan a solicitous look and moves quietly away from the table again.

'And I don't think,' I say, 'that Takuma is a kidnapper but I feel sorry for Gita too. Neither of them planned this. I think someone else forced these women to play these roles.'

Milan looks up at me. 'Who?' he says at last.

'I don't know,' I say. 'It's hard to know who would force a mother to abandon a small child and go to live in a foreign country. One of the men, perhaps, or perhaps it was a consensus of opinion. Who knows what they thought your parents would encounter when they journeyed to that foreign land? A land where women didn't have pierced ears, where people ate beef. The truth of the matter, I suppose, will never be known. People will just tell stories about it.'

The waiter reappears at my elbow. He holds a plate of biscuits and a small silver tray on which he has placed our bill. Tactfully he places them both in the centre of the table and gives an awkward smile.

'Thank you,' he says and gives us a quick nod.

I pick up the piece of paper on the silver tray and turn it over.

Under the amount of $12.50 it says, 'Your waiter for today.' Written next to this there are just two words: *Riddhiman Singh*.

CUT GLASS

The next day Milan and I go shopping in Singapore. In Little India we find a shop that sells Indian bronzes. In the window of one shop there is a small bronze statue of the elephant-headed god, Ganesh. It is about a hand–span in size and already mottled with verdigris. The Remover of All Obstacles stands with one foot resting on the back of a small mouse. He has four arms. His lower hands hold a pen and slate because he is the god of scribes.

We go into the shop and speak to the owner, who is keen to sell us anything he can. As he is wrapping the Ganesh up he notices the gold brooch that Takuma gave me which I am wearing for safekeeping.

'Nice brooch,' he says. 'Would you like some earrings to match?'

'No thank you,' I say. 'I have all the jewellery I need.'

I buy some newspapers and we sit in a quasi Italian cafe in front of one of the shopping malls and drink cappuccinos. We look like the perfect couple on a holiday.

The *Straits Times* has a story about a woman who has died after falling down some stairs at the Jantir Mantir observatory in Jaipur in India:

> *Today a woman fell from the Jantir Mantir observatory. The woman, who was with her family, was, according to the testimony of her daughter, afraid of heights, and it would seem likely that she lost her balance. The district commissioner reports that handrails have been suggested for the staircases in the observatory but that no further action has been taken up to this present moment.*

Several locals then gave their opinion that visitors to Jantir Mantir should be warned of the possibility of accidents, particularly in inclement weather.

I wonder if that is the full story or if, behind the newspaper summary, there is another more poignant story of a woman who, frightened and out of her familiar environment, lost her sense of who she was and why she was there and just fell.

Back in our hotel room in Singapore I take Takuma's brooch off and walk over to the light of the window to look at it more closely. On the face of the brooch there are two gold spirals inter-twined. Along each of the spirals the stones are set. As I hold it up to inspect it, however, I realise, with a jolt, that something is wrong. In one place where there should have been a stone there is a minute hole. A tiny stone has fallen out. I stare at it for a long time then I look away. I read once that a bro-ken stone meant death. Then, as I look at it again, I realise that it is not actually a broken stone. There is simply a gap where a stone is supposed to be.

I take the brooch downstairs to the hotel jewel-ler, who looks at it under an eyeglass.

'These are American diamonds,' he says.

'What sort of stone is that?' I ask.

'Cut glass, madam,' he says and shows me his teeth. 'It's not really worth fixing.'

'No,' I say, forcefully, 'it has great sentimental value for me. You must put in another piece of glass to cover up the hole.'

♦

AUTOMATIC TIMER

Just before we leave Singapore I discover that there is some film still left in my camera.

'Let's take a photo of ourselves together,' I say. 'We can use the automatic timer.'

I set the camera up on the dressing table of our room. I put the camera on automatic and slip the view-finder cap over the eyepiece of the camera to protect it from the light. After the timer switch has been pressed we stand together in front of the dressing table mirror and smile at the red pulsating light which flicks on and off until the shutter clicks and the flash illuminates the space around us for a second.

Milan holds me around the waist for the next picture and as the flash goes off the telephone rings. When he picks it up it is clear from the way he is speaking that it is from overseas. Later, after he recounts the conversation, I hear what the caller had to say to him:

'Hello, Babu, this is your Ma calling. Did you see your grandmother?'

Twenty-three

SLIDE NIGHT

A week later we hold a slide night at our house in Dight's Falls. The slides are of our trip. The entire Chaudhari family, with my mother and I, sit in our lounge room under the gaze of the fish-eyed goddess and watch scenes from our journey. The first one shows a vulture perched on a tree in Kashmir. The bird and the tree are just a black shape silhouetted against the fading light. Everyone admires it and then after that they fight over who is in each photograph and where each photograph was taken. When we come to the slides of the Taj Mahal, Milan says, 'It's been ruined. It's full of holes where the British removed the jewels from the walls. It looks dreadful.'

His father sucks on his pipe and then shakes his head.

'No, you're wrong. They've filled up the holes with glass.'

Milan picks up the remote control device.

'No, Baba. They haven't.'

To prove his point Milan clicks the slide back a frame to show a wide-angle shot of a wall of the Taj pitted with holes. His father ignores the shot and goes on:

'No, this restoration work was done some time back. You don't know. I've seen Taj maybe eight, ten times. This is what I am telling you—they have replaced the jewels with glass.'

Gita looks at him impatiently.

'OK, OK,' she says in Bengali. '*Tik ache*. These people have just come back but you won't listen to them.'

She turns to her son.

'Why are you bothering? You know your Baba is always right.'

A picture of Middle Auntie comes up on the screen.

'Who's that fat hippo?' Jyoti asks.

'That's your aunt,' I say.

My sister-in-law laughs.

'You know, Tilly, how you're not allowed to bring ivory into Australia? You could have brought her instead.'

She laughs again.

CLICK, CLICK.

When the slides of Takuma come up on the

screen there is a rustle, a murmur, an infrasound almost inaudible but running like an undercurrent through the family, because on the slides they can see that Takuma has held out her hand and touched me.

THE HAND AND THE THUMB

'You know how it is for me,' Gita says a week later. 'For a mother it is just too hard.'

We are travelling together in Gita's car to Victoria Market to buy some food for a family party. We have not spoken since the slide night. On that evening when the pictures of Takuma were shown, Gita sat very still, very calm, like a subject herself, posing for a photograph. For the occasion she wore a pale coloured sari with a red line of vermilion in the parting of her hair, and a red coral bangle and a white shell bangle on her arm. Her face seemed more lined than usual and in her eyes there was a tired expression. She looked like a woman I had seen in an Indian film a long time ago. It was a black and white film and Gita's character was playing the role of the mother.

At the slide night my mother had sat ramrod stiff, in an after-five dress and too much jewellery, trying to make conversation.

'Aren't you glad that you are here?' Mother said finally, indicating a slide of some desolate landscape outside Mumbai. 'I'm sure you wouldn't want to go back there.'

Gita looked as though she was not sure what to say.

'Jiban always thinks this is the country for him,' she said finally, 'but, you know, I miss Calcutta. That is where I grew up.'

There was a pause.

'But my children are here and I always try to be a good wife and a good mother. For me, my husband is my god and my children are my godlings.'

'I can't imagine what it would have done to my husband's sense of self-importance,' said my mother, 'if he thought that he was a god. I shudder to think.'

I remembered Gita coming to our house at weekends just after we were married with a chicken curry for her son. She would arrive at our front door with the curry in a Crown Corningware dish. There would be two elastic bands around the dish to keep the glass lid from falling off.

'This is for you and my godling,' she would say, pointing at Milan.

On the occasion of the slide night, Gita turned to her son: 'I always know what you are thinking, Milan, because I am your mother.'

He winced when she said this but she continued: 'You cannot escape my eyes. I see into your thoughts because we are one. I am the hand, Milan,' she said, 'and you are the thumb.'

During our visit to the Majestic Fort at Jodhpur, I noticed there was a row of handprints on the wall beside the Iron Gate. Each hand was a raised-up sculpture standing out in bas-relief from the wall. A rectangular box framed each one. The collection of boxes side by side looked like a cartoon of different hands, each picture showing the same object, a hand, but each hand slightly different.

'What are they for?' I asked Milan.

'They're *sati* marks,' he said.

I imagined each woman passing through the gate for the last time. As she passed she placed her right hand in some yellow clay and stamped the final outline of her hand and thumb on the sand-stone walls. Having made this contract it must have seemed almost impossible to turn back when she finally saw the flames of her husband's funeral pyre leaping into the sky.

'What are godlings?' asked my mother, interrupting. 'Are they some kind of elf or sprite?'

As we are driving to Victoria Market, Gita turns to me and says, 'Did you have a chance to speak to Takuma when you were in India?'

'Yes,' I say, 'we had a good conversation.'

'How did she find Milan? Was she pleased to see him?'

'Very.'

I can see the answer causes her pain but she continues as though, by asking, she is taking a hot knife to a wound and cauterising it.

'She has had a hard life too. She is Dadu's third wife, you know.'

'No,' I say, shocked. 'I didn't know.'

'Yes, his first wife died of cholera, the second of smallpox. Takuma is her sister. Some say that *she* only survived because she was an *ojha*.'

There is a pause.

'I have a gold ring at home. I am keeping it for you.'

'Oh?' I say, genuinely surprised.

'Yes,' she continues. 'It was Milan's when he was a little boy. It is inscribed with the letter M. When you have a son, I will give it to you.'

I look at her. I don't know what to say. Having had one son wrenched from her, is she making sure that the next boy will wear her signet ring, just in case anyone else may try to claim him? I want to say something but I restrain myself.

What makes you believe that his name will start with M?

But the expression on her face makes me contain myself.

In the black and white film there was a scene where the unwed daughter announced to her family that she was pregnant to her lover. To create the right mood violins wailed and a harmonium played up and down the scale. The distraught mother clutched her throat in grief and fell down dead. The look on Gita's face has the same desperation. I feel, suddenly, immensely unkind, as though I have caught a butterfly and I am pulling off its wings one by one. I feel ashamed.

'I am sure your grandson will love to wear his

father's signet ring,' I say. I look at her profile as she sits at the wheel. It eases slightly, her mouth relaxes as I speak.

'Pray God,' she says, 'that you have a son. Without a son a mother cannot die. It is as simple as that. Only a son can light the burning torch which is placed in the mouth of the dead.'

I had not thought of this aspect.

'I never imagined when I was a young girl that I would have to go through all this. But somehow, when you are faced with an ordeal you find that you can bear it and you survive it. I know now that I can survive anything because I survived that terrible pain. Coming to this country was not so terrible as having a child taken away like that. We are all so proud of you—what you went through. You could have been killed, of course, and then we would have lost our precious gem, our daughter-in-law.'

Gita stops at an intersection and while we are stationary a man in a car next to us winds down his window and yells at her: 'Get off the road, you stupid lubra!'

She does not say anything but she turns to look at me for a second and I see her eyes flicker. Then she puts her hand on the gear shift, moves into gear and drives on.

THE GIFT OF THE PAINTING
The package arrives in the mail a few weeks later. The familiar pink and blue postage stamps alert us,

even though we cannot read the postmark, that it is from India.

Inside there is a large flat plywood box and inside this, wrapped in several sheets of paper, is the gift. I unwrap it and lay it on the kitchen table.

It is a painting about the size of a large poster, drawn with indigo and pink ink, of a woman wearing a necklace of small skulls. Her large fish-shaped eyes are opened wide in a drunken ecstasy and from her mouth her tongue appears dripping with the blood of life.

The faint shaky writing on the piece of paper that accompanies it can only have been made by an old woman. I cannot read it because it is in Bengali.

Milan translates it with some difficulty.

This is my last painting, done in the Kali Yurg. At the end of the Kali Age, the cycle of death and rebirth will end. Until then here is her image to protect you.

Twenty-four

THE LETTER

It is almost a month after our return that another letter arrives. It is from Middle Auntie. She writes that Ranjit's body has been found on the road just outside Dolali. He has been shot in the head.

There are no traces of the Contessa. We can only imagine that the dacoits, having discovered that Milan's childhood stones were not what they thought, took their revenge on an innocent man.

Middle Auntie's letter is written in the ornate copperplate that is typical of Indians of her generation and education and for some inexplicable reason, known only to the Indian postal service, has taken over a month to reach us. She writes that the crime was discovered on the fourth, only a week after we left India.

With the arrival of her letter we are forced to

reconstruct our lives over the previous month. What were we doing on the fourth, the day he was found? What were we doing on the fifth, the day of his cremation? We saw ourselves then as characters who thought they knew the story, when all along there had been another ending which no-one had told us about.

Among the photographs I brought back is the snap I took of Ranjit the day he drove us, unwilling passengers, to Malabar Hill. After admiring the lights on Nariman Point I remember the shy young man whose photograph I took and who accused me, playfully, of stealing his image.

When the stones did not hold up to the magician's promise, Ranjit must have realised that Muni and the Kashmiri would turn on him. But perhaps he had hoped this would be after he had left their company. For someone, then, who always relied on timing, this magician's trick of his had fallen very short of the mark. In our hearts, however, we knew that it was not his fault. It was ours. We should never have left him.

Middle Auntie emphasises in her letter that none of our possessions have been found. She seems almost more concerned about this than she is about our driver's death. In India, it seems, life is cheap. It is belongings that are costly.

Milan puts his hand on my shoulder as I read out from his aunt's letter:

Dear Babu,
Please accept the blessings of the goddess Durga
through us. I write to you with a heavy heart of events
that can only remind us of our past ordeals. We have
come to know of the untimely death of your driver . . .

The formal, almost Victorian manner of speech
that she adopts in her correspondence seems quite
comical to us and gives to the news a more
grotesque quality.

On the morning of Ranjit's funeral Milan and I
were at the supermarket. Perhaps I was standing at
the check-out as his body lay on the pyre waiting
to be burnt. As I counted out the coins in my hand
and gave them to the girl, did his young son take
the burning torch and place it in his father's mouth
as the last act which begins the cremation?

THE HORSE SACRIFICE
The calendar that I bought at Chuckles has a painting in it of *The Horse Sacrifice*. The horse sacrifice
was an ancient ritual that required the sacrifice and
cremation of the most precious possession that a
king could have: his vehicle, the horse.

A white stallion was chosen and set free to roam
the countryside for one year. At the end of the year
an elaborate celebration was performed in which
the stallion was ritually sacrificed to the sun god by
a group of Brahmin priests who also ate the
cooked and sanctified flesh.

I take the calendar illustration to the framer to have it put under glass. I hang it up in our lounge room next to the picture of the goddess and then I place a blown-up picture of Ranjit on Malabar Hill next to them both on the wall. I feel so bereft I cannot say anything about him. I did not realise that his loss would mean so much.

I tell Milan, 'At least we can give him some immortality, hanging on a wall in Dight's Falls in Melbourne. It may not have been what he ever imagined, but he entrusted me with his image. I have to look after it.'

'Why have you hung them up like that?' Milan asks me.

'They are hung like that because they tell a story,' I say.